AS SERIOUS
AS DEATH

By Quintin Jardine and available from Headline

Bob Skinner series:
Skinner's Rules
Skinner's Festival
Skinner's Trail
Skinner's Round
Skinner's Ordeal
Skinner's Mission
Skinner's Ghosts
Murmuring the Judges
Gallery Whispers
Thursday Legends
Autographs in the Rain
Head Shot
Fallen Gods
Stay of Execution
Lethal Intent
Dead and Buried
Death's Door
Aftershock
Fatal Last Words
A Rush of Blood
Grievous Angel
Funeral Note
Pray for the Dying

Primavera Blackstone series:
Inhuman Remains
Blood Red
As Easy as Murder
Deadly Business
As Serious as Death

Oz Blackstone series:
Blackstone's Pursuits
A Coffin for Two
Wearing Purple
Screen Savers
On Honeymoon with Death
Poisoned Cherries
Unnatural Justice
Alarm Call
For the Death of Me

The Loner

Quintin
Jardine

AS SERIOUS
AS DEATH

headline

First published in 2013 by
HEADLINE PUBLISHING GROUP

1

Cataloguing in Publication Data is available from the British Library

9 780 7553 5712 3 (Hardback)
9 780 7553 5713 0 (Trade paperback)

Typeset in Electra by Avon DataSet Ltd, Bidford-on-Avon, Warwickshire

Printed and bound by CPI Group (UK) Ltd, Croydon, CR0 4YY

Headline's policy is to use papers that are natural, renewable and recyclable
products and made from wood grown in sustainable forests. The logging and
manufacturing processes are expected to conform to the environmental
regulations of the country of origin.

HEADLINE PUBLISHING GROUP
An Hachette UK Company
338 Euston Road
London NW1 3BH

www.headline.co.uk
www.hachette.co.uk

During the calendar year in which I wrote this book, my lovely Eileen and I have spent more time than either of us would have liked in the precincts of Edinburgh Royal Infirmary.

For the record, I am happy to say that all the care that she and I have received has been exemplary, and for that reason *As Serious as Death* . . . a wholly inappropriate title in the circumstances, but that's what it has to be . . . is dedicated to ERI, and all its caring staff.

One

I don't know how I'd have managed if it wasn't for my kids.

How can you be depressed when you live in one of the most attractive places on the planet, and you're wealthy enough to be in complete control of your life for ever? Good question, but lately I've known times when I have been.

Most of them came during the night, after Liam left St Martí d'Empúries and Spain, heading off to finish his travel book. He didn't say that he wasn't coming back, but I had no expectation that he would.

When did the shine start to wear off?

For certain it happened one early summer Wednesday evening, on the terrace of my house, looking down on the village square watching the restaurants begin to close up for the night, as the last few punters finished their pizzas. We were alone, as next day was a school day and the kids had gone to bed.

Out of the blue, Liam used the 'M' word, asked me to marry him, and I told him, rather more bluntly than I should have, as now I realise, that I didn't want to be Mrs Matthews, or Mrs Anyone Else for that matter. It wasn't the answer he'd been expecting.

'But you are already,' he pointed out, quietly. 'You call yourself Primavera Blackstone. It's not your birth name: that was Phillips. It's Oz's name, your former husband . . . your late former husband.'

He was speaking the plain truth, but I flared up at him, I'm afraid. 'That's different! I do that for the kids' sake, not for Oz's. They're all Blackstones, so it makes life easier if I'm one as well.'

'Does it? Does it make the slightest bit of difference to them? Have you ever asked any of them?'

'I don't need to,' I pouted.

'What do Janet and little Jonathan call you?' he asked, but didn't give me the chance to reply. 'They call you Auntie Primavera. You're not their natural mother; you're not even their real aunt. You adopted them formally when their mother's death . . . and by the way, Susie was Oz's widow, not you . . . left them orphaned, but neither of them call you "Mum", do they?'

'I don't expect it of them, nor will I ever. But Tom does.'

'Yes, in a fine baritone. Primavera, have you taken a look at your kid lately? He isn't a little boy any more.'

I couldn't argue about that. My son was into his teens and making a good job of puberty. Out of nowhere, he had a couple of inches on me, his frame was thicker and his voice had broken more or less overnight. He was taller than the best footballer on the planet and as big as its best golfer.

'Clearly not, but what does that have to do with it?'

'He knows who he is, and he knows who you are. Like you say, you're his mum. Do you think that if you married me his nose would be put out of joint? Do you think he still dreams that his father faked his death and that he's out there waiting until it all blows over, so that he can come back one night, under another name and with maybe a little plastic surgery? I don't believe he does, that's for sure, just like I don't believe he'd mind if you and I got married. In fact I know he wouldn't.'

'Oh yes? And how do you know that?' I challenged.

'Because I asked him.'

I stared at him. 'You what?!?' I exploded. 'You asked my son for my hand in marriage?'

'If you want to put it that way, I suppose I did.' He grinned at me. That made it worse; my glower became a full-on glare.

'How dare you do that?' I protested. 'What were you thinking about? I suppose you asked Janet as well.'

'As a matter of fact I did. She beamed, all over her face, and said that would be great.'

'And wee Jonathan? Did you ask him too?'

'No,' he conceded. 'He's maybe a little young for that sort of question.'

'Small mercies,' I muttered. 'What the hell are you trying to do, Liam, force my hand? I won't be railroaded into marriage, not by you, not by my kids, not by anyone.'

'I'm sorry if I was presumptuous,' he replied. His tone was distant, like I'd never heard it before. I'd hurt him, but at that moment I didn't care.

'I'd call it manipulative,' I snapped. I could see him withdraw further into himself.

'It wasn't meant to be,' he murmured. 'It was meant to show you that there's nothing in the way of us getting married . . . only you.'

'See what I mean by railroading?' It was time to cool it a little. 'Sorry, Liam, I appreciate your proposal, but I don't want to do that. We're fine as we are. We've been fine for a year now. So why change things? It's obviously important to you. Tell me why.'

'It's complicated. Let's leave it at that.'

'No chance. I'm a bright girl; I can process complicated issues. Try me.'

'Okay.' He took a deep breath. 'Oz was my best friend, but he's dead, and I'm alive. So why doesn't it feel like that? Primavera, I want to be the only man in your life.'

'But you are,' I protested.

'No, I'm not. That dream I mentioned, Tom's dream: he told me that he doesn't have it any more, but I'm sure that you do. You've never buried Oz Blackstone. You mumble his name in your sleep, but never mine. You look for him in the face of every forty-something male stranger who strolls alone into that square down there. Primavera, your thirteen-year-old son has come to terms with the fact that his father's gone, and he's ready to get on with his life. But you, you haven't, and you're not. You fantasise that he's out there somewhere. The worst part for me is knowing that you're thinking of him when you fuck me.'

4

'If any of that was true . . . which it isn't . . .' I lied, 'how would being married to you make any difference? You make it sound like you're trying to brand me. I never figured you as insecure, Liam. That's certainly not how Oz saw you.'

'Then maybe you've made me that way . . . or you both have.'

'That's arrant nonsense,' I insisted. 'You have no reason to doubt me, and you haven't from the day we got together. We have a great relationship, so why should we change it?'

'Do you love me?'

'Of course I do. I'm sharing my life with you, aren't I?'

'Not all of it; that's my point.'

That set me off again. 'Christ Almighty, man, listen to yourself. Don't you have a little place inside your head that's all your own? Of course you do, yet here you are trying to control my thoughts.'

'I'm not.' Goddammit, why did he have to be so calm? 'I'm simply suggesting that you get on with your life, and I'm asking you to share it with me.'

'As I've just said, I'm doing that already,' I insisted, 'and I'm happy with things as they are. I see no need for us to get married, so thanks, but no thanks.'

He shrugged his shoulders, and finished his mineral water.

'I'm sorry, love,' I said, feeling that a little contrition was in order. 'Come on, let's go to bed and I'll make it up to you.'

I did just that, and next morning we made it business as usual with the kids, getting them off to school . . . Janet and wee Jonathan have adapted well to the Catalan system, with the aid of some intensive private tutoring, and with Tom looking out for them. An outsider would have thought that everything was fine and dandy, and so it was, almost.

Liam was as loving as before, and I'd like to think I was too, but things had been said that couldn't be unsaid. There was a distance between us that hadn't been there before. It was imperceptible, or so I thought until three weeks later, when Janet asked me if everything was all right.

'Of course,' I replied. 'What makes you ask that?'

'I'm not really sure. It's just that you seem a little quieter than usual.'

'Do you know what the menopause is?' I asked her.

'Ah,' she murmured, and dropped the subject. As it happened, I haven't reached the change yet, but I hadn't lied to her, as I had lied to Liam about that damned dream.

I knew without him having to tell me that Tom dreamed about his father when he was younger . . . because he was only too ready to tell me himself . . . but I never discussed mine with him, or anyone else.

It visited me often for a year or so, maybe once a week, and it was always the same, more or less. A man appeared out of the blue. The first time, it was in Susie's house in Monaco, after her death, but usually it was right here in St Martí. He was always the same in every appearance. Facially, he wasn't Oz; his nose was broader, and his cheek-bones higher. His voice was different; it had a pronounced Western drawl. His hair was mostly grey, and close-cropped in military style. He was narrower in the waist and his muscles were different, though just as formidable, not gym-enhanced like Oz's but the result of hard physical work of some kind.

But he couldn't hide those eyes, not when he took off his Ray-Bans and looked at me as he stepped towards me.

I always woke up then, crying out, whether in fear, panic, or frustration I know not, but I imagine that's when Liam would have heard me calling Oz's name.

I wasn't surprised when he broke the news that he was leaving to finish his magnum opus, one morning in the square, when we were having a coffee at Meson del Conde. I couldn't really complain either; his book pre-dated me in his life, and he had put it to one side.

After the injuries that are an inevitable part of a very rough profession caught up with him, he developed a second career as a writer and photographer. His travel book was a long-term project, going back to his days of fame as a professional wrestler . . . sports entertainer, they call them sometimes, but he didn't like that, for he was the real thing, not a body-builder or failed US footballer. It was going to be a photographic guide to all the places that the global grappling circuit had taken him, complete with anecdotes. Not quite an autobiography, but not far off.

He had put it on hold when we paired up, only taking on work that could be done from Spain, apart from a stint at the Olympics as a commentator for Irish TV, but it had always been there in the background.

'How long will you be away?' I asked him.

'I can't say for sure. Most of the locations are in the US and

Canada, but I'll need to go to Japan as well, and Mexico, South America and Australia. It's not a personal project any more; I've sold it to a publisher in New York, so I'm working to a delivery deadline. I'll do my travelling and my photography and when I'm ready, I'll sit down and write the text.'

'Will you come back here to do that?'

He gazed at the table as he replied; that's when I twigged that it was probably more than a business trip. 'No, I plan to hole up in my place in Toronto to do that. My new editor says that's what I should do. Writing's a solitary profession, she tells me.'

'How long will it take you?'

'I'm not sure,' he said.

'What's your deadline?'

'End of March next year.' He smiled and looked towards me once again, without quite meeting my gaze. 'But hey, I don't plan to use every minute of it. I need to spend the rest of the summer and autumn doing research and taking pictures; I should be able to start writing by the beginning of November. Of course, whenever I have a gap in my schedule, I'll come back here.'

'Of course,' I repeated.

I knew that he was being less than truthful, because honest men are always terrible liars, but who was I to complain?

Looking back on it, I know that I lied to Liam about more than just the dream.

I didn't love him. I've only ever loved one man in my life, in a way and with an intensity that almost destroyed us both.

Liam was comfort, Liam was shelter, Liam was company, by day and by night, but ultimately he was right. He could never compete with Oz, alive or dead.

And he is dead, make no mistake about that; I can fool myself no longer.

After Liam left, I decided that I had to confront that dream, and all the other things that had been nagging at me. For example, there was Brush Donnelly.

Oz's nephew, Jonathan Sinclair, is a professional golfer, and a fairly successful one at that. By chance he played in (and won) his first pro tournament at the PGA course at Girona. It's less than an hour away from St Martí, and naturally I took him under my wing. He lived with Tom and me for a while, until he bought his own place, on his adopted home course of Pals.

When he turned pro after finishing his college degree in the USA, he did so under the management of a man named James 'Brush' Donnelly, whom he described as a former tour player himself, who hadn't been very good at it, and had disappeared off the radar for a few years, before re-emerging under a new guise. But Brush . . . he earned the nickname by sweeping up every detail of business . . . was something of a recluse. He and Jonny did all their early business by corre-spondence over the phone and email, and never met face to face.

I've always had a fertile imagination. The mysterious Brush made me wonder and I began to look for little anomalies in his story. I found a couple too. For example, his correspondence address was in Chicago, but the one time that he and I spoke, when he called one day looking for Jonny, it turned out that he was calling from his home in Arizona.

That was enough: I got it into my head that Brush was Oz, taking care of his nephew. That illusion was shattered when he and his client met up for the first time, in Chicago. I had Jonny send me a photograph. Okay, maybe if he decided on a completely new look, my ex might have tried to appear ten years older than he was, but no way would he have had his legs shortened by six to eight inches.

I didn't give up on the idea though; for little Brush to have a winter home in Tucson and a town house in Chicago, he must have been a man of substance, yet he had very few clients and his abortive golfing career had probably cost him money rather than earning him any.

Instead, I decided that he was a front. For whom? There could be only one candidate in my sad mind. I didn't pursue the notion though, not until Liam left. When I did, I didn't mess about; I hired Securitas, the biggest detective agency in the US, to investigate and report on Mr James Donnelly.

It didn't cost me much, for it only took them a day. They reported back to me that Brush was the son of a Mr Andrew Donnelly of Las Vegas, Nevada, a heating engineer until his death in 1962, and the nephew of Mrs Violet di Luca, the widow for twenty years of a Mr Antonio Luca, from whom she had inherited twenty-four per cent of one of the earliest and biggest casinos built in what had been the unspoiled Nevada Desert. I knew the place; they'd pulled it down for rebuilding in the brief period in which I lived in Las Vegas, but I'm sure that Brush hadn't cared about that when Auntie Vi had snuffed it herself in 2009 and he, her only living relative, had inherited the lot.

He used his new wealth to support charities in general and, in a way, through his role as a golf agent, for all six of his clients, four male, two female, had been hand-picked from the college system and had been helped financially at the start of their careers. For example, a couple of perks that Jonny thought had come from sponsors had been funded by Brush himself.

The report also revealed that his reputation as a recluse flowed from the fact that he had suffered from agoraphobia. He had been treated for the condition, but still avoided crowds or wide open spaces, which explained why he was never seen at a golf tournament. Like many Americans he did not own a passport, a simple explanation for the fact that he had never visited Jonny, his star client, in Europe, not even when he won the German PGA last summer.

With Brush out of the way as a possible link to a still-living Oz, I had only one other avenue to explore. Roscoe Brown was his Hollywood agent, and still represents the children's interests as his professional executor. Oz didn't make all that many movies in his short acting career, not compared with the likes of John Wayne, but every one that he did was a major box office hit and even though he's no longer around to promote them, the estate continues to pull in substantial income from DVD and Blu-ray sales, and now from streaming.

One thing you should know; I wasn't the only one clinging on to the notion that he wasn't dead. A cult has grown around him, not quite of Elvis proportions, but significant enough to sustain three different 'Oz Blackstone Lives' websites. I forbid few things to the kids, but I've told them that going anywhere near them is absolutely off limits.

I'd wondered on occasion whether Roscoe might be behind at least one of them, given that he's one of the most commercially acute guys I've ever known, so after I'd washed the Brush option out of my shortish blond hair, I called him in Los Angeles . . . via Skype, so I could look him in the eye.

'I need to know, Roscoe,' I told him. 'Do you feed any of the legends that Oz might still be alive?'

I could see that he was offended. 'Absolutely not, Primavera; to do that would be to take financial advantage of deluded people's grief, and that runs against my moral code. I have never thrown out a single hint to any of them that my client is anything but dead. Maybe that means I'm not doing as good a job for the kids as I could, but I'm not going to apologise for it.'

'I wouldn't expect you to,' I said. 'It's just . . .'

Roscoe's black, and the light was behind him, making his eyes unnaturally bright as they held mine from the screen. 'You're a believer, aren't you,' he murmured. If my sound hadn't been turned full up I might not have heard him. 'You are one of those poor deluded people.'

'Maybe,' I conceded. 'Usually not, but there are times, when . . . I find myself asking, "What if?" Oz was a role player all his life. Very few people saw the real him. For those of us who did, him faking his death, that's not such a hard concept to take on board.'

'But why would he do that?' he asked.

'To protect the kids,' I replied.

'From what?'

'From him. Oz did a couple of things in his life that would have ruined him if they'd ever come out . . . and they might have. I could see him thinking that if they did, the effect on his children would be emotionally catastrophic. And I can see him looking to spare them from that.'

'I hear what you're saying, but that would mean abandoning them. He loved those kids, Primavera.'

'But if it wasn't for ever . . .'

'Death tends to be permanent.'

'But if you have the resources, you can be reborn. It happens all the time, to supergrass witnesses and the like; I've even met one of those.'

'Do you want him to be alive?'

'Of course I do.'

'Even if it means that you're never going to see him again?'

'Even if . . .' I paused. 'Are you saying he is alive?' I gasped.

'No,' Roscoe replied, instantly. 'I am not.'

'But do you believe he could be?'

'No. Primavera, I didn't want to get into this with you, but I think I need to. As you know, the official reports said that Oz died of an unsuspected heart condition while doing a stunt for a movie he was making in Ecuador, involving a bridge over a rocky river. He fell in and was pretty badly smashed up facially when he was pulled out. Hence the legend that it might not have been him, that the victim might actually have been a stuntman. There's even a name that the true believers latch on to: Gary Hazelwood. There was such a person, but he was fired three days before Oz died, for smoking dope on set. That's why Oz did the stunt himself. The websites believe that Hazelwood died in the river and that Oz took advantage of the fact to disappear. They argue that he'd had enough of fame and wanted out. Straws, Primavera, that's all; they're clutching at straws.'

'Where is Hazelwood now?'

'He died in a car accident in Quito two months later. He never went back to the US.'

'Was his body identified?'

'Only by his driving licence and passport, I'll grant you, but that's irrelevant. It was him in that car, no doubt about it.'

'How can you be so sure, and why is it irrelevant? Look, Roscoe, nobody outside that film unit ever saw Oz's body, before it was cremated to comply with Ecuadorean law.'

'That's true,' he conceded. 'But it was Oz.'

'How can you be certain?'

'Didn't Susie tell you?'

'No, we made a pact never to talk about Oz's death.'

'I can understand that,' he said. 'I don't suppose you've ever seen the death certificate.'

'No, I haven't. All I know for sure is that no autopsy was

ever done, although the press reported, wrongly, that one had been.'

'No,' he agreed. 'The Ecuadoreans forestalled that. The film unit doctor, who certified his death, in British form since it was UK money that backed the project, didn't even mention a heart condition. He said that death was caused by the trauma of multiple head injuries sustained in the fall. However he also said in a side letter that in his opinion the accident may have been caused by the rupturing of an aortic aneurysm, which he had been able to detect.'

I was a nurse in a past life so I know about those: a weakness in an arterial wall that can occasionally leak or burst, with consequences that are usually fatal.

'How could he be sure of that without a post-mortem examination?'

'He said it was so big that he could feel it. But he couldn't be certain, which is why the insurance company was wasting its time when it tried to reject my claim under the policy.'

'What insurance company?'

'The one that covered Oz, and all the other major people on the project; it insisted that everybody have a medical. That involved full body scanning. Oz's showed a previously unde-tected abdominal aneurysm. The unit doctor knew nothing about that, incidentally,' he added. 'The insurance company's own nominated surgeon said that given its size the risk of rupture was probably no more that one in a hundred, and they went along with that. He was advised to have it repaired surgically, and he said he would, after the movie was done. Nobody saw it as an issue, so when the company tried to use it to void the policy, my lawyer said, "Hey, it was your guy who made a mistake, not us who didn't disclose." They folded pretty quickly.'

'Mmm,' I murmured. 'Even so . . .'

'I'm sorry,' Roscoe said. 'There's more. At first, I was like you; I didn't want to believe. I wasn't happy with the situation, so I instructed Oz's assistant on the movie to take hair samples and swabs from the body and to have them couriered to me in Los Angeles. I had DNA profiles run and compared them with the Federal database. It was a match.'

'Oz was on the FBI database?' I exclaimed.

'Primavera, these days many of us get on to a DNA database, one way or another. Bottom line, there is no doubt. Oz did die in Ecuador and it was his ashes that Susie scattered. I'm sorry to end your hopes but, ma'am, I really do think it's for the best.'

I looked into his eyes again, and I believed him, on all counts.

'Don't be sorry,' I replied. 'You're right. Goodbye.'

I ended the call and leaned back in my chair. I felt physically exhausted and yet my mind was clearer than it had been for longer than I could remember.

There wasn't a single anomaly left for me to latch on to, not one last tendril that I might grab to sustain my fanciful hopes. I had reached the point of acceptance. Oz Blackstone was dead. The man in my dream was there and there alone;

he wasn't going to walk into the square in my village or anywhere else.

'Closure' has become a bit of a buzzword, but I realised that it was something I needed. I didn't have to consider it for too long before I knew what I had to do. The eighth anniversary of the accident in Ecuador was less than a week away. I didn't have to remind the children, but that night over dinner, I raised the subject.

'How would you feel,' I began, 'if we had a little ceremony?'

'A memorial service?' Janet asked. 'In the church next door?'

'That won't work,' Tom chipped in. 'The priest knows I don't believe in God.'

'I do,' wee Jonathan ventured. His older siblings stared at him. 'Mum and Dad are with Him,' he whispered. He looked up at me, in search of a seconder for his proposition. 'Aren't they, Auntie Primavera?'

The things kids throw at you. 'I'm sure they're with someone,' I said. 'If you want to call him God, that's fine by me. But I wasn't thinking of anything as formal as a church service. I thought we might go down to the beach on Wednesday, after it gets dark, and do something there.'

'What sort of something?' Janet asked.

'We'll light a fire,' I proposed, 'maybe play some music, and talk about him.'

'Can we do it for Mum as well? It's nearly a year since she died.'

That hadn't occurred to me, but I did my best to cover the omission. 'Of course we will.'

'Where on the beach?' I still hadn't gotten completely used to Tom's man voice. I close my eyes and it could be his father's, when first we met, before it was affected and altered by his later life experiences.

The answer was spontaneous; I didn't even have to think about it. 'Near the old Greek wall,' I said. 'He used to love that place. Whenever he wanted to go and think about anything, that's where he would do it. He reckoned that it's haunted, in a nice sort of way.'

'Really?' Janet exclaimed, her eyes lighting up. She's a romantic at heart, and I hope she always will be. So was her father, until life made him a cynic.

'Oh yes. Oz was more than a little fey. He used to say that he could feel thousands of spirits down there. He missed his mother a lot, just as you and wee Jonathan miss yours. He used to go down there when he wanted to talk to her.'

'You never told me that before,' Tom murmured. I sensed an accusation hiding in his statement.

'No,' I admitted, 'I didn't. Probably because I didn't want you to spend all your time down there trying to talk to him.'

If we hadn't been seated, his reply would have knocked me back on my heels. 'I don't need to,' he said. 'I talk to him anywhere I want, and he talks to me. He has done forever.'

'In dreams, I suppose,' I conceded. 'But didn't you tell Liam you don't have those any more?'

He shook his head. 'No, not only in dreams. When I feel like it, I talk to Dad in my head, when I'm awake, and quite often I can hear him answer. I feel sorry for all those people fooling themselves on their websites, kidding themselves that he's still alive, when I know he's not.'

'And you never shared this with me? I thought we had no secrets.' It was my turn to accuse.

'Would it have made you happy if I had?'

My son is thirteen going on twenty-five; his question didn't need an answer.

We had our little Wednesday ceremony, the four of us, after dark as I had promised to make sure that we had some privacy. Tom lit the fire; if the sun had been coming up, we'd have been in the shadow of the old Greek wall. It is exactly that, by the way, a relic of the ancients' first toehold in Iberia, and the place where the Olympic flame came ashore, in the year of Barcelona.

I put a photo of Oz on my iPad, and played a piece of music, a song called 'The sun's coming over the hill', which was as appropriate as you could get in the circumstances. If you don't believe me, find it and listen to the words.

When it was over, I delved into my bag and produced a shirt. Oz had left it by mistake, the morning after the last night we ever spent together, and I had hung on to it. It was the only thing that had been his that I still possessed. I put it in the centre of the fire and watched as the flames consumed it, watched as its ashes rose and were gathered by the breeze and floated off, out to sea.

We sat silent for a while, the four of us, until Janet took her little brother's hand and murmured, 'I'd like to say a poem for our mother.'

'Yes,' I told her, 'please do. She'd like that.'

She recited Christina Rossetti's 'Remember me when I am gone away'. She was word-perfect; she even smiled in the right place. As she finished, wee Jonathan stared at her as if she was someone he'd never met before.

I looked at Tom. 'Do you want to say anything?' I asked.

'Thanks.'

'Go on then.'

'No, that's it. Just "Thanks", that's all.'

I didn't ask whether he was speaking for himself; I didn't have to, for I could feel what he did, the sense of a spirit set free.

We stayed for a few minutes more, until Tom gave us our lead by standing up and kicking sand over the fire to douse it. When it was extinguished completely, we walked off the beach, and back up the hill towards our fine stone house, ready, all of us, to get on with our lives in the way the people we had celebrated would have wanted.

Two

So why did I let those two lost people down, by allowing myself to be depressed to the point that on occasion I would cry myself awake at night? Note: in all my years, some of which were spent on hospital wards, I have never seen anyone cry herself or himself *to* sleep.

Liam's absence may have had a little to do with it, I concede, but the truth was that I was busy enough looking after three kids without having an adult on my hands as well.

I have to say in his defence that he hadn't deserted me completely. (Not that he could ever have been accused of anything.) He'd call a couple of times a week, to give me an update on his current location. He sounded just the same, said all the right things, made all the 'missing you' noises, and so did I, but I wasn't a hundred per cent sincere and I doubt that he was.

Another Primavera might have wondered why he never used a landline, and come to suspect that maybe he wasn't where he claimed to be, but that version of me probably disappeared with the ashes of Oz's shirt. The revised edition didn't care all that much, for she was too down on herself.

The main reason for my mid-forties midnight blues was my life itself. I have never been idle, not once, not as a single woman, or as a single parent. I have always found ways to vary my existence, whether it was by nursing in hospitals, or even in an African war zone, as I did before I met Oz, or by helping out in the St Martí restaurants, or running an unofficial tourist information bureau, or being a trade missionary in Spain for Her Majesty's Government, or by getting into several scrapes.

Suddenly, out of the blue, it seemed clear to me that all those days were behind me, and that for the first time in my life I had a truly full-time, twenty-four seven, job.

I was a single mother of three, mother of two adolescents, and one troubled little boy who had done nothing in his life but mourn, and I had no time for anyone or anything else. I had chosen my new role when I adopted Janet and wee Jonathan, and I did not and never will regret it, but I had not imagined what a demanding existence it would be.

Yes, I had help around the house, a buzz-bomb of a cleaner called Terri, but nobody else. When Janet and wee Jonathan had become part of the family, I had considered bringing the Kents with them from Monaco. Audrey had been Susie's secretary, and while her husband Conrad had been designated property manager, he had been, in fact, the children's minder. Oz had been obsessive about security, and had fantasised about kidnap plots and the like, so he had employed a professional, ex-military bodyguard.

The sale of Susie's business, which the three children had inherited on her death, meant that there was tons of money around, so the idea of buying the couple a house near mine and moving them to Spain was perfectly feasible, but when the three of us sat down and talked it through it became clear that there would have been no job of any significance for Audrey, and that Conrad would have spent much of his time sitting on his hands during the school term time.

He was honest enough to add that the risk to the kids in Monaco had been mostly in Oz's mind, and that Tom and I had got by for years in St Martí without the need for personal protection. So we all shook hands, and they left with a severance payment, going straight into jobs in London with an exiled Russian oligarch, where security definitely was a major issue.

So there I was, after Liam left, utterly on my own, in terms of adult relationships, and emotional support. He had never tried to be a dad, or to assert any sort of authority over the children, and because of that, and of course because of the guy he was, the elder two had liked him and had given him that status, or something close to it. Wee Jonathan had kept him at a distance, as he did with everyone, other than Tom.

Terri kept the house as spotless as anyone could, given that it's almost directly above a beach, but all the rest, all the school stuff, all the kitchen marvel stuff, and all the other stuff that is the basis of large family living, was down to

Mum/Auntie Primavera. Liam had helped me in most of those things, giving me some 'me' time, but with his departure that went too.

I was too busy to be bored, but I saw myself in a deep rut, the kind left by giant tyres. My doleful vision was that I would be past fifty by the time the children were grown enough for me to begin the climb out. By the time wee Jonathan had flown the nest, I'd be fifty-five, facing the unknown and heading downhill towards it.

On some of those dark tearful nights, I did think about picking up the phone, calling Liam and saying, 'Yes.' A couple of times I almost did it, only stopping myself when I saw how selfish that would have been, and also how cowardly.

During the day, I tried my hardest to be the old me, but I couldn't always cut it. Occasionally I would snap at the kids for trifling things that, before, I wouldn't even have noticed. On the first day of the new school term, I bollocked wee Jonathan in the kitchen for putting on odd socks while getting himself ready.

His little face grew even darker than usual; he'd probably have cried if Tom, who had heard me, hadn't laughed, and said, 'Tough shit, Mum. He's only got one pair left upstairs, and they're the same as the ones he's got on.' Then he winked at his brother, and nodded towards the door. The sad little boy gave him a tiny grateful smile, and went off to rearrange his dress.

As the door closed behind him, my caring young man looked at me. He was frowning. 'What's up, Mum?' he asked.

'Why should anything be up?' I replied. 'He couldn't have gone to school looking like that.'

'Why not?'

'Because . . . because . . . because his teachers would have thought he isn't well cared for, and because the other kids would have made fun of him.'

He shook his head. 'His teachers would have thought no such thing, and they would have said nothing about it. And the other kids aren't like that.'

'There's always one, in every school.'

'Yes,' he admitted, 'two or three, in fact, in wee Jonathan's school; bully types. I know who they are and even though I'm in the secondary now, they all know that if they give him a hard time, they'll hear about it from me. I might not be there any more, but I still look after him.'

My son was growing up before my eyes, and for the first time ever I found myself afraid that he was growing away from me.

In all our time together after his father's death, I had seen us as a twosome, Tom and me, me and Tom. There was nothing about him that I didn't know, and I was determined that when I judged him old enough, there would be nothing he didn't know about me . . . well, apart from the story about the man I shot in Geneva, during my first outing with Oz. (The guy gave me no choice in the matter; he was quite determined to kill us both, and I wasn't having that.)

Yet there I was, face to face with an aspect of him that I hadn't known existed. I hadn't been in any doubt that he loved his siblings, but the way he looked when he told me about the potential bullies sent a shiver through me. Tom has studied martial arts since he was a nipper, a form called wing shun, wing tsun, or sometimes wing chun. He's a black belt, and Liam developed him further in the time he was with us, but they both insisted that it was all about self-discipline, deflecting aggression, and only when necessary, self-defence.

I tried to imagine him, my gentle son, taking wee Jonathan's potential tormentors into a corner and warning them off his kid brother, peacefully, but I couldn't. All I could see was his father, who had definitely not believed in turning the other cheek.

'What did you say to them?' I asked him, anxiously.

He grinned. 'Nothing,' he replied. 'I didn't have to. They know who I am. I don't have to tell them that I wouldn't like it if they picked on my brother.'

'You mean they're afraid of you?'

'No. I mean they respect me. Kid stuff's all about face, Mum. They know that if they picked on wee Jonathan and I got involved, they would lose face with their mates, and they're more afraid of that than of me kicking them into the middle of next week. Not that I would . . .'

'Not even if you had to?'

He shook his head. 'There isn't the slightest chance of that, not with those kids, nor anyone else I know.' He paused. 'Now, are you going to answer my question?'

'What question?'

'What's up with you?'

'Nothing's up with me.'

'Sure, and the sea is on fire. I can see it from the window.'

'Oh, it's nothing. Did nobody ever tell you that women get moody sometimes?'

'They don't need to; Janet's living proof of that.' *Bloody hell, he's telling me now his sister has PMT!* 'But you don't, and you never have. There have always been times when you've looked sad, but this isn't like that.'

'Then what is it like?'

'I can't put it into words. That's why I'm asking you. Is it Liam being gone? Are you missing him?'

'A little, I suppose,' I conceded, 'but not that much. I lived without him for long enough and I can do the same again.'

'Is it the service we had for Dad?'

'Hell no! That was cleansing, for all of us. I'm fine with that.'

'Then what?'

'My life!' My emotional outburst took both of us by surprise. I tried not to let him see the tears in my eyes, but I found that I couldn't look away from him for long.

'It's having three children to bring up, Tom, on my own. Don't misunderstand me for one second. I love Janet and wee Jonathan as if they *were* my own, as if I had given birth to them myself, but I worry if I'm doing it right, like I've never had to worry about anything before. It's tough. Can you understand that?'

'Of course I can,' he retorted. His sharpness surprised me. 'But I'm a bit pissed off by being called a child, and Janet will tell you the same thing. We're both thirteen years old; Janet's started her periods and I've got hair under my arms and in other places too. That might not make us adults, but it sure as hell means we're not children any more. I don't know what "bringing up" means to you, but it doesn't mean that you have to watch the two of us round the fucking clock!'

'Tom!' I gasped. 'Language!' I'd never heard him swear before.

He flushed a little, embarrassed by his gaffe. 'Sorry, Mum, but it's true.'

'It is, Auntie Primavera.' Janet was standing in the doorway. 'You worry too much about Tom and me. We are fine, we're doing well at school and we're happy. To tell you the truth, I miss my mother and father every day and I always will, but I'm happier here than I ever was in Monaco. I can go to school on my own without being taken, I have friends without having to tell Conrad all about them, and I don't feel that I'm shut up in a prison like I did sometimes in our house there.'

'But what about your brother?' I countered. 'You're not going to tell me he's happy.'

'He's okay,' she insisted. 'I know he doesn't say much and doesn't smile much, but that's because he's still getting over Mum dying. He was only a toddler when Dad . . .' her voice faltered for a second, '. . . when he went. After that, Mum was all he had, and he has trouble coping with her not being here any more.'

'How can I help him with that? What can I do?'

'Do the best you can to make him laugh. That's what Tom and I try to do with him.'

I managed a small smile. 'You mean like when he puts on odd socks?'

'Yes, things like that. Whatever else it's not your fault. That might have to do with him being colour-blind.'

'Eh?' was all I could say.

Janet nodded. 'He might be. Mum was, I know that, so he could be too.'

'That's right,' Tom chipped in. 'I've seen him get confused with colours. That might be why he's so keen on astronomy; that all tends to be black and white.'

Stargazing was the closest the wee chap came to having a passion for anything. He has a telescope that he brought from Monaco. I let him set it up on the terrace off my bedroom, which faces the sea so there's less light pollution.

'I never knew that about Susie,' I said. 'In that case,' I declared, 'I'll make an appointment, soon as they can do it, to have him tested. It can be inherited.'

'I don't have it,' Janet said.

'You don't necessarily know that you have it. There are various degrees of colour blindness: red, green, violet. You're being tested too.'

'Can it be cured?' she asked.

'No, but it can be a bugger if it's undiagnosed, especially for a child . . . sorry, young person . . . at school. I'll arrange it today.'

'Good. And will you cheer up, as well?'

29

I looked at her, and at Tom; their sheer youthful vitality washed over me and warmed me, as I realised that I wasn't alone, and that they were capable of supporting me as effectively as I looked out for them.

I found myself smiling. 'Yeah,' I said, 'I'll do that too. Tom, it seems as if you're wee Jonathan's real authority figure around here. Go and tell him I'm sorry, and that he can wear whatever colour socks he likes to school . . . and a top hat as well if it suits him to do so.'

My habit was to do a morning school run but let them come home on the bus. That day, I felt restored as I took them to their various places of learning. As well that I did, considering the morning I had ahead of me.

Three

Terri arrived, punctual as always, a couple of minutes after I got back from the school run. I left her to do her thing, and went off to do mine. First on the list was stripping the kids' beds and putting the sheets into the washing machine, then adding as many clothes as it would hold. I smiled as I finished, recalling my earnest discussion with Tom and Janet.

'They're not children any more,' I said aloud. 'In that case they can start taking turns to do their own laundry.'

I left the utility room and went up to my office, to check my morning email box. My morning newspaper links were in it as usual, *La Vanguardia* and also the *Herald*, to keep me in touch with Scotland. There was also one of my regular updates from my actress sister Dawn, in Los Angeles, and a mail covering a quarterly report from the general manager of the wine producing business that Miles Grayson, her hulky superstar husband, owns and of which I'm a director. After those I found a couple of junk items that had made it through the spam filter. I had just deleted them when an incomer popped into the box, from Mac Blackstone, Oz's father, Mac the Dentist, Grandpa Mac.

He's one link with my late ex that I don't mind at all, but I was astonished that he should be emailing me. He had a bad experience on the internet once, and as a result he doesn't trust it. He calls regularly, at least once a week, to talk to his grandchildren and to me, so why, I wondered, the change from the norm?

I wasn't prepared for the answer.

'*My dear Primavera,*' he began, Mac being one of those people who doesn't go in for messaging shorthand.

This is a letter that I hoped I would not have to write, and a favour I'd rather not be asking. I wonder if you'd mind if I popped over to see you and my grandchildren for a very necessary break. Things in Anstruther have taken a turn for the worse, you might say.

You may have noticed for the last couple of years that there has been a lack of communication from Mary. If so, the sad explanation is that throughout that time my poor old wife has been slipping further and further into the grip of the dreaded Alzheimer's disease. It has reached the stage at which verbal communication is gone, because she's forgotten how to speak, and even if she hadn't, it would be pointless, because she doesn't have the faintest idea who I am.

Your professional background will make you aware that her remaining lifespan is anyone's guess. I've looked at all options for her continuing care; trust me, I've been in every nursing home in the East Neuk of Fife, and in one or two beyond. They're all very good, but I can't bring myself to commit her to one, not yet at any rate. For now, she will remain where she is, with full nursing care, in my old surgery which has been lying empty since my successor in the practice moved out, and which I have converted into the sort of facility that she'd enjoy in a proper establishment, with all the hoists and toiletry they have in those places.

I have shared this only with my daughter and son-in-law; not even Jonny and Colin know of the situation. My own health remains robust, as it has done since I had my heart valve replacement, but our Ellie is now insisting that I need some respite care, and I gave up arguing with my dear daughter long ago.

She suggested that I go on a cruise, and get away from absolutely everything, but that would drive me out of whatever mind I have left. Instead I would like to spend some quality time with my grandchildren, or as many of them as I can round up in one place, Colin having taken himself off to university in France, and to live with his nerd of a father during vacation time, to help in his computer consultancy.

Don't worry about me getting in the way of you and Liam. I will blag a bed in Jonny's house, which is near enough to yours to make that practical, but I would appreciate it if you could let me spend as much time with

*the kids as I can. Please let me know if this is okay, as I'd
like to make arrangements with my oldest grandson and
leave in a couple of days.*

   Yours sincerely,

   Mac

'Oh dear,' I whispered, as I finished. I had indeed noticed that
Mary was rarely mentioned. My take on that was simply that
they weren't getting on but were too damn old to do anything
about it, like splitting up. The truth was a shocker; poor
woman, condemned to a life she didn't even know she was
living. And poor Mac, who loved her and was condemned to
watch it happen.

I hammered out an immediate response.

Mac

   *Why are you even bothering to ask that question? Of
course you can come, for as long as you like. But you
shouldn't stay with Jonny; he's in a newish relationship
and he travels a lot, as you know. I spoke to him at the
weekend; he's off the golf tour for a few days, but then
he's due at a tournament in the south of Spain, leaving
on Saturday. Liam isn't around just now, so you won't be
getting in the way of anyone, and even if he was, I've told
you before you will always have a room here. Before you
ask, my father has no plans to come over any time soon.
He's been lured to California by our Dawn, and one
foreign trip a year's more than enough for him. Let me*

*know your travel plans and I'll collect you from wherever
you need collecting.*

I hit the send button, then read my unopened mail, including
the bodega manager's report, which said that sales were holding up in spite of the continuing Spanish recession, although
profit margins were down, since we had absorbed tax increases
into our pricing, as most businesses have done to survive.

I had just finished when another message came in from
Mac.

Dear Primavera

*Thank you. Everything's sorted. I have found a
flight on Wednesday from Edinburgh to Girona, with
WeighleyAir. It gets in at ten past two, but don't worry
about picking me up. I've spoken to Jonny, and he'll be
able to collect me.*

*On reflection, it is better I stay with you, if you have
room. Jonny's lass is going to the next tournament with
him, so I'd have been on my own in Pals. Looking forward
to seeing you and the tribe. Sorry to miss Liam, or will he
be back during my stay?*

Love,

Mac

I shut down the computer and went off to find Terri, to ask
her to give the guest suite . . . we called it 'The Grandpa
Wing' . . . a good going over. While I was pleased that Mac

was coming to visit, I was still processing the reason for it, and coming to terms with the picture of the elegant confident Mary that I had known having been transformed into a being who still functioned physically as a human, but one bereft of a mind.

The thought was so grim that it pushed my caffeine button. Time for my mid-morning break, in one of the four cafés in the square that our home overlooks; that morning I decided it was the turn of Can Coll. I headed straight there, with Charlie, our dim but loyal Labrador; he's golden in his coat, and usually his disposition.

I didn't have to look too hard for a table, as can happen sometimes. Ten thirty on a Monday in September, and the village was very quiet. Most of the early customers were youngish women, gathered in twos and threes; my guess was that they were all mothers, liberated by the start of the new school term.

I chose a place in the corner, against the wall. Liam would have called it a 'gunfighter seat'; it gave me a view of everyone coming into the square from any direction. I asked for a cortado, that's an espresso with milk, and a croissant. I had to wait a little but I knew that was because my bun was in the oven being cooked, not re-heated. Meantime the waiter brought a bowl of water for Charlie, without even being asked. He's a popular dog, not least because he's placid and never goes off at other animals, unlike some.

When my order arrived, I picked my hot croissant apart and thought about Mac. He'd kept Mary's developing condition secret for two years, he said. He's a strong man, but

I couldn't help worrying about the effect that would have had on him. We'd seen him last at Easter, when I'd taken the kids to visit my dad in Auchterarder. He and Ellie had come across for a day. Mary's absence had been put down to a heavy cold, I recalled. He'd looked okay then, and had made a great fuss of wee Jonathan; maybe that had been a case of one troubled soul empathising with another.

I was buried so deep in my thoughts that I hadn't noticed the square fill up. Bus parties call at St Martí pretty much all year round, good business for the cafés, and for Ben Simmers, our local wine merchant. That particular crowd were Japanese, and typically, they were filming and photographing everything in sight, me included.

I'm used to that, so I didn't mind; indeed I welcomed the diversion, so I smiled at them and even made Charlie sit up, so that he was in shot too. One chap, clearly a movie-maker, even started to speak to me in what might have been Spanish, but might not. I replied in English, and he beamed.

'You tourist, too?' he asked, still filming. 'How long you in Spain? We here for seven days?'

'No,' I replied. 'I've lived here for seven years.'

'Ah, you lucky, nice place.'

It was only when he moved on that I realised there was one person among them who was not Japanese, or even Asian. I knew from his total lack of a tan that he was a northern European. He wouldn't see fifty again, but he looked in decent shape, and he still had most of his hair, even if it was mostly grey.

Two other facts grabbed my attention and gave it a squeeze: one, he was looking at me, not curiously, but as if he was weighing me up; two, he was more than vaguely familiar. I knew this guy from somewhere. I tried to work out the context; not Spanish, that was for sure. I could recall everyone I'd met during the time I did my trade ambassador job for the government out of the Barcelona consulate. Not family, no way; I only have one cousin, and he's not likely to show up anywhere any time soon. Not foreign, US or Canada. Not recent, but not childhood either. Not friendly; bad associations, but not a bad guy. Authority? Maybe. Scotland? Yes. Glasgow? No. Edinburgh . . .

Ricky Ross! It was Ricky bloody Ross, not a scrap of doubt about it. Slightly portlier than I remembered him and more casually dressed, in grey flannels and a white short-sleeved shirt that might as well have had M&S embroidered on the breast pocket, but that's who it was.

A name from way, way back in my past, more than fifteen years ago. Finally I remembered him. Oh, did I ever remember him. I'd met him on the very day that I met Oz, in a pub called Whigham's in Charlotte Square in Edinburgh. He'd been a detective superintendent then, the hottest cop on the local force, and a cert to be a chief constable, some day, somewhere, they said.

A day or so later, I'd seen him again, from a distance, and that was the last time I'd clapped eyes on the man.

That glorious career of his had gone swirling down the drain as a result of him making a complete Horlicks of a murder

investigation, one in which Oz and I were more than peri-
pherally involved. In fact, Ross had been fairly convinced that
we had done it, an idea that he could not get out of his head,
even after the victim's wife had been arrested for the crime.

It wasn't the wrongful accusation that did for him, though.
No, it was the fact that he'd been having an affair with the
lady in question.

That circumstance didn't just destroy his credibility. It
even had him added to the list of suspects for a while. Before
too long the chief constable of the day realised that his protégé
was beyond protection, and handed Ricky the pearl-handled
revolver and the keys to the library, in the form of a very early
retirement package.

It took him a little while, I'd heard, but he had rebounded
from the disaster, setting up a private security firm, one that
had probity written all over it, unlike some others in that
sector in Scotland.

Certainly, it had been respectable enough for Miles, my
brother-in-law, to hire him and his team to 'mind' a movie he
was shooting in Edinburgh. It was one of Oz's early film
ventures, and that's where he and Ross met up again.

They were never going to be bosom buddies, but as I
understood it they did become friends of a sort, and that would
have been why he'd been hired subsequently to look after the
Loch Lomond estate, while Oz, Susie and the family were
away, as they were quite often, either in Monaco, or when the
kids were pre-school and he took them all on location with him.

The Japanese were summoned back to their guide by a

whistle blast. As they moved away, the ex-cop came towards me.

'We're both right about each other, aren't we?' he said as he approached. 'It is Primavera . . . What do you call yourself these days?

'Blackstone. We weren't married when Oz died, as you'll know, but I kept his surname.'

'For sentimental reasons?'

'Possibly, but it's mainly for the children's sake. All three are under my wing now.'

'Well, I'm pleased to meet you again, Mrs Blackstone.'

'Primavera will do,' I told him, 'although I have to point out that our first meeting wasn't exactly the friendliest. But that apart, Mr Ross,' I continued, 'what brings you here? Are you a tourist like our Japanese friends, and if so is Mrs Ross back at the hotel? Or did you just get on the wrong bus at the airport?'

'That was another world, and I apologise for getting the wrong idea about you two.' He extended a hand, and we shook. 'Likewise, it's Ricky,' he said, then shook his head. 'None of the above, I'm afraid. I'm here on business and Alison, that's Mrs Ross, is back in Edinburgh.'

'But your business is security, isn't it? How does that apply here?'

'It's a long story,' he replied, 'and this looks like your coffee break. Plus I have to take care of some stuff, calls and the like. Would you like to have lunch with me, in a couple of hours? I'll explain then.'

Four

I spent the rest of the morning feeding sheets, pillow cases and clothes into the tumble dryer, and getting myself into a presentable condition for my unexpected lunch date. As I did so I realised that in my moodiness, I'd let myself go to seed, but just a little, nothing that couldn't be fixed quickly.

I didn't go too far, though, only some nail varnish and a very light application of lippie, plus I teased my hair just a little, to cover the fact that it was overdue a trim. I didn't overdress, but I didn't underdress either. Normally I'd have worn shorts in the warm September weather; that day I chose a skirt, but one that stopped just short of being frumpy.

I was at a table in La Terrassa d'Empúries, with a fed, watered and placid Charlie at my feet, when Ross came up the slope and into the square. He was still dressed in M&S finest, but the shirt had changed from white to pale green, and his eyes were shaded, by a pair of Ray-Bans.

'Are the sunglasses for work purposes?' I asked him, as he

took the seat opposite mine. 'To make recognition more difficult?'

He smiled. 'Sometimes,' he replied, 'but not today.' He glanced down at Charlie. 'Nice dog. Is he your minder?'

'He has enough trouble minding his manners,' I retorted. 'As a guard dog he's all sound and no substance, I'm afraid. My minder-in-chief is my son Tom, but this is one of his days for just being an ordinary kid. He's at school with his brother and sister.'

'You said you had them all, didn't you.' A frown showed above the shades. 'Susie's death was a real tragedy. It was big news in Scotland when it happened given her business profile, not to mention the fact that she was Oz's widow. I met her, of course, through looking after the Loch Lomond place for them, and the kids, although they were much younger then. How are they these days?'

'They're bigger, but wiser in too many of the ways of the world, unfortunately. They're okay, though. Their childhood's been a real mix so far, especially for Janet and wee Jonathan, from wealthy parents, yet losing not one but both of them.'

'But lucky to have you.' He glanced around. 'And to be brought up in this place; it's beautiful. A far cry from Loch Lomond.' He paused. 'I did not like that house, you know. There was something about it that gave me the creeps.'

'Me too.'

He stared at me. 'You were there? I thought that . . .'

'Was very definitely Oz and Susie's place? It was, but I did visit there once.' At once I wished I hadn't mentioned it, for that was not one of the happiest times of my life, or for that matter the smartest.

I was pleased when Ricky changed the subject. 'How's things now? Still single?'

I nodded. 'I reckon I always will be. There is a man, though, an old friend of Oz's, Liam Matthews . . .'

'I know him,' he volunteered. 'He had a part in that Edinburgh movie Oz did. He was a wrestler, wasn't he?'

'That's right, but not any more. He and I had some time together, but he's gone off for a while, to get on with his life.'

'Didn't fancy being a father of three? Was that it? As I remember he was a bit of a playboy. There was this woman, worked for me at the time . . .'

To my surprise, I found myself laughing. 'I don't think I want to know about that, Ricky. He still has clothes in my wardrobe. Anyway, he'd happily admit to having been all that and worse, but he's changed; he's much more responsible now. When the family grew, he had no problem with it, and the kids love him. But he's got commitments outside St Martí, and outside Spain.'

That was as far as I wanted to go, so I changed the subject. 'How about you?' I asked, just as Cisco, the proprietor, appeared at our table, wearing an expectant expression, and a uniform with a Saltire badge I'd given him fastened to the lapel. I know the menu by heart, so I ordered a salad, with pasta and smoked salmon; Ricky took a minute or two but settled on a pizza.

'And to drink?'

'Canya, *si 's plau*,' I replied.

'What's that?' my companion asked.

'That's a beer, to you.'

'Fine, that'll do me as well. About me?' he repeated as Cisco left.

'Yes. I know nothing about you, remember, other than that you once wanted to lock me up for a murder your fancy woman wound up being accused of. Do you have any kids?'

'She didn't do it either,' he said, firmly. 'Officially it's still an open case, and it'll never be closed; ancient history. As for me, yes, I have a son and a daughter from my first marriage. Richard's twenty-nine, and lives in Australia. Judy's twenty-seven and works in marketing in Edinburgh, for a big whisky firm.'

'You said this morning that your wife's name is Alison. So you didn't marry that harridan that may or may not have knifed her husband . . .'

'Linda Kane? Hell no. The last thing she ever said to me was, "I'll cut your fucking heart out," not the smartest remark from a woman suspected of stabbing her old man to death. No, a couple of years after that, Linda landed herself a big-bonus corporate banker and she's been making his life miserable ever since. Mind you, the view around town these days is that it serves the bastard right, given his profession.'

'So they never did find out who killed her husband?' I asked, hoping that I sounded as innocent as I had been.

'No, but the stockbroking firm he was with went down the toilet not long after that, and all sorts of stuff came out.

The guy who took over my job decided that an angry client was behind the murder, but he never did find out which one.'

I was very happy to move on from there, knowing that his successor couldn't have been further off the mark. 'It must have been tough to see someone in your old office,' I murmured. 'Did you ever think about trying to rejoin the police? I'm told that's possible now.'

'Yes,' he admitted, 'and I could have, once the martinet of a chief who crucified me retired and an old pal of mine took over. What stopped me was the fact that I was making more dosh by then as a security consultant than I ever did as a copper. It was the right call, for business has improved since then.'

'I'm glad to hear it. Which of your clients has sent you out here? And why?'

Before he could answer, Cisco's head waiter appeared at our table carrying a tray loaded with two round chilled goblets of golden beer.

As the man left, Ricky looked me in the eye. 'Does the name Jack Weighley mean anything to you? Living out here, I can imagine that it might not.'

'You must be joking,' I retorted. 'The Flying Scotsman? Who hasn't heard of him?'

'One Jack Weighley, there's only one Jack Weighley'. That's what they sing on the terraces of the football club he owns, and they are so bloody right. Oh, I knew of him all right: the whole world knew him as a Scottish business hero, the man who started his working life in his early twenties with one tour bus, grew it into a fleet, diversified into the motor trade, then sold out and took to the air, buying the remnants of a failed airline, rebranding it as WeighleyAir and turning it into one of the most successful low-cost carriers in the world, bigger than any of its competitors, even the one with the harp on the tail of its aircraft.

Jack Weighley: a man so outspoken that there was no middle ground when considering his personality. You either loved Jack, or you hated him. Most Scots were in the former group; I was among the minority, for personal reasons.

As I've mentioned, a few years ago, I was given a job by Her Majesty's Government, acting as an ambassador in Catalunya, for Scottish goods and services. They did it to appease the Nationalists in the Edinburgh parliament, rather than out of any Westminster commitment to the Scottish economy, but I didn't care about that, for I enjoyed the work, for a while, until I felt it was affecting Tom. As soon as that happened I quit.

Before then, though, I'd had the 'honour' of an audience with Jack Weighley, at a meeting in Barcelona with the state monopoly company that runs virtually all of the country's airports. I'd arranged the damn gathering, which was to confirm the granting to WeighleyAir of a couple of dozen European routes, out of five new Spanish bases.

I'd done much of the development work too, going way beyond my Catalan brief to spread the WeighleyAir message all across Spain and to escort the airline's operations manager all around the country to inspect the facilities on offer.

I met Weighley for the first and only time in his hotel in Barcelona in advance of the meeting. The guy is eight years younger than I am, and yet he treated me like some bloody agency escort woman.

When the local UK consul introduced me, his first words to me were, 'Get me a coffee, please, there's a good girl.' At the meeting he used me as a translator into Catalan, and that was all. I knew all the guys on the other side of the table; indeed, I was part of the reason for them being there, but Jack the Lad swanned in there, his fake blond Freddy Starr bouffant perfectly arranged, gave them his own sales pitch, screwed an extra five per cent discount in landing charges from them . . . I'd already negotiated thirty per cent, them having started at fifteen . . . signed on the dotted line, then swanned out again, straight into a press conference at which the deal was announced, to a fanfare.

I hadn't anticipated any thanks for doing my job, but neither did I expect him to hiss, 'Why the fuck didn't you get forty per cent out of them? I was fucking hamstrung in there!'

He was handing me a glass of champagne at the time, and pretending to smile, for the benefit of everyone else in the room. I took it from him, poured it into the breast pocket of his powder-blue suit, shoved the glass back into his manicured paw, and walked out.

The British Ambassador was there and followed me from the room. He wasn't pleased. I dared him to fire me, and handle the publicity that I'd make sure would follow. He didn't take me up on it.

'So,' I said to Ricky, quietly, 'Jack Weighley's your client?'

'Yeah.'

'How do you find him?'

'I find him guilty of being a chromium-plated shit,' he replied, comforting me at once. 'But the money's good, and Alison's firm has much of WeighleyAir's PR business, so I put up with him.'

'What does your outfit do for him?'

'We're responsible for the security of his offices in South Queensferry, and for his aircraft in the new operating base that he set up in East Lothian and in other Scottish airports. He also uses me as a troubleshooter; that's why he's got me over here.'

'Are you saying Weighley's in Spain just now?' I had a sudden vision of him walking into the square and seeing me there. I wouldn't have minded that, but Ricky knocked it on the head.

'Hell, no. This is the last place Jack would come at the moment. He's paranoid about his own safety . . . with some reason, for the little bastard upsets people everywhere he goes.'

'Are you saying he thinks that he'd be in danger here?'

My scornful incredulity must have been obvious, for Ross smiled as he shook his head. 'I don't believe so, not for a minute, but he does and that's all that matters. To be fair to him, there have been a couple of things happened recently that have wound him up. Two of his aircraft were vandalised on the ground at Girona Airport during the night. It was pretty crude stuff; both of them were graffitied, covered all over with

Catalan independence slogans, plus things like *"mierdas Escocés"*, whatever that means, and the second one had its tyres ripped as well.

'The local police reckon it was no more serious than an ex-employee getting his own back for being fired . . . and WeighleyAir does have a big turnover in staff, believe me . . . but in Jack's mind it was attempted sabotage, full-scale, an attempt by his competitors to scare away his customers.'

'And if he's right?' I asked. 'Oz's dad's coming out here in a couple of days. I don't want him at risk.'

'There is no risk, I promise,' Ricky assured me. 'Ex-Superintendent Ross is on the case. Weighley's sent me out here to take charge of the situation, as he put it. My instructions are to arrange to take over security for WeighleyAir within Girona Airport and at our other Spanish bases if necessary . . . although we've had no trouble anywhere else . . . and to make sure that the local bobbies are taking it seriously enough.'

'Take over security?' I repeated. 'The airport operators won't wear that for a minute, will they?'

'You'd be surprised what they'll wear, Primavera,' he said. 'I thought the same as you, but I was wrong. They gave me a warm welcome. You see, since the Irish operator took the huff and dropped Girona, WeighleyAir's had a very strong hand of cards, and believe me, our Jack knows how to play them.

'The airport people are quite happy for me to put a full-time manager on the ground to oversee their security staff. In fact they've even issued a press release to say that it's happening, and Alison's firm has done the same thing in the UK.'

'That's the airport, fine,' I murmured. 'I can see them going for it, if only so they can have someone else to blame for every wee incident from now on. But the police, they'll be another matter, surely.'

'No,' Risky insisted. 'The cops were more than happy to see me too. They've had the British Embassy giving them all sorts of grief. It seems that the government dances to Jack's tune just as lively as the rest of us. I saw the top man in the Catalan force . . . what do you call it again?'

'The Mossos d'Esquadra.'

'That's right: the Vulture Squadron, or something like that. I saw him in Barcelona yesterday morning. He practically rolled out the red carpet for me. They're going to help me recruit a man for the airport job. They've even given me a list of approved candidates from their own staff, people nearing or just past retirement.'

I frowned, and took a flyer. 'One of them isn't called Hector Gomez, is he?'

He looked at me, surprised. 'As a matter of fact there is one by that name. The boss man told me he retired early on health grounds a year ago, but that he's fit enough for the job, as long as it doesn't involve chasing people. Why? Do you know him?'

'Yup.' Intendant Gomez and I had met on a few occasions, not always on the best of terms. He'd been my friend Alex Guinart's old boss before his heart scare; Alex had stepped into his shoes when he'd taken early retirement. 'I do indeed,' I said. 'He's a serious man, is Hector. He's a very sound operator.'

'Does he speak English?'

'A lot better than you speak Spanish,' I chuckled, 'since you don't even seem to know that *"mierdas Escocés"* means "Scottish shit". No, seriously, his English is good enough for the two of you to be able to communicate as well as you need to.'

Ricky nodded. 'Thanks for that. I'll put him at the top of the list, then. To be honest with you, he was their top pick too; you've reassured me that they weren't just trying to palm a mate off on to me. I'll give him a call later on and ask him if he'd like to meet me to discuss it.'

I was sure that he would, even if I decided not to say so, in case it weakened Gomez's negotiating hand when it came to money. Alex had told me that his old boss hated retirement, not least because his wife didn't have a job, and was making it her full-time business to make sure he did healthy things, for example gardening and playing golf, both of which he also hated.

'That's fine for the two of you,' I said, instead. 'But it leaves one thing unexplained. Why the hell are you here? The people you're dealing with here are in Girona and Barcelona, yet you show up out of the blue in St Martí, and here we are parked at a restaurant table right in front of my house. That's no coincidence, chum.'

He smiled. 'No, it's not. Call it nostalgia, if you like, but while I was here I decided I'd like to see how you and your lad were making out. I saw a piece in the *Herald* business section a couple of years ago. It was about Susie, and it mentioned that she was living full-time in Monaco . . . with her two children, it said.

'From that I worked out . . . . old detectives never die, remember; they just don't have a clue any more . . . that Tom must be with you. Oz and I were maybe better friends than you know, and I just felt, well, that it's something he'd have wanted me to do.'

'How did you know where to find us?'

'I Googled you. There isn't a lot about you, you'll probably be glad to hear, given your brief difficulty with the law in Scotland, but there was a link to your sister, and her husband, Miles Grayson. That led to a report in a top people's magazine about him buying a wine producer in this part of Spain.

'Oz told me quite a bit about his past life, so I knew that this place had meaning for you. So I took a gamble, phoned the town hall in L'Escala and asked if they knew of you.

'They told me, politely, to eff off. To a guy like me that's as good as saying, "Yes, we know her," so I drove up here, and booked myself into a hotel on the seafront in the town, something Mar, it's called. I asked the people there if they knew you, and they suggested that I should come along here. I struck it lucky.' He smiled, quietly. 'I'd very much like to meet the youngsters again, by the way. They were all pre-school last time I saw them, in Scotland. Any chance?'

'I don't see why not. No dodgy stories about their father and me, mind. How long are you staying for?'

'I like the hotel,' he replied. 'They gave me a nice

suite with a sea view so I'm planning to stay there until I get Girona sorted out, and get that manager in place.'

'That'll give us a few days then. Come up for a drink one evening, maybe tomorrow. Mac's arriving on Wednesday, so they'll be fully occupied then. Call me tonight, once the kids are back from school, and we'll fix something up.'

'That would be nice.' He killed what was left of his beer, just as our lunch arrived. 'Which is your house?' he asked.

I pointed towards it. 'That's it, right next to the church, on the left.'

'Bloody hell! That's . . .'

'It's a nice big family home, that's all, and as of last year it needed to be.'

There wasn't much conversation over lunch. I didn't mind that because I didn't want to revisit most of the experiences that he and I had in common. There have been many times when I've kicked the thought around that if my flight home from my nursing job in Africa had been delayed by another few hours, I wouldn't have walked through that door at that time, I wouldn't have met Oz Blackstone, and my life would have been very different and probably very ordinary. I'd either have wound up bored, frustrated, and single, or bored, frustrated and married to some bloody doctor I'd found in some bloody hospital, with a couple of swotty kids at Heriot's or Watson's or Fettes if he was rich enough.

Given the choice? Don't be daft; I might do some things differently given a second chance, but I'll never regret walking through that door when I did.

'This has been a very pleasant lunch,' Ricky declared, as we finished, and he paid the bill. 'I hope it hasn't disrupted your day too much.'

'Not a bit,' I replied cheerfully. 'It's been good for me to learn that you're not the bogey man I thought you were.'

I put Charlie in our garden, where his kennel is, then walked with my visitor out of the village, past Ben Simmers' shop and down the slope, towards the park where he said he'd left his car.

'I can understand why you settled here,' he said, as we reached the road. 'In fact, I'm having trouble understanding why you and Oz ever left.'

'That's several long stories,' I replied. 'Yes, this might be an ideal place for a forty-something single mother who doesn't need to worry about money to raise her kids, but for the volatile couple that he and I were, there was never going to be a paradise, anywhere.

'We were fucked up when we were here, Ricky, both of us. Neither one of us had any sense of purpose in life, or any plan for the future. Now I do, and that makes all the difference. But I don't have him, and that's the only cloud in my sky.'

'That's interesting,' he murmured. 'You know the whole world thinks that you and he were a two-person disaster area, but that's not really true, is it?'

I disagreed. 'Oh no, we probably were, but what's also true is that once we met, I was never very good at living without him, not until Tom came along, and even then I made an arse of it for a while. It's a miracle he's growing up so well-adjusted.

'As for Oz, though, that's another matter. Maybe we couldn't keep our hands off each other whenever we were together . . . but when we weren't, the sod got along without me perfectly well.'

'Don't be so sure.'

I stared at him. 'What makes you say that?'

'Nothing specific,' he admitted. 'Probably nothing more than the way he looked and sounded when he spoke about you. Even when he was calling you all the names under the sun,' he chuckled, 'there was a something in his eyes, as if another part of him was saying, "Aye, but she's my scheming manipulative little bitch!"'

'There's an old story about an English footballer who was being kicked all around the park by his Scottish marker. After the tenth or eleventh time, the Englishman picked himself up and shouted at the guy, "See you? You're just a big Scots bastard!" and the Jock gave him a toothless grin and said, "Aye, and don't you forget it." That's the sort of look Oz had in his eye when he talked about you; pride of a sort.'

I felt myself go squidgy inside. 'Did he indeed?' We had reached the hut at the entrance to the car park, where they give out the tickets through a window and collect the money through a door on the other side.

'Yes he did,' Ricky said. 'You know what else I think?'

'Do tell.'

'I think that part of Oz, maybe the bit that was his mother's son, I don't know, thought he should have a nice, quiet, well-ordered domestic life, just like his mum and dad. He went for it with the first lass, Jan, the girl who died, the one who gave me the runaround in Edinburgh that time when I was after you two. Later on he did the same with Susie. He played happy families, but now I think that was like a part in a movie for him.

'Now, looking back . . . and remember, Primavera, it was part of my job to read people . . . I'm convinced that the real guy didn't want that at all, and that he never really fitted the part. The real guy wanted you all along, because you weren't safe and sound like that; you were the opposite. You gave him a buzz and he was hooked on it, till he died.'

'I'm like that now; nice and well-ordered; playing happy families and loving it.'

'Are you? Are you really?'

'What do you mean?'

'I mean that you've still got it, that air of . . . let's give it a shot!'

'No I don't,' I protested. 'I'm a middle-aged mum.'

His laugh boomed out. 'So was Maggie Thatcher, once. I'm telling you, Primavera, you've still got the spark about you that made you and Oz a couple.'

'Ach, away with you, man. Whatever you think, my wayward days are over.'

'Maybe that makes you even more formidable.'

I laughed at his insistence. 'Go on, Mr Ross,' I chuckled. 'Bugger off.'

The car park was busy, but not full, as it would be in July and August. I watched him as he walked across to his hire car.

It was a green Seat Ibiza. I've never seen anyone driving a green car that was their own; my theory is that they're all bought by rental companies, because nobody's going to nick anything that colour.

I smiled as he walked up to the passenger door, bent to open it, and then remembered that it was left-hand drive. He corrected his mistake, climbed in and switched on the engine. I waved to him and turned away.

I hadn't gone very far when I heard a shout from behind me. 'Primavera!' I looked over my shoulder to see Ricky trotting towards me. Behind him his car door lay wide open, I could see from the exhaust's slight emissions that the engine was still running.

'You said I was to call you,' he said as he reached me, 'but you didn't give me your phone number.' As he spoke, there came the sound of yet another mighty bang. 'Bloody hell,' he laughed, 'the people around here surely do like their fireworks. But during the day?'

He was looking at me, but I was staring back over his shoulder. My eyes must have been wide, and possibly my mouth was hanging open too, for his expression changed and he turned to follow my gaze.

The green Seat Ibiza was no longer green. It wasn't much of anything really, just a mass of twisted metal in the midst of a ball of flame.

We stood there in silence, the two of us, while people scattered all around us. Marc, the man who'd been on duty in the car park, was the only person who didn't run for his life, apart from us, that is. Instead, he produced a fire extinguisher from the hut and started towards the burning car.

'No,' Ricky shouted. He sprinted after him, with a surprising turn of speed for a man of his age, hitting him with an all-embracing rugby tackle and bringing him to the ground, just as the heat ignited the vapour within the petrol tank and a second explosion erupted, quieter than the first, but with a bigger fireball, engulfing the tree under which the Seat had been parked.

'Bloody hell,' he murmured as I reached the two of them, and helped the winded Marc to his feet. 'Okay, there was nobody around to give me a ticket when I drove in here, but that's a bit extreme. Couldn't they just use wheel clamps?'

Five

There was nothing to be done for the tree, or for a couple on either side of it, but fortunately no other vehicles were close enough to catch fire. I called the emergency services number from my mobile, and the police, both the municipals and the Mossos, were there within minutes.

The firefighters took a little longer, but our town's service is staffed by volunteers so that was to be expected.

When I told Ricky that the Catalan word for 'fireman' is 'bomber', he muttered something terse and appropriate. He did his best not to show it, but he was shaken up, no doubt about it. So was Marc; he's not a small man, but even so, Ricky, who, I recalled from the mists of time, had been a top rugby player in his youth, had fairly hammered him into the ground.

The first cops there cleared the area of the gawpers who'd arrived in their dozens from the beach and the village, so many of them that they were blocking the access road. It's funny, people's first reaction is always flight, but once the action's over they'll always come back to stare at the wreckage, and even at the casualties if there are any.

When I told the officer in charge that I'd made the call and whose car it was that had gone up, she asked me to take Ricky back up into the square and wait there until she was ready to speak to him. I did what she asked, but I knew that any investigation would be out of her hands pretty quickly, so I anticipated that by calling Alex Guinart, on his mobile.

Alex is a detective; as such he works irregular hours, and I happened to know that he had Monday off. He wasn't at home, though, when I called. No, Gloria had dragooned him into doing the supermarket run with her, so he was actually pleased when I broke into his day, just as he was getting out of his car outside Bonpreu. He drove her and my goddaughter Marte home, full of apologies no doubt, then headed up to St Martí.

The panic was over and the fire was extinguished by the time he arrived in the square with his uniformed colleague, the woman I'd spoken to earlier. We'd gone back to our earlier table. I'd reckoned Ricky needed another beer, but I was wrong. Actually he needed several; the reality of what had happened, and the shock, had caught up with him. He was on his third canya by the time the two cops arrived.

The uniform was a sub-inspector, by the name of Borras. She seemed keen and I got the impression that she would have liked to hang around after I'd made the introductions, but Alex wasn't having that. He told her to go back down to the park and wait for the scientific team that he'd summoned.

'Scientists?' she repeated, looking at him, eyebrow raised. 'Do we need them here, chief? We know what's happened. A car caught fire, that's all.'

'Do you have a qualification in any form of forensic investigation, Maria?' he asked her, patiently.

'No, but . . .'

'No, and neither have I. So yes, we need them here. Yes, it may be there was a spontaneous fire in the gentleman's car, probably was, but I can't look at it and tell one way or the other, any more than you can. Now do as I ask, please. Go down and wait for Gemma Sierra and her team.'

She looked disappointed, but she nodded and left. Ricky had been looking at them both, blankly. The conversation had been in Catalan, which more often than not confuses the hell out of tourists who assume that their Spanish phrase book will see them all right.

'So, Señor Ross,' my friend continued, switching to English as he settled into a chair at our table, 'who the hell have you pissed off?'

'Or could your colleague have been right,' I asked him, 'could it really have been spontaneous? An oil leak dripping on to a hot pipe, smouldering for a while then catching fire?'

Alex raised an eyebrow. 'A few seconds after your friend switched on the engine? You were looking at it, Primavera, from what you said to me when you called. Now, replay it in your mind and tell me. What do you see happen?'

I frowned and tried to recall everything I'd seen in detail.

'No,' I admitted, after not very long. 'It's unlikely, very unlikely, that it was just a fire, for one simple reason: the explosion came before the flames.'

'Thank you. So my question stands, señor. If you hadn't got out of that car to speak to Primavera, as she told me you did, you'd be a dead man and I'd have a murder investigation on my hands. Who'd want to blow you up?'

'I could give you the names of half a dozen people who'd like to see me dead, straight off the top of my head,' Ricky told him.

'You have that many enemies?' Alex's smile showed a little scepticism, but Ricky didn't seem to notice, as he nodded, vigorously.

'More than my share,' he declared. 'But so have you, I'll bet, for the same reason.'

My friend's expression changed, as if he'd just shaken hands with a brother mason. 'You were a police officer?' he exclaimed.

'Yes. For my sins and those of others, I was a detective, like you, in Edinburgh; that's where I met Primavera. I was a superintendent when I retired.'

'Then you were an important man; that's a higher rank than mine. When did you leave the police?'

'Around fifteen years ago: early retirement, they called it . . . very early.'

Alex's eyebrows rose. 'Indeed. You must have been very young to be pensioned off . . . unless of course you're older than you look.'

'I'm fifty-five,' Ricky retorted. 'Let's just say I had enemies within my force as well as on the outside, and I gave them an excuse to push me.'

'What sort of excuse?'

He smiled, amiably. 'Mind your own fucking business.'

Alex chuckled. 'Señor Ross, you are the very man who should know that in a serious crime investigation, everything is my fucking business.'

'Touché,' my compatriot conceded. 'I remember saying that very thing myself to reluctant witnesses. Okay, let's just say that my dick got me into trouble.'

'Your . . .' He broke off as the centivo dropped. 'You screwed your boss's wife?'

Ricky snorted. 'Hell no! I doubt that even my boss did that. No, the woman I was involved with was a murder suspect, or would have been if I'd been doing my job properly. But it's all ancient history, and there's no way it could have anything to do with what happened just now.'

'Okay, if you say so. But would any of those enemies within your force want to kill you now?'

'Nah, not a chance; there never was. There only were a couple and they're both in their seventies now; one was the chief constable, and the other was his deputy. They were just happy to see my bubble burst. They were old school and they didn't like cops like me, university types.'

He paused to drain some beer, and as he did his eyes narrowed. 'But outside, now, that's different matter. Over the last five years of my career we had major drug gangs operating

63

in the city, and I led the team that went after them. I put away five of the main dealers, for long stretches.'

'How long?'

'Between twelve and twenty years; they're all out now. The last of the five was released on parole two years ago.' He paused, and his eyes went somewhere else for a while. 'Not that I'm blowing my own trumpet too loud,' he added. 'There were bigger people than them, Ronnie Roy in Edinburgh and Kenny McLeish in Glasgow, that we never laid a glove on. They've moved on and up since then.' He hesitated again. 'In fact . . .'

'Do you know where they are, the people you did catch?' Alex asked, cutting off his reminiscence.

'One of them's driving a bus in Edinburgh. I know that because he had the cheek to ask me for a reference. I told him to bugger off but they employed him anyway.

'Another, a guy called Grant Donaldson, wrote a true crime book about his days as a dealer. He was stupid enough to name a couple of people and got himself shot as a result. He's not dead, but he might as well be; he's in a chronic vegetative state.

'A third was an informer, what the tabloids in Britain love to call a supergrass. He did four years out of the fourteen the judge gave him, in solitary all the time, then he was given a new identity and relocated to New Zealand. But he left with none of the proceeds of his crime, and I was responsible for that. He's on the other side of the world, though, unless he's managed to get himself a false passport, for he isn't allowed a genuine one.

'A fourth guy, James Cockburn, the one who was paroled last, he's different. He threatened my wife in the street, a week after he was released.'

'I assume that he was taken back to prison, and can be discounted.'

Ricky shook his head. 'No, I handled that in another way. As a result, I don't believe that he's a threat.'

Alex frowned. 'What did you do?'

'Let's not go there.'

'I may have to.'

'Then you'll be wasting your time. All I'll say is that I have friends as well as enemies, and they're a fucking sight more effective than parole officers.'

My friend drew a breath. 'In that case, why mention him to me at all?'

'I'm doing you the courtesy of assuming that you're a good detective, and that you'll be doing your own digging. If you ask the people in Edinburgh to compile a list of suspects, his name will be on it. I'm telling you to cross him off it, that's all.'

'Professional courtesy?'

'Yeah, you can call it that. The fact is, I don't believe that any of the four people on my list of five had anything to do with this. Indeed, I know they didn't.'

'And the other one?'

'His name is William Rodger: I have no idea where he is.'

'Then I had better find out,' Alex declared. 'Who would be the best person for me to contact in your former force?'

Ricky killed his beer and waved for another. 'Listen, Intendant, let's not go off at half cock here.'

Alex stared at him, bewildered, as his colloquial English failed him. 'He means that you shouldn't rush into things,' I explained.

'Ah,' he chuckled, 'I see. And why not, señor?'

'Well, first off, let's wait for your forensic people to determine whether you are looking at the scene of a crime or an accident. We all know which is the likelier, but you're in the business of proof. If they do determine that, the field of potential perpetrators may be a little wider than your first assumption.'

He glanced at me, as the latest beer arrived. 'Primavera, have you told your friend why I'm here?'

'No. That's your business, not mine.'

'Business that I did not take very seriously, until about an hour ago.'

He launched into the tale of the vandalising of WeighleyAir aircraft on the ground at Girona and Jack Weighley's extreme reaction.

'As of yesterday,' he concluded, 'I had all but finished my arrangements here, just one thing left to do, but after this incident I have to consider whether my excitable client might not be paranoid after all, and whether his airline is under a genuine threat. And if I have to consider that then, pal, so do you.'

Six

Ricky's bombshell . . . nice choice of metaphor, Primavera . . . rocked Alex, visibly. 'Surely that can't be,' he exclaimed. 'I know about those incidents at the airport; my colleagues in the Mossos d'Esquadra looked into them, and let me know their findings. They were acts of simple vandalism, they were certain.

'WeighleyAir dismissed a couple of young cabin crew, Spanish nationals, one for turning up too late for a flight on three occasions, and the other for being rude to passengers. My fellow investigators checked them both out when the damage was done. The sleepy one, Oscar Rivera, got himself a job straight away in a hotel in Andorra . . . for more money, too . . . and he was there when both incidents happened, so we can forget about him.

'As for the other, Gaizka Alonso, that's different. He was seen by a witness, in the airport groundside bar, on the night when the tyres were exploded. He was taken in for questioning. He denied having anything to do with it, and gave them a story

67

about having gone to the airport to see a woman he wanted to ask out on a date, only she wasn't there that night so he had a couple of drinks and went home. That's what he said.'

'And the investigators believed that?'

Alex snorted. 'No, not for a second. He couldn't even remember the woman's name. But there were no witnesses to place him anywhere but the bar that night, nobody to say he was anywhere near the aircraft. There wasn't enough evidence for the prosecutor to start a proceeding against him, although my colleagues were sure it was him who did the thing. However their opinion was that it was a small-time grudge; there was property damage, yes, but nothing that can relate to what just happened here.'

'No?' Ricky murmured.

'No, absolutely not. I read their report and I spoke to the guy who wrote it. They thought Alonso was an idiot, no more.'

'Well, something relates to it, for sure.' Ricky hesitated, as if he was choosing his next words and weighing them carefully, knowing that they were important.

'I hope it's not the case, Intendant,' he began, slowly, 'that your force is going to leap to the conclusion that this is something that I've brought with me, personally. If you do, I'm going to find that difficult to accept.

'Yes, I made enemies during my time in the police force, and one or two of them might want to see me dead, but only in their dreams, and I certainly wouldn't expect any of them to try it here. If anyone wanted to kill me, they'd do it in Edinburgh, but the fact is I don't actually walk around there looking over my shoulder. I might be careful using a street crossing in front of a bus, just in case the wrong guy's driving it and hits the accelerator instead of the brake, but honestly I don't feel at risk in my home city.'

'Señor,' Alex pointed out, 'you just told ne that a man threatened your wife.'

'That was a one-off, a nutter. As I told you,' he pointed in the general direction of the car park, 'that was not his doing.'

'How can you be so sure?'

Ricky looked him in the eye. 'What would you do if someone threatened your wife?' he asked.

Alex winced, and averted his eyes. 'I don't know,' he murmured.

'I fucking do. Trust me, Cockburn didn't plant that bomb, or order it done.' He paused. 'There's an officer in my old force, one of my protégés: Detective Superintendent Ron Morrow.' He dug out his mobile, fiddled with it, then produced a pen and scribbled a number on a paper napkin. 'That's his mobile number. Call him, tell him what's happened and ask him to look through my past history for a list of potential bombers.'

'Won't he need a more official request than that?'

'Not when you mention my name, he won't. He'll give it priority, and get back to you within twenty-four hours. Mind you, I still think he'll be back to you with fuck all. I was targeted here, not in Scotland, make no mistake about it.'

'But why? Why you? With respect, you're . . .'

'Not a likely target for a Spanish hitman? No, probably not, but my client, he could well be. He spends his life pissing people off. Most recently he seems to have pissed off this Gaizka bloke, if your guys are right about him having done the things at the airport. Yes it's a step up from bursting a couple of aircraft tyres to a car bomb, but if he is a psycho, in my experience it wouldn't be unusual for him to display a pattern of escalating acts of violence.'

'In mine too,' Alex conceded, 'but why you? Indeed, how did he even know you were here?'

'There's a simple answer to both. Jack Weighley isn't exactly reclusive, nor is he one for turning the other cheek. The story about the tyres made the press here and in Scotland. They'd hardly been replaced before he issued a statement to the press and on his website saying that he was sending his right-hand man . . . which I'm not, but he's a bullshitter . . . to Spain on the first plane to oversee the investigation and to take charge of WeighleyAir's ground protection at Girona Airport.

'He mentioned me by name, and since I arrived I've been quoted in a couple of newspaper reports including one yesterday that I am indeed assuming control of the airline's security. *La Vanguardia* even had a nice photograph of me getting out of my fucking hire car at the airport office, the same one that's lying melted down in the car park.'

He swallowed half of his beer in a single gulp. 'So my friend,' he belched slightly, 'far be it from me to lecture an officer of your rank, so all I will do is repeat what you will know already, that criminal investigation is about eliminating every possibility one by one, until you're left with only one, in which case chances are that's who done it.

'At the moment this disenchanted former trolley wally Alonso is the only fucking possibility you seem to have, so I suggest that you get on with eliminating him fucking toot sweet.'

My friend nodded, a little stiffly. 'You're correct, señor, that probably did go without saying. Of course I will do that, and a lot more. For example I will suggest to Superintendent Morrow that as well as trying to identify threats to you personally, he opens a second line of investigation into people in your country who might have a grudge against your client, and who might think it was easier to act against him here.'

'Fair enough,' Ricky said. 'I'll be calling Jack, of course, to update him on this thing.'

'Won't you be briefing him in person?' Alex retorted. 'I've been assuming that you would want to be on the first plane back to Britain. I'm even prepared to drive you to the airport myself.'

'Shit no,' he exclaimed. 'If this is an attack on WeighleyAir, it's imperative that I stay here. As of a couple of days ago, I'm responsible for the airline's safety at that airport, personally, until I make a permanent appointment. As of now, and until further notice I'd like a constant police guard on every WeighleyAir aircraft that's parked overnight in Girona, and in every other Spanish base that we have. Can you arrange that?'

Alex whistled. 'That's a lot of manpower, and it may well be unnecessary.'

'Maybe so, but now that the request's been made, do you want to be responsible for the potential consequences of it being ignored?'

That was a no-brainer. 'No. I'll speak to my director general and pass the parcel to him. I'm sure he will do as you ask.'

'That's good. By the way, do you know a man called Hector Gomez?'

'Of course. I worked for him until he retired.'

'Is he in the market for a job, and would you stake your personal reputation on him?'

'Yes he is; I know that for a fact. And yes I would. You're talking about the airport, yes?'

'That's right. In that case he might well be the man I want,' He flipped him a card. 'I'd be grateful if you'd ask him to call me to arrange a meeting, this afternoon if possible.'

'Of course. Where, at the airport?'

Ricky shook his head. 'No, at the Nieves Mar Hotel: I'm kind of stuck for wheels at the moment.'

'You're staying there? It's rather public.'

'It suits me.'

'I'll put a guard on it, and you.'

'If you want, but there's nothing to guard while I don't have a replacement car, and when I do I'm going to be pretty fucking careful for a while before I get in, am I not? Look, this guy's no close-up threat. He's a bomber, not a shooter. He's followed me up here from Girona, you agree?'

'So it seems.'

'And that was yesterday. The car was parked in front of the

hotel all night, under CCTV, so he must have tailed me here this morning and planted his device there.

'Your forensics people will confirm this or not, but if I'm right he probably stuck it under a wheel arch on the driver's side to make all the more sure it was lethal, secured by a magnet possibly, ready to be triggered by vibration once the car was started . . . as it was.

'I attended a lecture on car bombs once, on a security course. The lecturer said that was a favourite method and it fits what happened today. As it turned out, I was lucky, and the bomber wasn't. Now he won't come within a mile of me again. For one, he'll know that you people will be watching and, two, so will I.'

'But Ricky,' I interrupted, 'what if he's not alone? What if he's part of a gang?'

'Then let them try me. I've faced down people before.' He looked at Alex. 'A firearm would be handy, though, just in case.'

'Even though you were a police officer,' he replied, 'and, I assume, trained in their use, that would be very irregular.'

'So's a car bomb. Look, I won't shoot anybody who isn't pointing a gun at me, I promise.'

'I don't know . . . I would need permission from the top.'

'Then get it. Don't tell me there aren't precedents.'

'That's right,' I pointed out. 'There must be. You know,' I added, 'there's one word that hasn't been mentioned in this discussion, and that is terrorism. I've sat here and listened to you guys personalise this for all you're worth, cops both of you, and yet neither one of you seems to have considered the possibility that the target might not have been personal but institutional. In the past, when ETA was active, it was known to do stuff to discourage tourists, like plant explosive devices on beaches.'

'That's true,' Alex murmured.

'Well, could this not be another attack on the tourist industry? I'm not saying that this is ETA back in action, but let's use them as an example. A Spanish prime minister lost an election for even suggesting that they might have been behind the Madrid bombing, so I'm not saying they would actually blow up an aircraft in flight. But they wouldn't have to, would they?

'No, all they'd have to do would be target a company heavily associated with tourism, to create a climate of mass fear and drive its customers away. And what company would be better to hit than WeighleyAir, a big pushy outfit that's currently carrying tourists into Spain from all over Europe and one that's owned by a guy who has a reputation for shooting from the lip. Do I have a point?'

Both men nodded, like synchronised divers ready for the off.

'Yup,' Ricky murmured. 'You surely do.'

'So what do you say we do?' Alex asked.

'Give Ricky a gun and keep him safe,' I told him. 'But publicly, maybe it would be better to let this have been an accident after all.'

Seven

Anyone but Alex might have dismissed me as a silly woman with an overactive imagination, but he didn't. He knew I'd been right before, with even more fanciful guesses than that one.

He thought about it for a few minutes then nodded. 'It's worthy of consideration,' he agreed. 'But it is . . . there's an English phrase you use, Primavera, about responsibility. Remind me.'

'It's way above your pay grade?' I suggested.

'Exactly so. My director general in Barcelona will agree for sure when I tell him about this. Then he will pass the problem to the Catalan government, the Generalitat. They may even bring in people from outside, if they feel that this may have implications outside Catalunya. Whatever, I'd better report immediately and let them make that decision.' He glanced at Ricky. 'As for your weapon, if the chief agrees, I'll let you have one. If not, I'll recommend that we give you an armed bodyguard.'

'You fucking won't,' he barked. 'I'm not having a nursemaid.'

Alex's eyes went all steely. 'Señor, you are in my country, and you will have what we say you will have. The alternative will be to put you on the first flight home. Am I understood?'

'We'll see,' Ricky murmured.

'We will,' Alex replied, rising to leave. He looked at Ricky again. 'Thanks for the offer of your contacts, but I won't need them. We're not so backward that we don't know how to access criminal intelligence databases, even in other countries.'

'I didn't expect your friend to be so gung-ho about it. International databases, indeed,' Ricky murmured as Alex walked away.

'Then you need a perception change,' I told him. 'This is a front-line European nation.'

'With some very strange drug laws. I was at a beach bar last night and half the folk were smoking spliffs, as far as I could see.'

'Not quite half,' I argued, 'but quite a few, I'll grant you. Smoking cannabis is a public health misdemeanour here, that's all. Nothing strange about that either. You're still a British cop at heart, with a British cop's draconian attitudes.' An earlier exchange came back to me. 'By the way, that guy you mentioned, Cockburn: why don't you think he's a threat any more?'

'Like I told him, don't ask,' he said.

I persisted. 'I just did. Go on, you can tell me.'

He sighed. 'All right, but between us: I had a word with a

couple of Jamaican guys I know in Glasgow. Drug dealers from way back, business rivals of his, but they've never been done, not least because when I nailed Cockburn, they were the people who set him up. That was never mentioned in court, though. We caught him in the act, with vast amounts of gear; he took counsel's advice and pleaded guilty. He thought he'd get a reduced sentence, but the judge whacked him regardless. He'd a long time to nurse his grudge.'

'When he got out, and threatened Alison . . . how did he know she was your wife?'

'I guess he found out where I lived and watched the house.'

'What did he say to her?' I asked.

'Something along the lines of, "You tell your man that I'm going to have him, and you too if you get in the way." Not his exact words, of course.'

'But why . . .'

'. . . not come at me direct? He didn't have the balls. Remember that old telly series, where the guy gets shot in the end and as he's dying he says, "You never hear the one that gets you"? Yeah, well, criminals are like that. If someone really means it, the victim finds out when the knife slips between his ribs or the bullet goes in the back of his head.'

'So Cockburn wasn't really a threat,' I suggested.

Ricky's eyebrows met in the middle. 'He frightened Alison; that was enough for me. So I told the Jamaicans that he was out and making trouble. I knew how they'd take it. They'd assume they'd be well up the list of people he'd want to make trouble for.'

I stared at him. 'And they'd act accordingly. Are you telling me you had him killed?'

'No, no, no. I never suggested such a thing, nor did any money change hands. He hasn't been seen around for a while, that's all.'

'Sure, he's gone for a one-way sail down the Clyde. Christ, Ricky, you've just reminded me why you were a scary copper.'

He smiled. 'Maybe, but back then I was reckless as well. Not any more.'

'So now you're in debt to Yardie drug barons?'

'Hell no. It was the other way around if anything, and now we're square.'

He picked up his glass and looked at it, as if he was contemplating a refill. He decided against, and handed the waiter a twenty-euro note as he passed our table.

'So that's Cockburn out of the picture,' he murmured, to himself more than to me. 'But I suppose I should check on Billy Rodger, just in case.' He stood, and took his change as it was handed to him. 'I'll call Ronnie Morrow from the hotel.'

He looked down at me, and grinned, wryly. 'Well,' he drawled, 'it's been an interesting day. I'll bet you're glad you came to meet me. There can't be much excitement around here.'

'You'd be surprised,' I countered. 'And it's you who should be bloody glad I came to meet you. Didn't I just save your life, when I forgot to give you my number?'

The reminder made him shiver. 'Indeed,' he conceded,

then paused. 'Which reminds me, you still haven't given it to me.'

I have some printed cards that I carry with me, with my phone numbers and email address. I took one from my bag and gave it to him. He slipped it into the pocket of his shirt, then produced one of his own from the same place and handed it to me.

'Mind you,' he said, as he did, 'tomorrow might be a non-runner, as far as meeting the family is concerned. I'll call you if I can, but if I don't manage, apologies.'

'Are you kidding?' I exclaimed. 'Do you think I don't want to know how all this turns out?'

He grinned. 'Okay, I'll call you when I can, promise.' He paused. 'Do you think your mate'll get me a firearm?'

'Honestly, Ricky? Not a chance. Cops might be armed here, and some security people that I would not personally trust with a pea-shooter, but they take a dim view of civilians carrying guns.'

'I don't suppose you've got one,' he ventured. 'Home security and all that.'

'No, I don't,' I replied. 'I have a police-monitored alarm system that's so loud it would fry your eardrums if you tripped it, so I don't need one. Do you really think you're still a target?'

He shook his head. 'No, but better safe than sorry. To be frank with you, I like your theory that it's some sort of half-arsed terrorist group trying to scare off the tourists this summer, and that I was picked either at random or because of those press stories.'

'Nothing to do with old grudges, or new ones?'

'Nah,' he scoffed. 'Fact is, Primavera, most of my old customers from my cop days, apart from the six I mentioned, are probably shuffling around on fucking Zimmer frames by now. As for new ones, as far as I know I don't have any, other than Alison if I stay too late in the pub on a Friday night.'

'Still, if it made you feel safer, I could drive you back to the Nieves Mar.'

'As Intendant Guinart could have done,' he pointed out, 'but he didn't think it was necessary either. I'll walk.'

'What are you going to do about the car?' I asked.

He shrugged. 'Phone Avis,' he replied, 'and find out if they really do try harder. Hey,' he chuckled, 'I paid the extra charge for no excess on the insurance. In hindsight, was that smart or what?'

Eight

'What's happened in the car park?' Tom asked, as he and Janet returned from giving Charlie his early evening exercise, a jog along the path to El Riuet and back. 'They've got the "Complet" sign out, but it's nowhere near full.'

'There's been a fire,' I replied, factually. 'A car went up in flames this afternoon.'

'Maybe it was a gas bottle,' Janet suggested. 'I've heard of that happening. There was one with a faulty seal, the car it was in filled with gas and when the owner pressed the remote to unlock it, it caused a spark and "Pow!" up it went.'

'It was a car bomb,' wee Jonathan announced.

'Sure,' Janet laughed. 'Like this is Kabul.'

'It was a car bomb,' her little brother repeated, more than a little smugly, a sign that he was sure in his knowledge. 'Leo, the waiter in Esculapi, he told me. The police were there, and CSI people in white suits. He said you were there when it happened, Auntie Primavera, with the man whose car blew up. And Alex was there too.'

81

There are no secrets in St Martí d'Empúries.

'Yes,' I agreed, 'I was, and so was Alex.'

'Who was the man?' Tom asked.

'He's an old associate of your father's from Edinburgh. He looked after the Loch Lomond place when you weren't there. His name's Mr Ross; he's in the area and he looked me up. He might come and visit us here.'

'I remember him,' Janet declared. 'He came to see Dad sometimes when we were there. He was a great big man . . . or maybe he only seemed that way because we were very small. I think Dad liked him. Do you remember him, Tom?'

'I think so. Dad called him Rocky, didn't he?'

'No, daftie,' Janet laughed, 'it was Ricky. He brought us presents when he came to visit. Why would anyone want to blow him up?'

'Hold on,' I intervened, 'nobody's saying anyone did. Yes, Alex has forensic people looking at the car, but just to find out what did happen. Whatever it was, the car was empty when it happened, and there were no other cars next to it, so nobody was killed or badly injured or even mildly scorched.'

Wee Jonathan looked mildly disappointed. 'I still think it was a car bomb,' he insisted.

I beamed at him. 'My boy, if believing that will make your day, then just you carry on.'

Given the day I'd had, you might think it was a minor miracle that I was able to put anything on the table at all, but it's easy to buy four pizzas when the source is ten metres away, and just as easy to serve them when you cut them into wedges and tell everyone to eat with their fingers. Kids don't have a problem with that, and neither do I.

We had just finished, and the older two were about to fill the dishwasher . . . a new task I'd given them along with bed-stripping . . . when I remembered that there was a bit of news I hadn't broken, and that wasn't on the village grapevine.

'By the way,' I said, 'I forgot to tell you with all the excitement. Grandpa Mac's coming to visit. He arrives on Wednesday.'

Even the teenagers, who were becoming more blasé by the day, as they do at that stage, were excited by that. He's always been able to communicate with them in a way few other adults can. I asked Tom once why this was; his reply was very simple. 'He talks to us like we're grown up.'

That's a secret my own father has never mastered, not even with Dawn and me when we were young. He's always been more a doer than a sayer. If I'd told the family that Grandpa David was coming to visit, they'd have been pleased, because he'd have brought them things, special things that he'd made with his own hands . . . my dad's a craftsman . . . but they'd have understood that it would be more of a tour of inspection than an activity holiday.

Wee Jonathan isn't an enthusiastic fisherman, not usually. Tom has to persuade him to go with him when he goes out along the jetty, and he'd never set off on his own. But when Grandpa Mac comes to stay, the rods are ready before he steps through the door.

'That's great,' Tom said. 'He'll be able to come to our golf lesson on Saturday.'

'What golf lesson?'

'With Jonny, at Pals, of course. He says he'll take Janet and me out before he and Selina leave for his next tournament. Grandpa Mac can make up the four.'

'What about your brother?' Wee Jonathan has shown not one sign of following in his namesake's footsteps. He may become a poker wizard, or a chess grand master, but he will never be an athlete.

'He'll come too. He can caddy for Janet.'

'And how are you going to get there?'

He grinned. 'There's no chance you'll let me drive, so . . . Honest, Mum, I was going to ask you. I only just fixed it up by text this afternoon. Anyway, Grandpa Mac can take us all now. You don't need to come.'

'Suits me.'

Another four years and he will be behind the wheel, I thought. *And what will I be useful for then?* I felt a pang of the old sadness but fought it off.

'I will if I want,' I countered. I added, 'You don't get rid of me that easily. You know what? When you lot go to Girona University, I might come too. I've got a nursing degree, but doing a different one might be interesting.'

All three of them stared at me, even wee Jonathan. I'd been joking, and yet it didn't seem such a crazy idea. Fortunately, any discussion was forestalled by the sound of the doorbell. I headed off to answer it and found Alex Guinart on the step. He was still in plain clothes, but he had a work look on his face.

'Come in,' I said. 'I was just about to have coffee. Would you like one?'

That was a rhetorical question; Alex loves my coffee. Most of the time, I use a filter in a land where everything else comes from a percolator or espresso machine, apart from instant, and that tends to be foul.

I sent him up to my first-floor terrace while I returned to the kitchen and brewed some up. When I rejoined him, with two mugs on a tray, and a plate of Principe biscuits, he was settled into the guest chair, looking down into the square and surveying everything that was going on there. Suddenly I was glad he wasn't in uniform.

'Okay, pal,' I said, as I put his mug in front of him, and also a *chupito* of Limoncello in a frozen shot glass, 'nice to see you as always, but why?'

'I didn't want you to go to bed wondering about what happened with your friend this afternoon.'

'It wouldn't have kept me awake, and he's barely an acquaintance, let alone a friend, but thanks. What's the latest?'

'It was definitely no accident,' Alex replied. 'It was a bomb, beyond doubt. It only contained a small amount of explosive, but enough to have spread Señor Ross all over the inside of his car.'

I whistled. 'Then he was lucky, right enough. Could they tell any more than that?'

'The device used a compact high explosive, of a type used by the military or in mineral extraction. There are many quarries in this region, as you know, so it's possible it could have been stolen from one of them. That will be one line of inquiry.'

'What happens now?'

'Well, I have reported to Barcelona, and also, as I must, to the prosecutor in Girona. When I told him he almost wet himself. His first thought was the Basques, ETA, but I don't believe that for a second. They have been inactive for a while now, and even when they were setting off their bombs, they rarely did so in Catalunya. It wasn't unknown, but no; if they were to restart an active campaign, it would be in a higher profile place than St Martí, and the target would probably be someone like me, a cop, rather than a foreign civilian.

'As for the next stage, I am the senior Mossos detective officer in the province, so I may simply be told to get on with investigating the outrage.' He killed his *chupito* in a single gulp. 'But I don't know that I'll be trusted with it.'

'If not you, who?'

He shrugged.

'So what can you do for now? Anything?'

'I can keep an eye on Señor Ross, to deter any second attempt on his life. He's a security expert and now he's been alerted, it would be reckless to try again, but I will look after him. He has an armed officer with him in his hotel. I can't give him a gun of his own, but I've done the next best thing. He wasn't pleased, but he understands that I have to watch my back as well as his. Other than that, we can only wait and see what tomorrow brings.'

Nine

As it happened, the morning brought a phone call from Ricky Ross, on my mobile, just as Charlie and I were heading for the dog-friendly nudie beach beyond the little river, to swim and sunbathe before the September tourists arrived to fill it up.

'Can I come and see you?' he asked.

'Of course. When?'

'About an hour? How would that suit?'

It didn't really. It was ten o'clock on a beautiful morning and I had planned to stay there until midday, maybe even lunchtime.

I compromised. 'Make it an hour and a half. Come to the house.'

'Will do, thanks.'

'The kids are at school, Ricky,' I pointed out.

'This isn't about them; it's something else.'

'About yesterday? Are you all right? Or are you shaken up, after what happened?'

'Sure, I'm fine. There's no point in fretting about things

that have happened. It's being ready for the future that matters. No, there's something I need to talk through with you, that's all. And by the way, I may be bringing someone with me, a colleague.'

'Bring who you like, but not before eleven thirty. In fact, if you could make it twelve, that would be even better.'

'Whatever you say.'

'Fine, twelve it is.'

I swam for half an hour, then stretched out on my mat for another half, before crossing the iron bridge once again, with my faithful hound, and grabbing a quick iced coffee (and a bowl of water) at VaiVe, our friendly beach bar. Slightly annoyed at having to rush things, I did contemplate calling Ross and putting him off for another hour, until politeness got the better of me. I dug out my trainers and shorts from my haversack and we ran home along the path: Charlie likes to trot.

I showered quickly, washed the sand out of my hair, slapped on a little moisturiser and lipstick. By the time the church bell struck twelve for the first time . . . not a slip of the keyboard, it always rings again at two minutes past the hour . . . I felt ready for my visitors.

When the bell rang the quarter-hour I was still ready, but a little annoyed. When it rang the half-hour, I was moderately pissed off, and considering going back to VaiVe for lunch and writing Ricky and his colleague off to experience. If the other bell, mine, had rung more than a couple of minutes after it did, I would have been off, for when I heard it I was at the top of the stairs that led down to the garage.

Things often turn on a single moment, a single decision. The one I almost made was to pretend I hadn't heard and carry on regardless, but instead I chose the other option.

I was looking at my watch as I opened the door, so I didn't even notice that Ricky had brought two chums, not one, far less did I recognise either of them.

'I'm sorry, Primavera,' he exclaimed. 'Mr Weighley's plane had an air traffic control delay at Girona.'

My eyes widened. I stared past him at one of the men behind him: wearing a white linen suit, around five feet seven, with a slim ginger moustache and a mop of fair hair that might have been tinted, or might not. Jack Weighley, as I lived and breathed, the Flying Scotsman, king of economy-class travel but first-class arsehole, and he was standing on my front step! Not only that, he was smiling!

'What the . . .' I gasped.

'Mr Weighley wanted to surprise you, Primavera,' Ricky offered.

'He did? Well, that's excellent. I'm glad I've made his day. Now you and he can fuck off.'

Weighley laughed. 'That's not very ladylike, Mrs Blackstone.'

'I save my feminine side for gentlemen,' I shot back. 'Now hop it.'

He glanced at Charlie, who was dozing in his kennel. 'Are you going to set your dog on us?'

'No,' I told him. 'I have a friend down there who has a couple of much bigger dogs. Push comes to shove, I'll ask her if I can borrow those.'

'Primavera, give us a chance,' Ricky said. 'Mr Weighley did say you might not be too pleased to see us. But he has come all the way here to meet you, on his private jet. Give us a hearing, will you?'

There was something in his tone; he wasn't quite pleading, but it suggested that if I refused, his employment prospects might no longer be too rosy.

'And also, I've come to apologise, Mrs Blackstone,' Weighley added, his expression turned serious. 'You know what for.'

'You're a couple of years too late with that,' I told him. 'But okay, I'll talk to you. Not here, though. Ricky, you find a table at Esculapi, and I'll join you in a minute or so.' No way was I letting that man into my home. 'You'd better make it indoors; it's more private there at this time of day.'

I saw the three of them off the premises, then went back inside, not for anything in particular, simply to gather my thoughts. Jack Weighley had flown all the way to Spain to see me . . . on his private jet, as if I thought for a minute he'd be caught dead on one of his passenger aircraft.

'What the hell can he want?' I asked myself, then replied that there was only one way to find out.

It can be cool inside Esculapi's big stone walls, even on a warm day, so I picked a light shawl from the coat rack by the door and draped it round my shoulders, then headed out to catch up with the Flying Scotsman and his crew.

They had found a table upstairs when I arrived, and were the only people there; useful, in case the shouting started all over again. They all stood as I approached, very properly, and only sat again when I did.

I nodded towards the third man. 'Are you going to introduce your colleague?' I murmured.

'This is Mr Jenkins, Cedric Jenkins,' Ricky advised me. 'He's Mr Weighley's driver.'

He gave me the briefest of nods and made the briefest of eye contact. A man of few words; a prerequisite, I imagine, since his boss could talk for Scotland, and on occasion tried to do just that. The driver looked the part: very neat, if a little overdressed in a dark blue suit, white shirt and blue tie. Ties are a daytime rarity where I live; their wearers are usually bank managers or local civil servants.

'Would you like a drink, Mrs Blackstone?' Weighley asked. 'We thought sangria might be appropriate.'

I looked at him and smiled sweetly. 'Wouldn't that be taking a hell of a chance?' I replied. 'It would make a hell of a mess of your nice white suit.'

He smiled back, but it wasn't what you'd call full-hearted. 'Touché,' he murmured. 'That was what I want to apologise for. My behaviour that day wasn't very nice, I admit. You'd done a very good negotiating job, and you weren't even on a performance bonus. I should have recognised that and been more grateful.

'You were quite right to do what you did, even if it was embarrassing at the time, with the press being there, and TV. Our little incident made *Reporting Scotland*, you know, and STV, not to mention the papers.'

'No, let's mention the papers,' I chuckled. 'How many column centimetres did you generate out of it? Your PR people . . . Ricky's wife's firm, I understand . . . were into action quick enough. They described me as being annoyed that I hadn't been given more credit for the deal, and upset that you'd been able to negotiate a bigger discount on the airport charges than I had. With the spin you put on it, the coverage must have been worth the equivalent of a right few powder-blue suits.'

'That's what I pay them for,' he conceded. 'Yes, it worked out quite well, I admit. But we didn't drop you completely in it. None of the photographs or TV footage showed your face. Alison could have revealed your identity, but I told her not to.'

'Why not?' I asked, genuinely intrigued but trying not to show it. 'That would have put more spice in the story.'

'Yes, but I was feeling guilty by then, and also . . . I didn't understand this fully at the time, but I felt that you were someone I was much better keeping onside.'

'Oh yes?'

'Yes. Dead or not, Oz Blackstone still has a lot of fans, and many of them are my customers. Then there's your brother-in-law,' he chuckled, 'Grayson. He's richer than I am, and not a man to mess with, they say. But those weren't the main reasons, either of them. It didn't take me long to realise that you were someone I'd rather have on my side. Exposing you to public ridicule would hardly have achieved that, would it?'

'No, but what makes you think I'd ever want to be on your side?'

'Come on,' he retorted. 'You're Scottish, even though

you've settled in this beautiful place. And you must concede that I'm putting our country on the map, across Europe.'

'It's always been on the map,' I pointed out. 'But I admit that you're raising awareness of us.'

'Thank you.' He looked up and I realised that a waiter was standing behind us. 'Let's have lunch,' Weighley said, 'then we can get down to the reason for my visit.'

I had a momentary vision of me with a long spoon, and the Flying Scotsman with horns and a tail, but my morning exertions had left me starving, so I pushed it away and asked for a house salad. I passed on the sangria, though, and settled for sparkling water. I know how strong sangria can be and they didn't; if that gave me an advantage later, then no harm in it.

Our lunchtime conversation was sparse; I asked Weighley what kind of a plane he flew. 'A Gulfstream,' he replied, as he forked up some of his pasta.

'Mmm,' I murmured. 'I flew on one of them, once upon a time.'

'I'll bet you enjoyed the experience.'

'Yes, I did,' I said. 'Right up to the moment it crashed.'

His fork stopped halfway to his mouth. 'Seriously?'

'Yes. Come on, Mr Weighley, you've checked up on me for sure. You must have known I was in a plane crash.'

'Yes, I did,' he agreed, 'but I didn't know it was a Gulfstream.'

'Well, it was, but don't worry. It wasn't mechanical failure that brought it down. It was sabotaged. One of the other passengers was on somebody's hit list.'

'Did he survive?'

'No, she was killed. If she'd chummed me to the toilet she might still be alive, but you know aircraft; there just isn't room for two.'

'Fucking hell, Primavera,' Ross exclaimed. 'That's pretty cold-hearted.'

'That's how you've got to be after something like that,' I retorted, 'if you want to survive emotionally as well.'

'No bad dreams?' Cedric Jenkins asked, proving that he wasn't mute, and also that he was allowed to speak at the great man's table.

'I did look into the other part of the plane,' I replied, 'and that revisited me a couple of times. Otherwise, no. Should I be guilty about that? I don't think so. Anyway, that's not the worst thing that's happened to me.'

'Then what was?' Weighley chipped in.

I looked at him. 'Your mother's still alive, isn't she?'

'Yes, but what . . . Oh, I see. Yours isn't. I'm sorry.'

'Me too; she'd have been a terrific granny, but she never got the chance.'

That put the kybosh on the small talk for a while. We ate in silence, and I watched as Ricky and his boss guzzled a litre of sangria between them, quicker than they should have, judging by how little ice had been in the jug. Jenkins abstained, and stuck to water, like me. He was a driver, after all.

We all passed on dessert and went straight to coffee. Jenkins and I had Americano, while the other two had carajillos, recommended by me, just in case there hadn't been enough brandy in the sangria.

Weighley's eyes widened as he tasted his. 'To business,' he declared.

'If we have any,' I said, 'although I can't see what it might be.'

'I'm concerned about Spain,' he began, 'particularly this area. Catalonia is politically volatile just now and Ricky's unfortunate incident yesterday has really focused me on it.'

'Hold on,' I interrupted, 'you're calling it an incident? What have the police told you?'

'Not very much. I've spoken to the boss of the Catalan force, the Mossies, or whatever they're called, but all he would tell me was that his top man in the Girona area had reported to him and that it was under consideration.'

I knew a lot more than that, but I wasn't going to let the volatile Mr Weighley in on it. 'Under consideration by whom?' I asked.

'He didn't say. I pushed him as far as I could, but he wouldn't go any further.'

'When did you speak to him?'

'Last night. I called him again this morning as soon as my plane landed, but he wasn't any more forthcoming. I threatened to go to the president of the Catalan government; he told me to go ahead if I wanted. I did just that, but his office said he wasn't available.'

'No, he has more important things on his mind right now.'

Weighley bridled, visibly, at the idea of anything being more important than WeighleyAir or its owner. 'Such as?' he challenged.

'Such as getting re-elected. It's a problem that many governments face every so often, and it's getting worse.'

'Still . . .'

'It's a fact of life, Jack. Now, can we get to it, please. What does any of this have to do with me?'

He nodded. 'Okay. As I said, I'm concerned about Spain and my operations here. Mr Ross has told you about the attacks on my aircraft. I responded appropriately by sending him across to take charge of airport security, in the belief that would put an end to the whole business, and yet a day later his car gets blown up.'

'Gets blown up?' I repeated.

'Come on, of course it was. Sure the police haven't confirmed it yet, but going by what he's told me, it doesn't look accidental. Come on, Primavera, you were there, you know it wasn't.'

'I'm not a ballistics expert.'

'Neither am I but I've seen what the explosion did to the trees around the vehicle.'

'There were two explosions,' I pointed out. 'The petrol tank going up accounted for the trees.'

'Irrelevant; they're charred skeletons, regardless. Look, Primavera, I could have a business crisis here. I've asked Mr Ross to remain here for a while, at least until all his new security arrangements are up and running, but I feel that I need another representative on the ground. I'd like that to be you.'

I stared at him, not trying to hide my incredulity. 'Me? Why me? I know nothing about the airline industry.'

'Irrelevant: I have other people here who do. They keep my planes in the air and on schedule, but that's the extent of their knowledge. You know Catalonia; you know how its government works, and you know its institutions. You're forceful and you don't let people stand in your way. You're the ideal person to look out for my interests.'

'I've got a job already; single mum, three offspring.'

'I'm not talking about going to an office,' he countered. 'This isn't a nine-to-five thing. You'd be a presence on the ground, not an employee, a consultant; I'll give you a retainer of ten grand a month sterling, paid any way you like. Offshore account, Swiss bank, you name it.'

I played my last card. 'Jack, I don't even like you.'

He laughed; I wondered idly whether he was half-cut from the sangria. 'Primavera, nobody fucking likes me, other than the punters who believe Alison's PR stories. I'm not here to be liked, I'm here to run a successful business, not to get myself elected to anything.' He looked at his driver. 'Do you like me, Mr Jenkins?'

'Not very much,' the man replied, straight-faced, in a tone which might have implied that he didn't like anyone very much.

'How about you, Mr Ross?' Ricky hesitated. 'Go on,' his client insisted, 'it won't come back to bite you.'

'No,' he said, finally. 'But so what? I spent an entire police career confronting people I didn't like, and working under quite a few. The colleagues I did like were those I chose myself, but I didn't give a damn whether they liked me or not.'

Weighley turned back to me. 'See? As for Alison, Mrs Ross, she'd tell you the same. She has the toughest job of anyone around me. She has to make me seem likeable to people who don't know me, in spite of my big mouth and all the difficulty it puts in her way. And she's a genius at it, for our tracking polls show that most of our customers think I'm Mr Nice. A couple of months ago, I came second to Lorraine Kelly in a newspaper "Nicest Scots" reader poll. Alison got a bonus for that.'

'I'll bet she cast a lot of votes,' I retorted.

He laughed again. 'I don't give a bugger. If she did, she didn't get caught at it, that's if the paper even bothered to check.' Then he frowned. 'I know you'd never vote for me, but I don't give a bugger about that either. I want you on my side because I believe that if I ask you to do something for the good of my business, the business that will be hiring you, and you accept that it's kosher, you will follow it through until you get a result.' He paused. 'But I believe also that if I ask you to do something and you have a problem with it, you will challenge me. Am I right?'

'Be sure of it.'

'I am, and I'll be fine with it.' He glanced to his right and to his left. 'I have enough "yes" men around me. Don't need another.' He slapped the table. 'So you'll do it. That's excellent.'

'Did I say I'd take the job?'

He nodded. 'Yes, you did. When you answered my last question.'

Ten

He was right, the little bastard; in effect I had. He'd got to me and we both knew how, even if he had the sense not to say it. He had tapped into my vanity. I've always been aware of its existence, and tried to keep it under a stone, but it's always been there for people perceptive enough to spot it, and to take advantage of it.

I gave in. 'Very well,' I said. 'I'll do what I can when I can; if you want to pay me silly money for that it's down to you, but it has to be legit and declared in Spain.'

'Excellent,' Weighley beamed. 'I'll have my office send you our standard consultant contract this afternoon. Please let me have your email address.'

I took a card from my bag and handed it to him. 'Where do we begin?' I asked him.

'First and foremost, I'd like you to find out where we are officially with the incident yesterday. We'll see where we take it from there.' He stood up, suddenly, abruptly. 'Right,' he said. 'Got to get back to Edinburgh so Mr Jenkins and I will leave you and Mr Ross to get on with it. I'll expect an update in twenty-four hours. Mr Ross will give you my contact details.' He glanced at Ricky. 'Take care of the bill, there's a good fella.'

And then he was gone.

As soon as the top of his mullet had disappeared from sight down the spiral staircase, I looked at Ricky. 'He really is a fucking twat, isn't he?' I murmured.

'Absolutely,' he agreed. 'But his business does what it says on the tin, and that's what counts to most people.'

He turned, waved at the waiter and made a 'Bill, please' sign.

'Will you get that on expenses?' I asked.

He shrugged, and smiled. 'Maybe yes, maybe no. It'll depend on how Jack's feeling. Nothing's delegated, you know; he checks all his consultancy invoices personally.'

'We'd better get a result for him, in that case.'

'A result being?'

'Finding out who tried to blow you to bits.'

'If anyone did. We don't know for certain.'

'Oh, someone did all right.' I told him about Alex Guinart's visit, the night before.

He stared at me. 'Then why was the Mossos director so fucking coy about it when Jack asked him?'

'That's a very good question. I haven't a clue what the answer is but I bet we're not going to like it. You square up here then we'll go up to the house and I'll call Alex from there.'

I went to the ladies' room while Ricky paid the bill, then we walked the short distance to my house. I was reaching for my keys when a voice called out to me.

'Primavera.'

It was Alex, in civvies; he was seated at a table in La Terrassa d'Empúries, with only a coffee in front of him, no lunch. At once, I knew he'd been waiting for me.

He rose, and approached. 'I've been here for ten minutes,' he began. 'When I got no answer at the door, I asked Cisco if he knew where you were. He said that he'd seen you going into Esculapi. I need to talk to you, but I don't want to be seen. Let's go inside.'

The look in his eyes told me not to question him. There was something there that I'd never seen before: anxiety. There was also the fact that he was speaking Catalan, meaning that Ricky Ross was not meant to be part of any discussion. I unlocked the place, then led the way through the hall and into the kitchen.

'Beer?' I asked, still in his language. 'You look as though you need one.'

'You're right but no thanks; water will be fine.'

I took a bottle of Fonter from the fridge, uncapped it and handed it to him. 'Okay,' I began but that was as far as I got.

'The other two men you were with, who were they?'

'How did you know . . .'

'Cisco told me. Also I saw them leave: white suit, dark suit, yes?'

'Yes.'

'Who were they?'

'White suit was Jack Weighley, of WeighleyAir. Dark suit was his driver.'

He swore, softly. 'Primavera, please tell me you didn't talk about my visit last night, and what I told you.'

'No, but I need to talk to you about that. Weighley said that your boss gave him the runaround this morning when he asked about it. I decided that he wasn't hearing the truth from me. Ricky knows, though: I've just told him.'

'Can he be trusted to keep it to himself?'

'Let's ask him.' I switched to English. 'Ricky, from the sound of things, although he hasn't explained it yet, Alex has got a problem. He needs you to forget the version that I just gave you of what happened yesterday.'

Ross frowned at him. 'Have you been talking out of turn? Saying things you shouldn't?'

Alex nodded. 'I didn't know it, but yes. The director general called me this morning. He asked if anyone had seen my report. I told him no, which technically was correct. He said that was good, because Gemma Sierra, the forensic team leader, had changed her mind. They are now saying, officially, that the explosion was caused by oil leaking on to the hot exhaust and being ignited. In other words, that the car caught fire spontaneously.'

'Do you believe that?' I gasped.

'Of course not. They've been told what to say. The whole business has been taken out of our hands; the politicians are involved. For the first time in recent memory the presidents of the Madrid and Catalan parliaments are in agreement. The explosion has been declared accidental, and any further media questions will be handled not by us but by the Guardia Civil.'

'The Guardia? But this is Catalunya; the Mossos are the law around here. How can they get away with that?'

My friend smiled. 'Come on, Primavera. The politicians can get away with anything they damn well want. The car is registered in Madrid; that means that any follow-up investigation into its condition and its road-worthiness . . . not that there will be one . . . will be carried out there, where the Guardia Civil are the law, as you put it.'

'So it's a cover-up,' Ricky exclaimed. 'But why?'

'I don't know,' Alex confessed. 'The director general was not in the mood for discussion. Maybe he doesn't know himself, not for certain.'

'What's your guess?

'The best I can offer is that Primavera was right yesterday. They're afraid it's the work of terrorists, targeting you because of your recent publicity and because of who you work for, and they want to keep a lid on it.'

'But I thought ETA had given all that up,' Ross countered.

'Not ETA,' he declared. 'The big unspoken fear is that Catalan nationalism will turn violent. You talk in English about the Monster in the Cupboard. That's ours, and they don't want anyone opening the door.' He drained his water bottle. The bubbles made him belch slightly.

'Bottom line, Alex,' I murmured.

'Bottom line is that I'm putting my career at risk by being

here. I've been specifically forbidden to speak to you, Señor Ross; my orders are to refer you to the *jefe* in Barcelona if you approach me. If that cupboard door is opened and it gets back to me, it will definitely be over, and they might even find a way to put me in jail if they have a mind to do so. So you see, Primavera, I need you, and I need you, Señor Ross, to forget that you have ever heard this truth.'

'What truth?' I said, and looked up at Ricky.

'Once a cop, always a cop,' he declared. 'No way will I hang a brother officer out to dry. So you can relax.' He paused. 'That said, being a cop, there's no way I could ever be expected to swallow that bollocks story about hot exhausts. That just doesn't happen in a modern car. Somebody tried to kill me, Intendant Guinart, and I can't be expected just to overlook the fact. But don't worry, anything I do will be discreet and will not involve you or any of your colleagues.'

'I understand that,' Alex replied. 'I'd do the same myself in your shoes. But suppose you find the person who planted the bomb. What then?'

The former detective superintendent smiled, without humour, and for a moment I was back in that pub in Edinburgh, all those years before. 'In that case,' he chuckled, 'something else will never have happened.'

Eleven

'What do we do about Weighley?' Ricky asked, as the door closed on Alex.

I frowned at him. 'Is there any part of "fuck all" you don't understand? You heard what Alex said. If one word of this gets back to that man he'll probably go ballistic and start screaming at the government, in Barcelona and in Madrid. If that happens, his source will be very obvious. I have to report to our Jack, not you and when I do I will give him the official version.'

'But we don't have it yet,' he pointed out.

'True,' I agreed, 'so you'd better make that call to the Mossos director and tell him you were referred to him by Intendant Guinart. Hold on, I'll get the number from the website.' I picked up my iPad from the kitchen table, where I'd left it that morning, and found what I was looking for inside a minute. 'There you are,' I said, as I handed over the tablet.

'Will he speak English?'

'Probably, but if he doesn't, there will be someone who does. He'll be expecting your call. But use your mobile; I don't want my landline number logged in there.'

I watched and waited as he keyed in the number, then listened as he tried to make himself understood by the switchboard operator. It didn't take long, so they must have been primed that a Señor Ross would be on the line.

He hadn't put his phone on speaker mode so all I could hear were Ricky's responses, but they told the whole story.

'So it was an accident? Your forensic people are certain?'

'They are? That's good. It's a relief to know that nobody was out to get me.'

'Yes, I'm quite happy now. No, no need for me to call the people in Madrid. I understand why they're involved, but I won't be making a complaint against the hire company. I'd like to thank you, sir, for taking such a personal interest in the incident. I appreciate that, and so will my client, Mr Weighley, when I tell him.'

He ended the call and pocketed his phone. 'Bullshit,' he grunted. 'He sounded desperate to be sure that I bought it. Did I sound as if I did?'

'You almost convinced me that it was an accident,' I replied. 'Now all we have to do is convince the Flying Scotsman. I'll wait until tomorrow morning before I give him his update. After that,' I continued, 'what do we do? If you were serious in what you hinted to Alex, about looking into it yourself, where do you begin?'

'To be honest, I don't know. If the cupboard monster

theory is right, it's not my territory at all. I'll get nowhere without the locals on my side.'

'In that case, you'd better recruit one. Have you seen Hector Gomez yet?'

'No. The guy never called me. The police office in Girona gave me his number, and I rang his home this morning, but he was out and his wife doesn't speak a word of English.'

'Let me try to contact him,' I said. 'We haven't always been the best of friends, but we're cordial now. I don't have his number, though. Do you have it on you?'

He nodded, and retrieved it from his mobile's contacts list. I recognised it as a Girona number and dialled the nine digits as I read it. Hector's wife answered again, in a cautious tone. Given his former profession I guessed that she had been his gatekeeper for most of his career.

I introduced myself and asked if I could speak to her husband. Strangely, she repeated my name, aloud.

'Si,' I said. A couple of seconds later, Gomez came on line.

'Señora Primavera, how good to hear from you,' he exclaimed in Catalan. 'It's been a long time. You are behaving yourself, I trust.'

'As best I can.'

'Alex told me you have a new partner. I was pleased to hear that.'

'Because it would keep me out of mischief?'

'No, because I believe you need someone. Behind all that energy, I always thought that you were a very lonely lady.'

'I have my children,' I said, knowing that I sounded

defensive. His unprecedented frankness had caught me off guard.

'A woman needs more; so does a man, for that matter. Children grow up, and eventually they move on . . . or they should.'

'I know all about the growing up part. As for moving on, it's not just kids who do that.'

'Ah. If I understand properly what you're saying, then I'm sorry.'

'I'm not.' As I said the words, I realised that they weren't exactly true. Our informal committal on the beach had cleared some space in my emotional life, and I was beginning to miss Liam after all: a little, but not enough for me to ask him to come back.

'Then what can I do for you?' Gomez asked.

'I'd like you to meet someone.'

He was silent for a few seconds. 'Let me guess. A Scottish person.'

'Yes.'

'I'm not sure I want to meet him. I was in when he called earlier, but I told my wife to say that I wasn't.'

'Then you know what it's about?'

'Of course. Barcelona asked my permission before they gave him my name. I said yes, but now I'm hesitating. I don't know if I want to go back to work.'

'This will be an office job, Hector. Management.'

'I know,' he said, 'but I have seen the man I'd be working for on television.'

'Ricky Ross?'

'No, the one who owns the airline. He has the phoniest smile I have ever seen.'

'Granted, but you can say that about most presidents and prime ministers.'

'Do you know this man yourself?'

'Yes, but I'm not trying to sell him to you. All I want is for you to meet Señor Ross, and hear what he has to say.'

'Mmm. For you, I'll do it, but only for you. Where and when?'

I hadn't thought that through, but the answer was obvious. 'At the WeighleyAir office in Girona Airport. Tomorrow morning. Would ten thirty suit you?'

'Make it eleven. I'm not such an early riser these days, another reason why I'm hesitating about meeting your friend.'

'Lucky you,' I laughed. 'I don't have the choice. Eleven it is.'

I ended the call. 'You get that?' I asked Ricky.

He nodded. 'Yes, thanks. Does that give you time to get there, getting the kids off to school, and all?'

'Me?'

'Absolutely. I'd like you to be there, and I'm sure Weighley will expect it.'

I threw him a sceptical look. 'You just want someone else to blame, in case he doesn't perform once he's appointed.'

'Maybe, but I'd like your input as well. If Gomez joins us, Jack might be paying him but in practice he'll be working for me, and I'll define his remit.'

'What do you mean by that?'

'You'll see tomorrow. Would you like a lift down to the airport?'

I smiled. 'Ricky, if you think I'd get in your car after what happened yesterday, you're crazy. I'll drive myself.'

Twelve

Ross had barely left to return to the hotel . . . 'I suppose there'll be no nursemaid outside my door tonight' . . . before the kids arrived home on the school bus.

'Have they caught the bomber yet?' That was wee Jonathan's first question, as soon as the door had closed behind them.

'There was no bomber,' I told him. 'The police say that it was a spontaneous explosion, an accident.'

'You're kidding!' Tom exclaimed.

'No, I'm not. That's what they told Mr Ross, and it comes all the way from the top. If any of your friends ask you, that's the official verdict, and you can tell them that. In fact you should tell them, to dampen down the gossip and stop stories from spreading. We don't want people to be discouraged from using the car park, do we?'

'I suppose not,' he conceded.

Wee Jonathan looked disappointed. Clearly the idea of a mad bomber on the loose had appealed to him.

Later, when we were round the dinner table, tucking into Janet's expertly poached peaches in cinnamon, with a couple of figs . . . they are irresistible in the autumn, plus they . . . well, you know . . . and a spoonful of soya yoghurt, I told them about Jack Weighley's visit. I didn't have the option not to; St Martí is not designed for secrecy, and Tom and Janet know all the staff in Esculapi.

'That man,' my son growled. He knew about the affair of the cava and the powder-blue suit, and he hadn't forgotten; my name might not have been in the press but all of my friends and neighbours knew who the 'angry blonde lady' was. 'What did he want?'

'He wants me to work for his company, as a representative in this part of Spain.'

'Doing what?' Janet asked.

'Looking after its interests, wherever necessary. I'd be a sort of troubleshooter . . . not that there'll be any trouble to shoot, you understand.'

'Are you going to do it?'

'Well, it would be part-time. I'd work from here and I'd be on call . . . but it wouldn't affect you three in any way.'

'She's going to do it,' Tom said, casually. Then he beamed. 'Liam was right, Jan.' He's taken to calling his sister Jan, for short; I've never asked him why.

I sat up straight in my carver chair, my spoon stopping halfway to my mouth. 'What do you mean, "Liam was right"? Right about what?'

'He's always asking if you've found a job yet.'

'He is? When?'

'Mum, you're not the only person Liam keeps in touch with. He phones us on our mobiles, and sends us emails, with photographs of the places he's been. The last one was yesterday, from Caracas, in Venezuela; it's a big city with mountains around it. And every time he does, he asks if you've got a job yet.'

The revelation shook me. I had no idea he was staying in touch with the kids; and the bugger never sent me emails! Occasional phone calls were all I got, not bloody photographs from Caracas bloody Venezuela. 'Why the hell should he ask that?'

'He says you're like a fish. You've got to find fresh water or you'll drown.'

'That's silly,' wee Jonathan muttered. 'Fish can't drown. Liam's silly.'

His sister looked ready to slap him; I stepped in. 'He might be silly, Jonathan, but he's right. If the oxygen in the water where they're swimming gets too low, it's the same in effect as a human falling in and drowning. But he's wrong about me; just being around you lot gives me all the oxygen I need.'

I looked at my youngest and wondered. 'Why do you think Liam's silly? Is it because he keeps in touch with the others and not you?'

He gazed at the table for a while, but eventually, he nodded.

'But he can't, can he, not in the same way?'

'Maybe not,' he admitted.

So why can't he send him the odd postcard? I asked myself. *Because like many people, it doesn't occur to him any more,* I answered.

'If I got you your own mobile, and kept it in credit, you wouldn't be silly with it, would you?'

His eyes came up to meet me; I read caution in them, as if he thought it might be a trick question. 'No,' he murmured. 'I promise.'

'And if I get you your own computer, and set up an email account for you? You'd use it properly?'

Those doubting eyes started to shine in a way that made me forget everything else that had happened that day. 'Yes!'

'Okay, we'll do that. You're ten now; let's say that's old enough. One condition: I have to be able to look at both of them and see what you're doing there. Only I get to clear the history on them. Agreed?'

'Yes!'

'Okay, you're on. Once we've got them I'll give Liam all the details so he can keep in touch with you as well.'

But not with me, the son of a . . .

As soon as the children had loaded the dishwasher and gone off to take care of their homework, I sent Liam a text.

'*What sort of fucking fish would I be? Barracuda, perhaps?*'

I didn't expect a speedy answer; indeed I didn't expect one at all, but my phone buzzed a couple of minutes later. I was still bristling as I looked at the response.

'*I was thinking more of an angel fish. Love u, miss u.*'

'*Miss u 2. Why no pretty pics of Caracas?*'

'Been giving u ur own space.'
'Tks, but u always did, till u used the M word.'
'Sorry. Can I come back November?'
'U better u sod.'
'Got a job yet?'
'Yes! Now eff off. xxx P'
Maybe I did love him after all.

Thirteen

I called Weighley next morning, on his direct line, before I left for Girona. By that time I'd read his 'standard consultant contract', and a side letter confirming the money, and replied, changing 'monthly' to 'monthly in advance', then telling him that it should be paid not to me, but to the lawyer in Figueres who manages my private client account and keeps me square with the Spanish tax authorities.

I gave him a factual outcome of the situation as it had been explained to us. I had anticipated that he might question it, but he didn't . . . well, not much.

'That's what he said?'

'Word for word.'

'Are you happy with that?'

'He's the top man in the Catalan police force, and he's taking the trouble to deal with the incident personally. If you weren't involved, via Ross, they'd have put out the fire, towed the car away and that would have been that.'

'When you put it that way, yes, I suppose I should see it as a compliment. Anyway, if it's been passed to Madrid, that suits me fine; the further away from Girona the better. Ross isn't going to make a complaint against the company, is he? If so, stop him. You've got general authority over him in Spain.'

I couldn't stop myself from laughing. 'Does Ricky know that?' I asked.

'If he doesn't he should. I'll send him an email advising him of it.'

'That's your privilege,' I told him. 'As long as I'm not in the room when he reads it.'

'If he doesn't like it he can do the other thing. Primavera, my priority is to stabilise the Girona situation, but to do it discreetly. That's what I sent him out there for, but it wasn't meant to involve him getting his name in the Spanish papers. Keep a lid on it, and him.'

'I don't think you need to worry about Mr Ross,' I said. 'He knows what he's here to do. In fact he's doing something about it this morning. He's interviewing a candidate for the security manager job at Girona Airport, and he's asked me to sit in on it.'

'Mmm. That's good to hear. I'd have asked you to do that, even if he hadn't. Who's the bloke you're seeing?'

I gave him a quick rundown of Hector Gomez's career, leaving out the fact that he'd retired early on health grounds. He'd recovered well and Alex had told me he'd quit smoking, so I saw no reason to share his medical history with Weighley, even if he was going to wind up employing him.

'I've got to leave for the airport now,' I said. 'That's where we're interviewing him; it wouldn't impress him if I was late.' Actually I had plenty of time in hand, but Jack wasn't to know that.

'On your way, then. Ross and I haven't discussed salary for this post, but if you think he's a top man, and right for the job, pay what it takes to sign him up. I like the idea of having senior ex-cops on my payroll. Favours repaid cost a lot less than bungs, if you get my drift. While you're on your way down there, I'll call our Ricky and mark his card, make sure he knows you're in charge.'

He'd got the message by the time I walked into the WeighleyAir office at the airport: I could see it in the way he looked at me when the operations manager showed me into the room in which he was waiting.

'Good morning,' I said, politely.

'Mmm,' he grunted, as the other guy left us. 'And to you, ma'am.'

'Oh, come on,' I sighed. 'Don't show me your petted lip, Ricky. I didn't ask Weighley to put me in charge, and I'm not going to pay any attention to him either. This is your area, it's your interview and your decision.'

'Which you have to confirm and report to the bastard.'

'You could always quit,' I suggested, a little archly. 'I saw on the departures board that there's a flight leaving for Edinburgh this afternoon. I'm sure I could fix you up with a seat.'

'That will be fucking right!' he snapped. 'Weighley would like that, I'm sure. No way am I giving him the satisfaction. Besides, I've got unfinished business here. I don't believe for one fucking second that a bunch of Catalan extremists picked me as a target just because I'm foreign and my name was in the local paper the other day. We both know those forensic people didn't make any mistake. That was a car bomb, and it was aimed at me because of my past career or my present connection with WeighleyAir. It didn't work and now it's been hushed up. What do you think that means? That they'll go away? No, they might lie low for a bit, but sooner or later they'll come up with a Plan B . . . unless I get to them first.'

'Ricky . . .' I was stopped from going any further by a knock at the door. It opened and the operations guy appeared again, stepping aside for Hector Gomez.

I won't go as far as saying that I almost didn't recognise him, but he cut a different figure from the man I'd last seen leaning against a tree at a murder scene, dragging on one of the cigarettes that had put an end to his career. He was a little greyer around the temples, and he had a few more lines on his face, but they were due to weight loss, ten kilos, maybe fifteen, rather than ageing. His tan was deep and he radiated fitness. If anything he looked five years younger than Hector the cop, and five years younger than Ricky Ross, although they had to be around the same age.

He extended his hand. 'Señora Blackstone,' he said as we shook, 'good to see you again.' He spoke Castellano.

'And you,' I replied in the same language. 'You're looking well.'

He laughed. 'For a man whose heart put him out of a job? I'm glad you think so, for I agree with you. I'm feeling well too. I had a check-up last month and the cardiologist said I was fine.'

'You've been spending more time outdoors, that's for sure.'

'I've been fishing: not just from the rocks, out on boats, big boats like my father.' I recalled him telling me that his dad had been a trawler skipper. 'Just for fun,' he added. 'Not regularly and never more than overnight. My wife would draw the line at that.'

I sensed feet shuffling beside us. 'Erm . . .'

'Sorry,' I exclaimed, switching to English, 'we were just catching up. Intendant Gomez, this is Mr Ross, formerly Detective Superintendent Ross of Lothian and Borders Police in Edinburgh.'

'Always good to meet a fellow cop,' Ricky said. 'I'm glad you could spare the time to meet me.' I noted the singular, but let it lie. 'Have you been retired long?'

'A couple of years, but I'm sure they told you that.'

'Yes, they did,' he admitted. 'It's just that you look young enough to be in the job still. Why did you quit?'

As Ricky asked the question, I understood why Hector had spoken in Spanish and not in the Catalan that he and I would normally have used. He wouldn't have expected his interviewer to know anything of that language, but he'd been checking out his fluency in Castellano. Clearly, it was lacking.

We took seats around a small table, and Hector explained the reason for his early retirement.

'But you'd be fit for an office job?' Ricky asked him.

'I am, I believe; and so does my doctor. What is the duty?'

Ricky explained what the job entailed; responsibility for the safety and security at Girona of all WeighleyAir aircraft and installations.

'What about the other companies who fly out of here, and the private owners?'

'I don't give a shit about them, personally, but if the man we appoint does the job as I expect it to be done, clearly they'll benefit also. In practice there are very few other operators, and not a lot of general aviation either. WeighleyAir won't be employing the security people here, that will continue to be done by the airport owners, but the WeighleyAir security manager will plan and oversee their operations and will determine the adequacy of the security equipment, camera, motion sensors and all that stuff. If he sees an area where there's a weakness, the airport owner will plug the gap. What I'm saying is that he will have total . . . I stress the word . . . responsibility for everything affecting the safety of the WeighleyAir operations.'

'I understand,' Hector said, quietly. 'And if I was fortunate enough to be offered this position, who would be my manager? You, Señor Ross?'

'Technically, no, you wouldn't be my employee. Technically you'd be responsible to Mr Weighley, the owner. In fact, you would report to anyone he nominates.' He glanced at me. 'Probably that would be Primavera. She's now working as a general consultant to the company.'

He smiled. 'That would be an unimagined situation for me, but it would give me no difficulty.'

'If I were to offer you the post, Señor Gomez, what salary would you expect?'

Hector frowned, stared at the ceiling for a few seconds, then looked back across the table. 'It's a responsible position. Would sixty thousand euros annual be acceptable to you?'

Ricky glanced at me. I guessed that Weighley had told him I had authority to close the deal.

'Normal employment conditions, but on call twenty-four seven?' I put to Hector.

'Of course.'

'That would be acceptable,' I told him. 'If you give me a moment, I'll arrange for an employment contract to be issued.'

I went into the corridor and called Weighley. I told him that we were going to appoint Gomez and what the salary was.

'Sounds cheap to me,' he said. 'I'll have the paperwork faxed across to you, if you give me his details.'

I stepped back into the room and asked Hector for his second surname . . . Spanish people use both parents' surnames but usually answer to their father's . . . and his tax identification number. He wrote both down for me; to my surprise I saw that his mother's name, and thus his grandfather's, was Sierra. I knew that I'd come across that handle recently, but I couldn't pin it down, not then.

Contracts arrived by email from Edinburgh ten minutes later; in Castellano and in English. As the two men read them through, I took the precaution of making sure that each version said the same thing. My name was entered as company representative, and so when we were all satisfied, Hector and I signed three copies of each document and he was on the payroll.

'Excellent,' Ricky declared. 'Now . . .'

'Now we should walk round the airport and look at the current arrangements, yes?'

'Yes, but there's something I want to discuss with you first, before we get down to that. You'll have noted that there's a confidentiality clause in there; it binds you to secrecy over anything of a sensitive nature that you may hear in the company's employment.'

'Of course,' Hector replied. 'I was expecting it, and I don't have a problem with it.'

'Good, because there's something I have to tell you.' He turned to me. 'Primavera, you can leave us now if you'd rather.'

'I'm staying,' I told him firmly. 'Remember what Jack said?'

He frowned, and grunted, 'Okay, if you insist. Señor Gomez, there's a situation I want to tell you about.'

I listened as he talked our new colleague through the events that had brought him to Spain, the spray painting and the punctured aircraft tyre. That I'd expected, prior to any tour of inspection, but when he added, 'On top of all that some bastard tried to kill me on Monday, by blowing my car up in St Martí,' I was rocked back in my seat.

I was almost knocked off it when Hector Gomez nodded, and said, 'Yes, I know of that.'

'You do?' Ricky and I exclaimed, simultaneously.

'Yes, that is to say I know of the incident. I had no idea until now that you were the intended victim of the attack.'

'Has Alex Guinart been talking to you?' I asked.

'No, no, not at all: Alex is much too conscientious ever to share a professional secret, unless it was absolutely necessary. I have another source, one I can vouch for, and one I am going to protect.'

And then I worked out where I'd come across his second surname before.

'She wouldn't be called Gemma, would she? The forensic team leader, by any chance?'

He looked at me, then at Ricky, and I saw a little of the tough, unsmiling cop he used to be. 'And that confidence remains within this room also, yes?'

'Of course,' I assured him.

'I should have known you would make the connection between her name and mine. Gemma is my cousin, the daughter of my mother's brother, as I imagine you have worked out by now. She came to see me last night, looking for advice. She said that she had been called to the scene of an explosion and fire, a car in the public park just outside St Martí d'Empúries. Normally she would have taken her two colleagues with her, but one is about to have a baby and the other had called in sick that morning. So she went alone. It did not stretch her skill, she said, to know that the initial explosion had been caused by a bomb. She described the type of device to me in detail, that's how certain she was. She ordered that the car be transported to the Mossos office in Girona for further examination, and she reported her findings to Alex Guinart.

'She was at home on Monday evening when she had a visit from two men. They were unknown to her and they were in plain clothes, but they told her they were colleagues, not Mossos but another department. They showed her their identity cards but kept their names concealed. I might not know who they were, but that behaviour tells me what they are. I believe that in the Reino Unido, Señor Ross, you have a network that you call Special Branch. So do we; we call it something else, but its task is similar and it behaves in similar ways.'

Ricky nodded. 'Fucking spooks: we call them that as well. I was one myself when I was a detective sergeant.'

'Then you will know that they hadn't called on Gemma for a beer and a friendly chat. They told her that they had been sent to tell her that her report to Guinart had been mistaken and that the explosion had been spontaneous. They even showed her a statement that explained how it had happened, and they told her . . . told her, they didn't ask . . . to sign it.'

'Which she duly did,' I murmured.

'Of course; she was frightened, she did it to get them out of her house. We live in a country, Primavera, where a couple of generations ago, people might disappear with no questions being asked.'

He seemed a little offended. 'I'm not having a go at her; I'm not criticising,' I said quickly. 'I'd have done the same thing . . . although I might have used magic ink that disappeared as soon as they were out the door.'

He smiled. 'They'd have come back, be in no doubt about that.'

'What about the person who tried to kill me?' Ricky asked. 'Will he come back?'

'He'd be taking a risk if he did, don't you think, now that you have been alerted to his existence.' Hector paused and scratched his chin. 'Of course there is another possibility.'

'What's that?'

'Do you believe that the person who planted the bomb was trying to kill you because you are Señor Ross, or because you are a public representative of the WeighleyAir airline?'

Ricky shrugged his shoulders. 'I don't have a Scooby.'

'I'm sorry? I don't understand this saying.'

'It's slang, rhyming slang,' I explained. 'Scooby means Scooby-Doo, and that rhymes with clue.'

He stared at me as if I had gone mad. 'Scooby-Doo?' I ventured. 'The cartoon character?' Not a flicker; I gave up. 'He's saying he doesn't know. Go on with what you were about to suggest.'

'I was going to propose that if the bomber is a personal enemy, that is one thing, but if he is someone who has targeted WeighleyAir . . . then more than one of its employees might be at risk.'

I got the drift. 'In which case Madrid is putting all of them . . . us . . . in danger by pretending that this never happened and trying to cover it up.'

'Exactly.' He smiled. 'Now that I am an employee of the company, that makes me a little angry.'

'Go back to your cousin,' Ricky said. 'What did she do after the spooks had left?

'She lay awake all night. Next morning, she went to the depot where the car should have been taken. It wasn't there. It had been taken away, by a scrap metal company. They arrived with a certificate of permission from the Guardia Civil, and the person in charge let them have it. When her day was over, she came to see me and told me the whole story.'

'So what did you tell her?'

'Are you crazy, señor? What do you think? I told her to forget that any of it had ever happened and to get on with her job. She's a working cop, but a specialist and they shouldn't interfere in things that happen outside their . . .' He looked at me. 'How do you say it?'

'Area of expertise.'

'Exactly.' He leaned forward. 'Now, Señor Ross, why don't you get round to what you were going to tell me.'

'Okay,' Ricky replied. 'We all know what really happened on Monday, and, Mr Gomez, I agree with your proposition that in theory we might all be in the firing line. I don't really believe for a second the thing was personal either. Chances are, anyone with a grudge against me would have had a go at me in Scotland a long time ago, and nobody ever has.

'So where does that put us? I'll tell you. The Mossos d'Esquadra may have been sidelined by Madrid, and a cover-up may have been staged, but that means fuck all to me, as the guy who might have been on his way home right now in a cardboard box. If nobody else is going to get after these people, I am, and as a fellow target, so to speak, I'd like you to help me.'

I held up a hand. 'Hold on a minute, Ricky,' I exclaimed. 'Before you go any further, I have to remind you that when Hector signed up, he didn't know any of this background. It might be company business, but if he wants I'm going to let him walk away from this thing right now, by tearing up those contracts we just signed.'

Both ex-cops looked at me, Ross frowning, Gomez smiling.

'That is very generous of you,' the latter said, 'but I will not be doing that. You're paying me a ridiculous salary for a simple job, and I'd be a fool to walk away from it because of a little risk, after spending a career, like our friend here, facing dangers that were probably much more real. How can I help, Señor Ricky?'

'Two ways: first, are you able to pull some favours by accessing your national crime computer . . . if you have such a thing in Spain . . . to draw up a list of known criminals with expertise in bomb-making?'

'It's possible,' Hector admitted, 'but I'll need to be careful. If I'm too direct, word might get to the wrong people in Barcelona, worse still, in Madrid. I don't want the guys who visited my cousin to turn up at my door.' He paused. 'However, there is another way, so leave that with me. Now. What's the other thing you have in mind?'

'I want to trace somebody, an individual. There's a suspect for the nonsense that happened here at the airport, a man named Gaizka Alonso. I only know that he used to work for the airline until he got sacked, and I have no idea how seriously to take him but his is the only name I have, and I want to put a face to it and if possible find out where he was on Monday, to cross him off the suspect list, if nothing else.'

'What do you know about him?'

'Only his name and the fact that he was WeighleyAir aircrew until he was fired for being rude to the punters.'

'Mmm,' Gomez murmured. 'That first name sounds Basque . . . but these days that doesn't mean too much. When he was let go by the company, would his personnel record have been destroyed?'

'Yes, I'm afraid it was,' Ricky confirmed. 'I've checked with the Human Resources people in Edinburgh. He has a file, but it's very small; the only things on it are three records of complaint by the customers he was rude to and a statement by his cabin team leader. It says that there had been previous incidents that she had managed to smooth over, and that she had warned him about his future behaviour before the final episode, when she recommended him for dismissal. The only other item in the folder is his formal termination letter. It's in Spanish and English like the company contract. But that's it; those documents were kept as a defence against any legal comeback, but everything else went into the shredder.'

'So we don't have a direction for him?'

'A what?'

Hector raised an apologetic hand. 'I'm sorry, an address.'

'No, otherwise I'd be there right now, banging on his door.'

'However, the incidents, the painting the aircraft, the vandalism; they happened here, in Girona, yes?'

'Yes, and he was seen here on the night the tyres were done. The police interviewed him but he spun them some story about waiting for a woman who didn't turn up. He couldn't prove it but they had nothing on him either.'

'Ahh, he was interviewed by the Mossos?'

'Yes.'

'Then they will have a record, and an address.' The sudden light in his eyes vanished almost as soon as it appeared. 'But of course if I ask anyone what it was, even Alex . . .'

I finished for him. 'You'll put him in a difficult position. As you said earlier he's too much cop to share that information, and he might even report your interest to Barcelona.'

'Yes,' Hector agreed, 'that is true and so that channel is not open to us. But there are others, public ways in which I can trace Señor Alonso. That he was seen at the airport and interviewed here suggests to us that he does live in this area. If he does and he owns property then his name will be on the register in Girona. The contract I have just signed says that legally I am employed in Spain and not through WeighleyAir's head office in Scotland. If the same is true of flight crew as well as ground staff, then social security payments will have been made on his behalf. Indeed if he is still unemployed, he will be receiving payments from that department. Like you, I am sure, Señor Ross, I have made many friends during my career, in many government departments. It won't be difficult for me to trace our friend Gaizka, if he is still in this part of Spain.'

'How quickly?' Ricky asked. 'I want to move fast on this.'

'Let me do what I have to do at the airport for the official part of my new job, for I am responsible here even now. As soon as I can I will get on to the other thing. Maybe this afternoon, maybe tomorrow morning, but soon, I promise.'

We all rose from our seats and as we did, he put a hand on

Ricky's shoulder. 'Tell me, Ricky, do you really believe that this man Alonso could have tried to kill you?'

'Honestly? No, I don't. Blowing up aircraft tyres with a penknife, that's small-time. Blowing up cars with specialist explosive, that's right at the opposite end of the scale. And something else; if he does have bomb-making skills, why didn't he just blow up the bloody plane? However, Hector, as I said earlier, his is the only name I have, so I need to sit down with him, have a serious talk with him and look him in the eye, before I cross him off my list.'

'I know. I hope I can make it possible for you to do that before tomorrow is over. Until then, take care, look out for anyone or anything unusual around you . . . as will I, now that we are colleagues, although . . .' His voice trailed away as if he'd decided to leave something unsaid.

Ricky wouldn't let him. 'Although what? Come on, what weren't you going to say?'

'Okay. The theory, the Madrid theory, that the bomb they are trying to deny might have been a Catalan nationalist terrorist thing, I would not rule it out. However, I do not believe that all of the WeighleyAir employees are in danger.

'I need to check the files but I am sure that nearly all the people employed here in Girona will be Catalans themselves. As such, they are not going to be targets. But you, Señor Ricky, you may very well be.' He looked at me. 'As for you, Primavera, I think you should keep word of your new employment out of the papers.'

Fourteen

He had a point. I called Weighley again, on his direct line. He was tied up in a meeting, but his secretary, whose name was Gemma, took my call. When I asked her to pass on a request that my appointment should be kept private, I didn't like her reply.

'I'm sorry, Mrs Blackstone, but a press release has gone out already. Alison Ross issued it this morning, here and in Spain, through her associate company there. That's not a problem, is it?'

Potentially it was, but I couldn't let Jack know that without him wanting to know why. 'No, it's not,' I told her, 'as long as it didn't contain my home address.'

'It's all right,' she assured me, 'it didn't. Only your company mobile number and your company email address.'

'I don't have a company mobile. Or an email address.'

'Your phone's being couriered to you from our Spanish supplier. As for the email address, all employees have those.'

'But I'm not an employee,' I pointed out.

'You are, technically.'

'Technically, nothing. My tax status is important, to me if not to Jack. I'm not having anything that will cause me problems down the line. That includes benefits in kind, so you can put a stop on the phone as well. I will send you a standard monthly invoice for my fee and expenses. That's what I do for the directorship I hold in my brother-in-law's Spanish wine business. If Jack doesn't like that, he can do the other thing.'

'What other thing?'

'He can go and . . .'

To my surprise Gemma laughed. 'I like you already, Mrs Blackstone. I've been longing for someone to tell him that. Would you like me to send you a copy of the press release?'

'Yes please, in both languages. Things can get lost in translation.'

I hung up and headed out to the concourse to catch up with Hector and Ricky on their security tour, but by that time they were at the northern end of the airport, and so I let them get on with it. I was about to head back to L'Escala when something clicked. I'd told Ricky earlier that he was welcome to catch the afternoon flight to Edinburgh; that was the return leg and it was Wednesday, so Mac Blackstone would be on the incoming aircraft.

I called Jonny on my mobile. 'Hi, Auntie P,' he exclaimed as he took the call: I've tried to get him not to call me that but he insists. 'Pleasant surprise. I'd feared it was Grandpa calling to say his flight had been cancelled. It wouldn't surprise me, given the lot he's flying with.'

'Don't be rude,' I chided him. 'WeighleyAir has a very good punctuality record.'

'Yeah, sure. But don't trust them with your golf clubs. A mate of mine did and he had to tee up in Portugal with a borrowed set.'

'That can happen with any airline. It's down to the baggage handlers.'

'Jesus, you sound as if you're on their payroll.'

I laughed. 'As a matter of fact I am.'

'For real?' he asked, astonished.

'Yup.'

'When the hell did that happen? How did it happen?'

'When, yesterday. How … that's a complicated story. The point of my call, Jonny, is that I'm at the airport now. I can hang around and pick up Mac, rather than you taking a big chunk out of your day.'

'Oh.' There followed a few seconds' silence, during which I'll swear I could hear him think. 'Could you really?' he resumed, eventually. 'This is going to sound terrible, and please don't tell Grandpa, but that would suit me. I sent my short game coach a couple of video clips last night. We're trying to sort out a problem I've had for the last couple of weeks, and he's come back to me this morning with some suggestions. I'm on the practice ground now with Logan, my caddie, and it's going well, so if I could carry on for another couple of hours . . .'

'You do that. You must see him before you leave at the weekend, though. How are you and Selina placed tonight? Could you come and eat with us?'

'Yes, but you'll eat with me, all of you.'

'Don't be daft.'

'No, it's the least I can do. How about that restaurant where you took me once, the night you gave me a pep talk I will never forget?'

'Can Roura?'

'That's it. Book there for seven of us . . . or eight, if you want to bring someone.'

I smiled at his thoughtfulness. After Selina, I'm Jonny's biggest fan, and I know it's reciprocated. 'I'll do that, but it'll be seven. I'm not giving up on Liam yet. See you tonight, around seven thirty. School day tomorrow; the older two keep big people hours now, but I don't want your namesake to be up too late.'

I closed the call and let him go back to whatever golfing intricacy he was sorting out. I had almost two hours before Mac's flight was due, so I drove up to Girona and did some shopping in El Corte Ingles. I was slightly spooked on the way up when I realised that I was looking in my rear-view rather more often than was usual, just to check that I wasn't being followed.

'Bloody hell, Liam,' I murmured to my empty car, 'where are you when I need you?'

But I wasn't blown up, or shot at or abducted, or anything else nasty, and when Grandpa Mac wheeled his case through the doorway that leads out of the baggage hall, I was there waiting for him.

My first thought was that he hadn't come a moment too

soon. He was pale and drawn and tired, looking every one of his years for the first time since we'd met. I hoped that my concern didn't show as I gave him a welcoming hug.

'Hello, Primavera darling,' he murmured into my ear. 'Great to see you. Has that grandson of mine let me down?'

'No he hasn't,' I promised him. 'I had to be at the airport on business, and so there was no point in him breaking into his practice session. You amateur golfers,' I scolded. 'You don't realise that being a pro is a full-time job. They spend more time on the driving range than they do on the course in tournaments.'

He laughed. 'Ellie told me you treat him like a mother hen. This girlfriend of his; what's she like? I've never met her.'

'Selina's lovely. She's as Catalan as you can get; she's teaching Jonny the language and introducing him to lots of people his own age. He has a life outside golf now; that's something he was needing.'

He was silent as we crossed the road to the car park, and loaded his case into the boot of my beloved old jeep. 'Jonny: his career still comes first though?' he ventured as he strapped himself into the passenger seat. 'He's not being distracted, is he?'

'Definitely not,' I assured him. 'He's not here because he wants to get his game one hundred per cent right for next week's tournament. If anything he's even more ambitious. When he turned up here two years ago to play in his first pro event, it was as if he was just giving it a shot. But when he went and won that, everything changed. He's proved to himself that he's got what it takes to be one of the best, but he understands that getting there involves hard work. He doesn't drink, he doesn't smoke and he's in the gym every day.'

'I noticed that a few months back, when he visited his mother and Harvey. The lad's built like a brick shithouse or *casa de mierdas*, if that's what it is in Spanish.'

I laughed. 'Near enough. Liam was his fitness coach while he was here; he gave him proper workout and weight routines, so that he developed the muscles he needs for his game, without restricting his movement.'

'Aye, Liam.' Mac glanced at me as we rolled out of the car park and into traffic; again, I couldn't help glancing in the rear-view mirror to see if anyone was exiting behind me. My paranoid side had actually checked under the wheel arch on the driver's side, while Mac was loading his luggage. 'Will I be seeing him?'

'No, not this visit.'

'He will be back, though?'

I nodded, and caught his eye, briefly. 'Yes, in November. Ach . . . we hit a bump in the road, Mac, and he went off to finish a book he's working on. But I've got my head right now, and I really do want him back.'

'Are you going to marry him?'

'Don't you start,' I snorted. 'That was the bump in the road.' Then I softened. 'But you know, I just might, if he still wants to. It's not like with Oz and me; I don't feel the same,' I looked for a phrase, 'the same dangerous excitement with him, but he's a good guy and he loves me and I love that

137

about him. It's only very recently that I've come to terms with this, but I'm getting too old for passion and adventures and all that shit. It's only very recently I've accepted my present and my future, and realised that being a mother of three is the best job I've ever had.'

Mac laughed. 'Bloody hell, Primavera, you're far too young to be having a mid-life crisis.'

'Thanks, but if I was I've got over it. How about you, how are you handling things?'

I sensed the laughter leave him. 'As best I can, lass. Mary's away with the fairies and she'll never be back; I've known that for a while. The person I married no longer exists; I'm looking after the thing she lived in, but it's empty, devoid of personality, devoid of coherent thought, devoid of soul. I've been far from perfect in my life, Primavera, and if this is a punishment so be it, but Mary never did anything to deserve it.'

In fact she did, if you believe in retribution. Mary had a secret that only Oz knew about, until he told me, the last time I ever saw him; it involved Mac but she had kept it from him, until she was beyond sharing and confession.

'That's too bad,' I told him. 'You're a brave man, Mac. Most people would have put her in a care home.'

'That's what I have done, in effect, Primavera. She has everything at the house that she would have in one of those places, and a wee bit more, because she has the same faces around her all the time, including mine, for what that's worth.'

'It's worth plenty, I'll bet. Mac, you have no idea what's going on inside her head.'

'Ah but I do,' he said gloomily. 'I've seen the brain scans.'

There wasn't anything I could say after that, so I kept quiet for a while.

We were north of Girona before Mac broke the silence. 'And you, madam,' he exclaimed out of the blue. 'You said you were at the airport on business. What was that about? You haven't started doing taxi runs, have you?'

'Hell no! That'll be the day. You know that airline you've just flown on?'

'Of course. A great Scottish business success story; probably our biggest. The only airline I can think of with its own airport. They call it Edinburgh East, even though it's in East Lothian, and who the hell cares, because it has its own direct rail links from just about anywhere, and its own station. I caught the train at Kirkcaldy, changed once and I was there in just over an hour. I couldn't have driven there that quickly. So? What about it?'

'If you know all that you'll have heard of the man who founded it.'

'Jack Weighley? The Flying Scotsman? Who hasn't? He's a bloody hero back home, Primavera, and a nice guy too, by all accounts.' I fought to keep a smile off my face. 'I saw him on telly a week or so back, on a chat show on STV. He came across very well. They're saying he'll be Sir Jack before too long. Some guy. Started the business with his own money and look at him now.' He glanced at me. 'What about him? Why are you asking?'

'Because it was his business I was looking after at the airport.'

'You're kidding me! You're working for WeighleyAir?'

'In a manner of speaking.' I explained that I was a consultant to the company, and that in my eyes that made me an adviser and not an employee. 'In other words, I give them my advice and opinion. Whether it's accepted or not, that's up to Jack.'

'First-name terms,' Mac murmured. 'I always knew you were important, Primavera, but you never cease to impress me.'

'Flattery will get you anywhere,' I chuckled. 'Sarcasm will get you dropped off on the hard shoulder and left to walk the rest of the way.'

He patted my shoulder. 'I'm guilty of neither, my love. All I was doing was speaking the truth. How did this come about?'

Good question, for the whole truth wasn't an option. I tried to recall the wording of the press release, which I'd had emailed to me and had studied on my phone's small screen in the ladies' in El Corte Ingles, with the aid of my hated reading specs.

'Catalunya is a very important part of WeighleyAir's business,' I parroted, 'and Girona is its principal hub. The political situation here is complex and ever-changing; the company needs advice on that and on the state of the tourist industry, since obviously that's its main customer base. They're calling me a public affairs consultant; that's as good a description as any.'

'Very good; you might even pick up some other clients, and have a nice wee business on your hands.'

'I don't want any more,' I said, firmly. 'I've told Jack what

I'm able to do for him and he's okay with that. But I will not have time to do it for anyone else . . . not for a couple of years anyway, when the kids are a bit more grown up . . . although . . .' I stopped, surprised by my unexpected prevarication but also as I recalled my recent bollocking from Tom and Janet for treating them like children.

'What?' Mac prompted me.

'Oh, nothing. You haven't seen the kids since Easter, have you? Don't be surprised when you find the older two have grown eighteen months older in those six.'

He looked at me, sideways, across the car. 'It must be an odd situation for you to have a brother and sister in the same family who are practically the same age. My promiscuous, prolific son has a lot to answer for.'

'But he never will, Mac, will he? Anyway, it's not a problem; I treat all three as my own, and I treat Janet and Tom as twins. So do they, although they haven't defined it that way, not yet.'

'I'm looking forward to seeing them again anyway. How's the wee chap?'

'Most in need of a grandfather figure to take him under his wing.'

'Then I'll do just that for as long as I'm here. What's he interested in?'

'Astronomy?'

'For real? Then let's hope for some clear nights.'

Having Mac in the car made me feel safer, somehow: I realised that I hadn't even thought about being tailed for a while. Then we drew up at the autopista pay station, and involuntarily I found myself checking the mirror. It was unlikely, I decided, that I was being pursued by a man in a dirty white pickup with hens in crates loaded on the back.

We had only just joined the L'Escala road when my phone sounded in the cradle on the dashboard. 'Ricky Ross' showed on screen: unthinking, I took the call, then realised that it would be on speaker for Mac to hear. 'Ricky,' I exclaimed, before he could get a word out, 'I've got Oz's dad in the car. Did you ever meet?'

'Once, when I was looking after Loch Lomond. How are you, Mr Blackstone? Richard Ross here.'

'I'm very well thanks, Ricky, and don't be so bloody formal.'

'Glad to hear it, Mac, sorry about the formality. I take it you're on your way back to L'Escala, Primavera.'

'Yes.'

'Me too. I was going to ask you if you wanted to have dinner tonight, but I guess you'll be busy.'

'Afraid so.' Not that I would have anyway.

'Okay, we'll catch up tomorrow. I'll be in touch once I've had feedback from Hector. Oh yes, and one other thing. I finally got around to making that call to Ronnie Morrow in Edinburgh. As I thought, he hadn't heard from the locals, but that's not surprising, given subsequent developments. He's going to check out those names on the list we discussed with your friend, and get back to me as soon as he can.'

'Fine, let me know when he does.'

'You don't need to be involved from here on in, you know.'

'Maybe not, but I want to be informed, at the very least.'

He laughed. 'Just in case you have to pick up the pieces?'

'Don't say that!' I snapped.

'Kidding, only kidding. That said, there was a time when you wouldn't have minded at all.'

'Not any more.'

'Nah. You got any ideas of places I might eat? Maybe out of town, but not too far.'

I looked at a road sign as we passed it, and had an idea. 'There's a village called Ventallo, about halfway between L'Escala and the autopista, with a restaurant called La Bassa. It's a very nice place, with a garden. If you take a jacket, you might be able to eat outside.'

'I'll give it a try, thanks. Speak tomorrow. Cheers.'

The loudspeaker buzzed as he ended the call. 'What the hell's he doing here?' Mac asked.

'He's on the WeighleyAir payroll as well,' I told him. 'He's Jack Weighley's security consultant.'

'Why does that bring him here?'

'There was a job needed doing at Girona Airport. He and I have just appointed a man to do it.'

'Mmm,' he grunted. 'Oz trusted him but I was never sure of that fellow. He's fifty per cent bullshit, I always thought. But maybe I'm wrong.'

'Yes, you are,' I said. 'In reality it's only around twenty-five per cent.'

'And how about Jack Weighley? How's he?'

'Jack? Oh, he's one hundred per cent, but not mere

bullshit, beyond that. He's a complete arsehole, with very good PR people around him.'

Mac sighed. 'There we go. Another idol brought crashing down . . . and believe me, when you get to my age, there aren't that many left.'

Fifteen

By the time the kids got home from school, their grandfather was installed in the guest room.

'My goodness, Primavera,' he exclaimed when he saw Janet and Tom . . . his language always improves when the kids are around, 'you weren't kidding about these two. Lass, you look more like your mother every day, and you, Tom, you'll need to be careful soon, or people will be taking you for Oz Blackstone.'

'I wouldn't mind that, Grandpa,' my son replied.

'Maybe you should. He'd have been nearer fifty than forty by now. From the way you're growing you're going to end up bigger than him. How tall are you now?'

'One metre seventy-three; Mum has a chart that says I'll be around one metre ninety-five when I stop.'

'What's that in language I'd understand?'

'About six feet four.'

'At least, I'd say. Are you still doing that martial arts stuff?'

'Yes, I'm a second dan black belt now; with another grading

coming up at the weekend. Liam says that fifth is probably as high as I'll get.'

Mac smiled. 'Who's Dan, when he's at home?'

Tom looked at him blankly; he isn't up to speed with Scottish colloquialisms. 'It's the grading system,' he replied.

'Ah, stupid bugger that I am. How's your golf? What are you playing off these days?'

'Six handicap at Pals, as of last month, after I won the adult medal; Jonny coaches me when he's at home. Janet too; she's off twelve and she's only been playing seriously for the last year.'

'They've left me behind, Mac,' I told him, 'both of them.'

He turned to wee Jonathan, and ruffled his hair. 'And how about you, my man, how's your game?'

'I don't play golf, Grandpa.' He said so in a guilty tone.

'Thank God for that. At last I've got one grandchild that isn't going to kick my arse around the course. Your Auntie Primavera says you like astronomy; me too, but I don't know much about it, so you can give me some tips. How about fishing?' he asked, even though he knew the answer.

The wee chap treated him to his widest smile. It transforms him, but we don't see it often enough. 'I like fishing,' he said, nodding vigorously.

'Even better. I'll tell you something, Jonathan; my best golfing days are well behind me, but I have a feeling that my finest fishing years are still to come. Have you got a spare rod?'

'We've got a garage full of them,' I said. 'I'm short of bait just now, though. All I have is stale bread.'

'That'll do fine,' Mac chortled. 'In my experience sea fish are completely fucking . . . oops, sorry, Primavera,' he said as all three kids giggled, '. . . stupid. Come on, wee Jonathan, let's go; and anyone else who wants to come.'

Janet isn't big on angling; she doesn't like what happens after you catch them. Tom might have stayed behind too but I gave him a nod that he read correctly. Wee Jonathan would want to fish off the jetty that extends from below our house, and parts of it are very rough indeed, till you get to the end. He isn't allowed out there on his own and I doubted that his grandad would be much use in an emergency. Tom, on the other hand, is a water boy, and has been since he was a nipper. He is also not slow to stop his kid brother from doing anything risky.

I told them to be back by six forty-five at the latest, on pain of me having to come and get them, and that threat worked, for they reappeared on the dot. The boys were pleased and Mac looked as if Christmas had come early as they presented me with three large sea bass, properly cleaned . . . by Tom, I guessed, for that's his job when I fish with them.

By the time Jonny and Selina arrived, just after seven, we were all presentable, ready to be seen in public. But it wasn't just Jonny and Selina; we were to be an eightsome for dinner after all. They had brought Selina's mother, Anais, a very attractive woman, just short of the sixty mark. She had been widowed eighteen months before. She'd taken it hard, and had coped by throwing herself into the family business, a hotel in Figueres. I was glad to see her beginning to emerge into the world again, although I was a little surprised to see her doing so that evening.

I poured some drinks on the terrace to give Mac some catching up time with Jonny, while I talked to the ladies and the two boys told Janet about the ones that had got away. At seven thirty on the dot we left, and walked the fifty metres from our house to the restaurant. As we got there I whispered to Mac, 'Does Jonny know about Mary?'

'Yes,' he replied, just as quietly. 'I told him the whole story on Monday, over the phone.' I found myself wondering whether that explained Anais' presence.

The weather was warm enough for us to sit at a long table in its rear courtyard. Señor Joan, the owner and chef, had brought out a space heater, just in case, but it stayed unlit. Eight people, under an awning, give out quite enough heat. The tasting menu was excellent, as it always is there, a series of creative dishes, tapas-sized but enough to leave you feeling satisfied when it's all over. Jonny and his lady sat alongside Mac and Anais, with Janet and me flanking them at one end and the two boys at the other.

I was amused by Tom; he spent the evening talking to Selina, and hardly at all to his cousin. In fact Jonny is one of his idols, but nowadays he's far too cool to let it show. In any case, Jonny was busy making a fuss of his much smaller namesake. At one point, I heard him say, 'You have to get out more, be more gregarious.'

'What?'

'Gregarious. It means mix more, be more sociable, meet

more people, make more friends. You can't live within your-self; it's bad for you. My agent, Brush, he did that and it got to the point where he couldn't mix with other people without starting to panic. Do you know what a phobia is?' he asked.

'It means you're afraid of something,' the wee man told him, promptly. 'My mum was afraid of spiders. I killed them all for her.'

'Right. That's a very common one, maybe the most common, but there are millions of them, waiting to trap you if you stay too wrapped up in yourself. And not just people. There's a belief that elephants are afraid of mice.'

'No,' wee Jonathan protested, scornfully. 'They could just squash them. Like I did with the spiders.'

'But you weren't afraid of the spiders,' Jonny countered. 'Your mum was, and she was much bigger than they were, so why shouldn't it be the same with elephants and mice?'

'I suppose,' his cousin admitted. 'But I don't have phobias. And I don't not mix with other people. They don't mix with me.'

'Are you sure that you don't encourage them? I know you've lost your mum, and your dad, and that's terrible for a boy. You'll always miss them, but you don't need to show it all the time. You have to learn to smile more. Smiles are great things, they're like yawns.'

'What do you mean?'

I was at the other end of the table, but I was tuned into the discussion, fascinated.

Jonny grinned, and my heart gave a small jump. There's

one thing he shares with his late uncle, and that's charisma. But always it takes me by surprise when it hits me; you can be too close to something to see it properly.

'Have you ever noticed that when you're in a bunch of people and somebody yawns, pretty soon everyone else is doing it too? It's the same with smiles; they're just as infectious. So the next time you feel one coming on, don't smother it, let it out and let others catch it.

'You know, my brother, Colin, your other cousin, when he was your age, he was a right wee toerag, an imp of concentrated mischief. He was always up to something, inquisitive, a cheeky little bugger and always laughing. And then something happened to him. I don't know what it was; it was as if he caught the gloomy bug. He stopped smiling, he turned serious, he avoided all his friends and he spent all day face to face with his computer, and those never smile back at you. In short, he turned into the dour little bugger that he is to this day.'

He patted the wee chap's shoulder, man to man. 'I tell you this; I am not going to allow that to happen to you. I can't. We have the same name, and I simply will not have people saying, "See that Jonathan? A right miserable sod he is." Others might think they were talking about me.

'So stop hiding your real self in there. Let him out and people will love him.' He paused, then turned his cousin's head, gently so that he had to make eye contact. 'Trust me on this,' he continued. 'Give me a smile and see what happens.'

Neither of them realised it, but the other six of us had fallen silent, and were gazing at them as, slowly but steadily, a grin spread across the sad little boy's face, widening until it turned into a gentle laugh, and then a full-on giggle. The terrace lighting had been adequate, but suddenly it seemed twice as bright.

'That's it,' Jonny said. 'When you've got a smile like that, kid, it's a crime to lock it away. Look around you.'

He did as he was told, and saw six smiling faces, all looking back at him; at least one had a lump in her throat.

'Do you see?' Grandpa Mac said. 'Jonny's right, it works. He's right about his brother too. He needs bringing out of himself. There's some excuse for him, though. He takes after his father.' He glanced at Jonny. 'Sorry, son, but you know it's true. What you've got to make sure, wee Jonathan, is that from now on you take after yours. And I can tell you that when he was your age, he was the toerag to end them all.'

'And he never changed,' I added, 'not completely, at any rate.'

Anais was smiling with the rest of us, but I could tell that she wasn't following all of what we were saying. I suggested to Mac that he explain, which he did, very happily, it struck me.

Dessert was on its way when my phone told me I had a text. *Not bloody Weighley*, I hoped, as I took it from my bag. It wasn't; it was from Alex Guinart, and it read, 'Where are you? I am at your house and need to see you. *Urgente.*'

My friend isn't a man to overstate a situation, and so when he says something is urgent, I believe him. I sent a quick reply, 'Can Roura. See you outside, now.'

I excused myself to Jonny and Mac, telling them that I had

to see someone, but would be back in a minute or two.

As I stepped out into the square Alex arrived at the restaurant door. 'What are you doing?' he asked, quietly.

'I'm in the middle of a family dinner,' I replied, just a little annoyed. 'Oz's dad's here, and Jonny's entertaining us. Where's the bloody fire?'

'It's not here, but I would like you to come with me.'

'I can't, Alex, it would be rude. Or are you telling me I'm under arrest?'

'No, of course not, but please, come with me. I don't want to go into it here, because I don't know all of it, but it is important and you will want to be involved. If you wish, I will make your apologies to your nephew.'

I had a choice, and yet friendship meant that I didn't. 'No,' I said. 'I'll do that.'

I went back inside and told everyone that I had to leave. 'Alex Guinart says he needs my help.'

'Then go help him,' Jonny replied at once. 'He's your pal. I think Tom and I can manage to get everyone home safe.'

'Thanks, you're a love. Good luck next week. I'll bet on you to win.'

He smiled. 'I fancy my chances, but backing me each way might be safer.'

As I left, I gave wee Jonathan a kiss on the cheek; he beamed again, and turned pink.

Alex's car was parked in front of my house; not everyone is allowed to bring a vehicle into the village, but cops can do anything they bloody like, can't they? I didn't ask any questions as we headed off. I knew that whatever it was that he had to tell me, he would when he was ready. Instead I let him concentrate on the road ahead, for he was travelling at a fair speed, and his blue lights were on. We turned right on to the main road, away from L'Escala. I thought that he might turn into Viladamat, but he didn't. He kept straight on, cruised through the first junction and took the bridge that crosses the main Figueres road.

It was when he zoomed through the roundabout on the other side and headed for Ventallo that I began to get a bad feeling.

'Alex,' I murmured, 'are we going to where I think we're going?'

Sixteen

We took the first exit into the village. It was unmarked, but there were signs there advertising its restaurants and one of them read 'La Bassa'. I looked ahead as Alex made the turn and saw more blue lights off to the right, pulsing.

'Shit,' I murmured.

He drove on, past the little nursery and the village hall on the left. The road forked but we drove straight on until we reached a police car, slewed sideways and barring our way. As Alex drew to a halt, a cop approached.

'You'd be best to go on foot from here, Intendant,' he said. 'It gets narrow, and there's a fire tender up there already . . . not that there was ever much of a fire to put out. An ambulance is on its way from Figueres, but they ain't going to need that either. What a bloody mess.'

Alex killed the engine and we both got out. The officer glanced at me. 'Do you really want to take the lady in there, sir?' he asked.

'Of course I don't,' Alex snapped back at him. 'I don't want to be going in there myself. I'd rather be at home with my wife and daughter. Wouldn't you?'

'Of course. Sorry, boss.'

We left him and headed towards the restaurant; the fire engine was parked there sure enough, we saw it as soon as we cleared a curve in the road. It sported the blue lights I had seen earlier; they were quite unnecessary, but the firefighters in our part of the world are all part-time volunteers, and they like to play with the toys whenever they can.

The crew were standing around, looking sombre, every one of them. Their chief started towards us; he was carrying his helmet, another sign that their job was done.

Before he reached us, two couples passed by, or would have if Alex hadn't stopped them. 'Excuse me,' he asked. 'I assume that you've come from La Bassa.'

I'd made the same assumption on the basis that all four of them looked shocked and ghostly white, even under the yellow-hued street lighting. The two men had taken off their jackets and draped them around their ladies' shoulders, but both women were still shivering.

'Yes,' one of the guys replied. 'We got to get out of here.'

'I'm sorry,' Alex replied. 'I have to ask you to wait. I've only had the most sketchy report of what happened in there. I'm going to need your statements as witnesses.'

'But we didn't see anything,' the man wailed. He was a chunky bloke, but nonetheless seemed on the edge of hysteria. 'We only heard it. My wife was sitting nearest the door, and she's deaf in her left ear now. Look, it's bleeding.' He took his arm from around her shoulders so that we could see. The nurse in me recognised a perforated eardrum.

'She needs to go to hospital,' I said. 'All the more reason for you to wait here, since there are paramedics on the way.'

'Okay,' the potential witness said, grudgingly, 'but we're not going back in there.'

'You can sit in our tender,' the fire chief told him, as he arrived in time to pick up the last of the exchange. 'We won't be going anywhere for a while.'

'Are there any other customers still in there?' Alex asked the shaken man.

'No. We were the only ones; it was a quiet night. Juan Manuel's still there though, and his wife.' I knew them; they ran the restaurant.

He turned to the fireman. 'Is it safe now? Should they still be there?'

'They wouldn't leave,' he replied. 'But I believe it's okay. There was a small fire but we put it out. The outbuildings, though, they're completely demolished. As of course is the poor guy who . . .'

'Yes, yes,' my escort snapped, forestalling him. I guess he did it for my sake, but I had worked out what had happened before we'd even reached the village.

'Let's go,' I said quietly, tugging at Alex's sleeve.

'You don't need to,' he murmured, speaking English for the first time that evening.

'Of course I do, or you wouldn't have brought me here.'

'I'm beginning to regret that now.'

'Tough.'

I turned away and walked towards the entrance to the narrow lane that leads into La Bassa, with Alex following me for a change. From the fire chief's description, I knew what we were going to find there, and as soon as we stepped out of the approach vennel, we did.

The building is large, stone and old. Its public areas are a long bar and a dining room, both of which open out into a garden, where most of the food is served in the summer.

It wasn't summer, though, and there was a chill in the air that I hadn't noticed in St Martí, so none of the tables were set. If they had been most wouldn't have been usable, for they were upside down, or on their side.

La Bassa has a peculiarity. As I said, it's an old building, with a couple of hundred years of history, reflected in the fact that the toilets, both men's and women's, are outside, with a small *trustero*, a store, between them. Those were the out-buildings the fireman had mentioned and he hadn't been exaggerating about their condition.

They'd been reduced to rubble. Stone, porcelain, paper, wood, slates, you name it, they were strewn all over the garden.

And one more piece of debris: a body. When I saw it, my stomach lurched, but I was able to keep its contents in place, and my mind as dispassionate as I could.

It was about twenty-feet away from what had been the men's toilet and appeared to be embedded its door. Maybe that's why most of it was intact, although I could see that a couple of parts were missing; to be specific, the feet. The arms

157

were still there but appeared to be impacted in the torso, hands together as if they had been holding something, as is often the case in a gentlemen's convenience. The head was still in place but it was well out of shape, and scorched with the rest of the . . . the thing.

I didn't want to go any closer . . . there would have been no point in a detailed examination, as there was nothing identifiable there . . . so I led the way towards the main building, picking my way through the debris. I was at the top of the short flight of steps that leads to the bar when something caught my eye. I bent and picked it up. Alex was ahead of me by that time, having hurried past the body, so he didn't notice.

It was a mobile phone and, amazingly, it was still more or less intact. The plastic casing was a little rippled, but the screen was unbroken. A modern design masterpiece and no mistake. I don't know why I slipped it into my pocket rather than hand it to Alex, but I did.

Juan Manuel and Tess, his wife, were sitting at a table in the empty bar as we entered, with a bottle of brandy and two glasses in front of them. She was in tears, and from the look of him, he had been too. They recognised me, as a regular customer, but not Alex. When I introduced him, they were too dazed to ask what the hell I was doing there.

'My sympathies,' he began. 'This is an awful thing to have happened.'

Tess nodded and tried to speak, but erupted into more crying.

'But how?' Juan Manuel exclaimed. 'That's what I can't understand. How did it happen?'

'I have a scientific officer on the way here,' Alex said. 'I'm sure that she will be able to give us the answer. The dead man,' he continued. 'How did you know who he was? Had he paid his bill?'

'No, he hadn't finished his meal. He asked where the toilets were, I told him, and he went outside. He'd only been in there a few seconds, and then . . . Boom!!!!' His eyes widened at the recollection. 'He booked a table for this evening, by phone, earlier, for one, and said his name was Ross. He was English.'

'Scottish,' I corrected him. It's a reflex with me, whenever someone makes that mistake.

'I'm sorry, Primavera,' he murmured. Poor bastard; he was in shock and there was I, giving him a lecture on European nationalities.

'It was lucky he had closed the bar door on the way out,' he went on, 'otherwise God knows what might have happened. As it was the glass was blown in. It was a small miracle that nobody was cut to ribbons, but Dolors, the customer who was nearest the door, I think she's injured. She was screaming, and said that she couldn't hear properly.'

Alex nodded. 'We saw her outside; the medics will look after her when they get here.' He glared at his watch. 'When!' he repeated, angrily. 'They'll be no use to Mr Ross, though.'

Juan Manuel bit his lip. 'I didn't go out there,' he murmured. 'I could see from here that it would have been no use. I should have covered him up, I know, put a tablecloth over him, but I, Tess, she was . . .'

'That's okay. As you say, it would have been no use. The only thing I can ask you is this. Are you certain that it was Mr Ross who went into the toilet? Was there anyone else out in the garden who might have beaten him to it?'

Tess looked up at us. 'No,' she mumbled through her sobs. 'It was him. I was at the other end of the bar from Juande, so I could see him as he went in. It was him; it's him who's lying dead out there.'

Alex's question had lit a small flame of hope with in me. Her firm answer blew it out again. That final reality turned my legs to jelly; I had to lean on the bar for support. I'd been doing my best not to connect the scorched, mangled thing lying out in the garden with the man I knew, the man I'd been with less than twelve hours before. Unable to hide from the truth any longer, I started to shudder, violently. Alex saw it, gripped me by the arms, and held me tight until the spasms subsided, and I was still again.

'Would you like a brandy?' Juan Manuel asked me.

'Thanks,' I replied, 'but no thanks. I never hide behind alcohol if I can avoid it, in case I never come out again. I knew Ricky. A long time ago, and then again very recently; we were colleagues of a sort. That's why Intendant Guinart brought me here. There's nobody else in Spain who's close to him, or responsible for him.'

'What did he do, this man?'

'He was in security; a consultant to the Scottish airline

WeighleyAir, as I am. Before that, though, he was a police officer.'

'Then I think I saw him on television,' the restaurateur exclaimed, 'a few nights ago. There had been a couple of incidents at the airport and he had arrived to deal with them. Is that correct? Was he that man?'

'Yes, that was him. There is a saying in English, "There is no such thing as bad publicity", but it's not always true.'

'There's such a thing as bad luck as well, in any language, and his was out tonight. What the hell could have caused the explosion?'

'Good question. It's time I tried to find out,' Alex declared, firmly.

He headed for the door, and I felt strong enough to follow him. When we were outside I was able to deal with what was left of Ricky Ross, not by thinking of the man I'd seen that very day, but of the ruthless ambitious cop I'd met for the first time in Whigham's Bar in Edinburgh, more than fifteen years before, to whom I'd taken an instant dislike. I went across to where he lay and made myself look, playing an Emeli Sandé song in my head, to help keep me calm.

He had died in a flash, literally, in mid-stream, so to speak. His hands, and what they had been clutching, were like charcoal, his clothes had been incinerated instantly and the wood against which he was plastered was scorched black. Most of his head had been destroyed by a piece of metal, which was itself embedded in the door. From my own visits to the La Bassa outhouse, I recalled that the ladies' had an old-fashioned high cistern, and guessed that something similar had remodelled Ricky's top-piece. He wasn't the first homicide victim I'd ever seen, but for sure he was the messiest.

'He couldn't have known a thing,' I said, as I rejoined Alex, who was surveying the ruins of the khazi. 'A millisecond, maybe, but not long enough to process what was happening to him.'

'Is that a nice way to go, do you think?' my friend wondered.

'I dunno,' I replied. 'What would you choose?'

'I don't know either.' He considered the question for a few moments. 'Having sex, maybe; you come and then you go. Perhaps that's how it should be.'

'In which case,' I retorted, 'many a woman would live forever.' He didn't get my drift.

He stepped forward, into the centre of the rubble, the obvious seat of the explosion. We were in the midst of a pond. The toilet fittings had been blown to bits and the water supply to the cistern and washbasin had been ruptured and was running freely. All the walls were gone, but Alex found a stopcock on an exposed dangling pipe. He turned it and the flow slowed then stopped altogether.

'What?' he whispered.

'Not really,' I whispered back. 'That's pretty obvious. How? One of the other customers might have gone for a leak. One of the ladies, even; we're never too fussy here which one we use. So how come the thing went off when Ricky was in here?'

'We'll get to that.' He stepped back, and I followed his lead.

I looked down at the floor. The water was beginning to clear and I saw that amidst the scorching there were two white footprints, a little apart as they would have been when a man was in the act. I thanked God that there was no sign of Ricky's feet, I couldn't have taken that.

Alex noticed too. 'Why should that happen?' he wondered. 'Why would his feet be blown off?'

I knew why. 'There was a gap at the foot of the door,' I explained. 'It didn't go all the way to the floor, stopped about twenty centimetres short. A design fault, you might say, and occasionally, when the tables outside were full late on a summer evening, a conversation piece.'

'How come?'

'People at certain tables might have a fine view of a lady's knickers around her ankles when she was in there. That's if she was wearing any, and if she wasn't, that's what the conversation would be about. Before you ask, when I was in there I never put the light on.'

I'd been speaking past tense, because clearly it would be some time before I was in there again. The other toilet was badly damaged too, although its back wall, and the one furthest from the seat of the blast were still standing. The toilet bowl had been smashed to pieces, the basin was cracked and the mirror above it wasn't going to be lucky for anyone, ever again.

Between the two cubicles, the storage space was just rubble. Anything that hadn't been blown out was buried, apart from one item, a tall LPG cylinder. It had been orange coloured once, but was as black as everything else. However, it was intact.

'What do you think?' I asked Alex.

'Speak Castellano, please.' The voice, in that language, came from behind us. 'We're having no secrets here.'

My friend stiffened; we both turned to see the interloper. In fact, there were two of them, two men. One was in his thirties, and from the sneer on his face we knew that he had spoken; the other, who was standing a little further away from us, looking a little less sure of himself, was probably a little short of that milestone. Neither was tall but both were scruffy, in need of a haircut and the advice of a decent tailor.

'Yes, we are,' Alex growled, still in Catalan, 'if I wish it.'

'But not if I don't,' the other guy replied, switching tongues easily and fluently. 'I speak your gutter language, but my sidekick here, he struggles with it, so I want us all to know what's going on.'

'What language would you like to be arrested and charged in?' Alex shot back. 'This is a crime scene and you are intruding into it.'

'We have authority. As for the status of this place, that remains to be determined.'

'Then who the fuck are you two?'

It was my night for being prescient; with another flash of insight, I knew who they were. I also knew where they'd been on the previous Monday evening. They'd been paying a call on Hector Gomez's cousin, leaning on her to change her version of the event that had happened in the St Martí car park.

The boss, as clearly he was, reached into an off-colour buckskin jacket; as he did so I caught a flash of a holstered pistol under his left armpit, and I was fairly sure that I was meant to. At the same time, his oppo went to the breast pocket of his checked cowboy-styled shirt, moving closer to us as he did so.

Each produced a photo ID badge and held it up for inspection; I was close enough to read 'Ministerio del Interior' and to see below it the Guardia Civil insignia, the old fascist sword and axe symbol with a crown on top.

Each held a finger over his name, but Alex wasn't having that. He grabbed the older man's hand before he could withdraw it and moved the obstruction aside, not gently. 'Luis Saviola, First Lieutenant,' he read. 'I am Alex Guinart, Intendant. That means I outrank you, chum.'

'I could give a shit,' Saviola laughed, switching back to Spanish. 'You don't outrank the people I work for.' He nodded in my direction. 'Who's the woman? Your girlfriend? Did you bring her along for a cheap thrill?'

My friend's eyes blazed. 'Whoever you work for, don't push your luck, or they'll have to put you back together again. The lady is a colleague of the dead man; I brought her along to confirm the identification.'

'And the dead man is from Scotland,' Saviola continued, in a matter-of-fact tone. 'Until now he was one of the luckiest people in the world, but tonight it all ran out.'

I gasped, and then laughed, in amazement. 'You cannot be serious,' I yelled, in a tone that even John McEnroe would have envied. 'You and your friends in Madrid might have got away with covering up an explosion and fire on a hire car, but not this. Look around you, man; consider where you are. This is a restaurant, in a village. By midday tomorrow everyone who lives here will know what happened, and it will not stay a secret. You can't put a lid on this.'

'You bet your pussy we can, lady,' he chuckled back at me. 'A bet I would be happy to cover, incidentally.'

I slapped him, almost hard enough to knock him down. Alex stepped between us, but Saviola didn't react. He put a hand to his scarlet cheek, and nodded an acknowledgement; he was smiling no longer.

'Let's look around here,' he said. 'What happened? A bomb went off, you say? Come on, let's get real. As you say, this is a quiet rural village. It is also the twenty-first century. Such things don't happen in places like this. Bombs aren't that obedient either. How did it know when to go off? Was there a processor in it that analysed your colleague's piss stream? I think not. The bomb theory is wild, so let's look for another explanation.'

He surveyed the scene and all of a sudden his grin was back. 'And there it is.' He pointed towards the ruin of the storage *trustero*. 'A gas cylinder exploded. Have you any idea what can happen when one of those things goes off by accident? No? Well, you're looking at the consequences.'

'You're crazy,' I scoffed. 'It's clear and obvious where the explosion happened. I'm no expert and even I can see that. Look at Ricky's body; look at the trajectory. It was blown twenty feet, with the door it's stuck to, in a straight line by the source of the blast.'

Saviola shrugged. 'That's not what the official photographs will show. Your friend isn't stuck down, he can be moved.'

He turned to Alex. 'Your technician's been headed off, Intendant. Mine are on the way here. You may want to protest about that, to report this to your director in Barcelona, but I doubt that you will. Well, no, maybe you might to cover your own arse, but you know what you'll be told, that this incident is a matter for Madrid, and that you have no locus here.'

Alex was frowning, but he wasn't arguing.

'This was a gas explosion,' the Guardia spook continued. 'Because it was, it is insured damage. The company will move fast, and the buildings will be reconstructed, exactly as they were, inside two weeks, and the unfortunate owners will be compensated for lost profits. They will also have a new and more adequate store for the gas bottles that they use to cook with. They'll be happy, the village will be happy, and the whole incident will be forgotten in a few months.'

'And what about Ricky?' I asked. 'What about him?'

Saviola shrugged and raised his eyebrows. 'He'll still be dead, and nobody here will remember his name, the few who ever heard it.' He glanced up at Alex, one officer to another for the first time. 'You know how it is, don't you?'

'Yes,' he sighed, 'I know how it is. The Interior Ministry wants to keep the spectre of Catalan terrorism firmly under wraps.'

'That's right,' the other man agreed. 'But not just them. Your Catalan government is even more keen. I'm told it was your own Interior Ministry who wanted the business handed over to us.'

Seventeen

It wasn't until we were almost back in St Martí that the full enormity of the situation hit me properly. It wasn't just Ricky's death, but the whole cover-up scenario.

Saviola had told us that we were never there, and that the Guardia Civil would take responsibility for informing the UK consulate in Barcelona that a British citizen had died in an unfortunate gas explosion in Ventallo. Then he had gone on to explain the official circumstances to Juan Manuel and Tess. We weren't part of that discussion but we could see them nodding. They'd go along with it for sure. Why wouldn't they, with guaranteed compensation and an expedited repair?

We left the spooks to deal with the witnesses in the fire tender, or not, since we didn't see any need to mention their existence. But the little sod was thorough; no way was he going to overlook them.

Alex dropped me off, not at my front door but at the top of the hill, next to the old foresters' house. 'Old' I say: it's probably the youngest building in the village, yet it adds to its distinction. By that time all but the last stragglers had gone home. Those that remained, mostly restaurant staff, were sitting at tables in La Terrassa, nursing wind-down beers.

I sat there in the dark in the passenger seat, feeling totally impotent . . . an unusual sensation for a woman, now that I think about it.

'What are you going to do?' Alex asked.

'I wish I knew. Right now I can't get past thinking about the practicalities. Ricky has a wife. She should know right now that she's a widow, but how long will it be before she finds out? Nobody's going to speak to the consulate until tomorrow morning. The people there will act as fast as they can, but it could take hours before she's notified.'

'Have you ever met her?'

'No. Funny thing, though, she was Oz's girlfriend for a while, before I knew him. He introduced her to Ricky, as I recall. The poor girl's going to be gutted. Maybe I can speed things up, though. I'll have to talk to the boss of WeighleyAir, Ricky's client and mine, to let him know he's a man down. I have his mobile number. I'll call it as soon as I get in.'

'Be careful what you say to him,' my friend warned.

'Oh, don't worry. I know what I can and can't say. If I tell him what we know to be the truth, he won't want to know. He'd a little security problem at Girona and it made the papers, so he sent Ricky out to sort it, as publicly as he could. The last thing he wants is for the world to think that he really is being targeted. When I told him that Ricky's car exploded spontaneously, he was only too pleased to believe me. When I feed him the Guardia Civil version of what happened tonight, he will react in exactly the same way. Then he'll put on his best black suit, and call on Alison Ross to break the terrible news. He'd probably take his PR person with him when he did it, only Alison is his PR person.'

'Will it be big news in Edinburgh?' Alex asked.

'Not as big as it would have been when Ricky was a cop, and famous, but big enough nonetheless.'

'Will people believe the story of the explosion?'

'Why should they not? The British government will be telling it, so will the Spanish Interior Ministry, and so, most tellingly of all, will Jack Weighley.'

I saw his smile in the light of his dashboard. 'And you, what will you say?'

'I'll toe the party line, buddy, strictly.'

'But what will you do? That's the key question?'

'What can I do?

'That's not an answer.'

'It's as much as I'm going to give you. Didn't you hear what Saviola said back there? The ministers in Madrid and in Barcelona see this as a public safety issue. The cover-up's only just begun. By the time the sun rises, there will not be a single piece of physical evidence of a bomb at La Bassa, just as there's no longer any evidence that Ricky's car was blown up. It's a cube of metal by now on its way to be recycled.'

'How did you know that?' Alex murmured. 'It's news to me.'

Me and my big mouth: but I covered up my gaffe. 'Maybe

it is, but surely it must be. One look at the thing would have told anyone what happened to it.'

'I suppose so.' He was silent for a while, then, just as I was about to bid him goodnight and get out of the car, he said, 'You know I can't help you, Primavera?'

I laughed. 'Help me do what, for goodness sake?'

'Whatever you're planning to do; I can have no part of it and I want no knowledge of it. Did it occur to you when we were with that untidy little man Saviola that the people who sent him might have a point? All that anyone needs to do is mention the possibility of an act of terrorism by the Catalan independence movement, and we would have a wave of hysteria. Worse, they might actually trigger it off.'

My eyebrows rose. 'Are you saying,' I asked him, 'you believe that might actually be the case? That Ricky was targeted by terrorists?'

He looked at me. 'If not, then who? Who else would want to kill him? He hasn't been a cop for fifteen years. The men he put away are either dead or senior citizens. You heard the names he mentioned the other day. They were the only people he could think of and even he conceded that none of them were real possibilities.'

'There was one he couldn't rule out. What was his name? Rodger; that's right, William Rodger.'

'So you aren't going to let it lie,' he said. 'You are going to rock the boat.'

'No,' I protested. 'I never said that. Alex, do you think I have super powers? I'm not an investigator. Suppose I did

171

want to follow this awful thing up? Suppose I did believe that Ricky's widow has a right to know that her husband was murdered and that he has a right to justice? Suppose I was unreasonable enough to believe those things, I wouldn't have the faintest idea where to begin. Even if I did, I would have access to nothing.'

'That's right,' he declared, 'not even to me, for we should never speak of this again. I can't afford to get sucked into your crusade.'

I smiled as I opened the door. 'Then it's just as well I'm not planning to start one,' I told him. 'Goodnight, chum. Thanks for the drive even though we never actually went anywhere.'

I went indoors, to a silent house. Jack Weighley's contact details were on my desk. I checked the time: twelve twenty-five, an hour earlier with him in Scotland. Sod it. I dialled his mobile number.

The phone rang for some time. Just when I expected to be picked up by voice message, he answered the call. 'Yes? Who's this and what's the panic?'

He sounded slightly out of breath: I found myself wondering about his domestic arrangements. I had no idea whether the man was married or single, or even if he batted for the usual team, the other one, or even both.

'It's Primavera Blackstone,' I replied. 'I have something to tell you. Whether you panic or not, that's up to you, but I thought you'd want to hear the news before morning. Ricky Ross is dead.'

I counted the seconds: one, two, thr . . .

'He's what? When?'

'This evening, about four hours ago.'

I counted again: one, tw . . .

'How? What happened? Heart attack? Stroke? Do they even know yet?'

'According to the policeman I spoke to at the scene, it was an accident. It happened in a village a few kilometres from my home, in a restaurant where he'd gone for dinner. A big gas cylinder, one of the kind they still use in a lot of places here, exploded and blew him to kingdom come.'

'You were there?' Weighley murmured. 'Were you eating with him? Were you and he . . .'

'Absolutely not. Don't even think that. I told him about the place, that was all.'

'So how did you come to be there?'

Good question, and my answer was not going to involve Alex; time to dilute the truth. 'I was called, after it happened. I know the owners; we eat there quite often. Ricky may have used my name when he booked a table.' I was pleased with myself; not a word of a lie.

'Was it,' he hesitated, 'was he messed up?'

'Oh yes.'

'But it was definitely him?'

'I'm absolutely certain that it was.'

'And that's what happened? A gas explosion?'

'That's what the police told me. There's no doubt, they said.'

Weighley reflected for a few seconds. 'Was anyone else killed?' he asked.

'No. Ricky was the only casualty.'

'That's a relief. Makes it less likely there'll be any publicity.'

'What?' I gasped. 'That came straight from the heart, Jack.'

'Come on, you know what I mean,' he protested. 'If there had been half a dozen deaths, that would have been front-page stuff. How much coverage do you think it will get out there?'

'Probably not much beyond Figueres,' I told him. 'Ventallo isn't exactly a metropolis.'

'His name was in the Spanish press last week,' he pointed out. 'Do you think the story might be bigger than otherwise because of that?'

'I'd be very surprised if the police even release his name.' In fact I knew for sure they wouldn't; Saviola had told me so.

'What about the Scottish media?'

I gave him the same answer that I'd given Alex earlier, but added, 'That's up to you, to an extent, and to Ricky's widow. You make the announcement of his death, with appropriate grieving noises, and it'll all go away in a day or two, once his old cop colleagues have paid their tributes. WeighleyAir doesn't even need to be mentioned.'

'Yes,' he said, softly, 'that's true. What do you suggest I do now?'

'The obvious. Someone's got to tell Alison; better someone she knows than she gets a call from a Foreign Office clerk.'

'Of course. I'll let her sleep, though, and tell her first thing in the morning. It won't break before then, will it?'

'No way.'

'Then that's what I'll do,' he declared. Then he hesitated, in contemplation. 'It is a hell of a coincidence, Primavera, is it not? His car blows up spontaneously on Monday. Three days after that lucky escape, he's killed in another freak accident.'

'Yup. I've met some unlucky people in my life, but poor old Ricky stands right at the top of the list.'

'You do believe it, don't you?' he asked. 'These were accidents, weren't they? There's no doubt in your mind?'

'Are you going to argue with the Guardia Civil?' I countered. 'Jack, I was at the scene of both events, and I saw what happened. There is absolutely no doubt in my mind.'

Yet again, I hadn't uttered a single untruthful word.

'No, good, glad to hear it.' He paused. 'The alternative wouldn't bear thinking about. Primavera, if Alison wants to talk to you, after I've broken the news, would that be all right?'

'Of course it would. The poor woman's going to be stunned. I'll do whatever I can to help her.'

'Thanks. We'll speak in the morning.'

I put the phone back in its cradle.

'Hi, Mac,' I said. 'Sorry, I didn't mean to wake you.' I'd been aware of him standing there for quite some time.

'You didn't,' he replied. 'I was sitting on the terrace, having helped myself to one of your very fine brandies. I heard you come in, and assumed you'd join me. Then I heard you speaking.'

'How much of it did you pick up?

'Enough. Somebody's dead; Ricky Ross. The same guy we spoke to this afternoon.'

175

'That's right.'

'The same guy somebody tried to kill in the car park down there last Monday.'

'How did you hear about that?'

'Wee Jonathan told me all about it tonight, after you left.'

'The police don't see it the same way he does,' I said. 'The car exploded of its own accord. Oil dripping on to a hot exhaust pipe.' I looked up at him from my chair, then started to rise. 'Do me a favour, Mac, go and find me one of those brandies, and let's sit outside for a bit.'

'Sure.' He went off to the drinks cabinet and I went off to the terrace. When he rejoined me he was carrying two glasses, and handed one to me. 'Carlos the first, Gran Reserva; no' bad, no' bad at all, considering it's Spanish.'

'You're a brandy snob, Mac,' I chided him. 'The French don't have a monopoly.'

'They'd like you to think that, though. They're the real snobs.' He took a sip from his replenished glass.

'You don't believe all that spontaneous combustion shite, do you, Primavera? Something like that might have happened to my old Reliant Scimitar forty years ago, but in a modern motor car, no way.'

'You didn't say that to the kids, did you?'

'No, I didn't want to start the debate, but Tom's not fooled either.'

'Do you know that after his next birthday, he'll be old enough to have a scooter . . . a motor scooter, that is. Same with Janet, of course, and if the one has . . .'

'Is that right?' he exclaimed. 'Seems a wee bit young to me. What are you going to do about it?'

'Wait until they ask then decide. I'm hopeful that they won't.'

'Aye, sure,' he laughed. 'There's as much chance of you getting away with that as there is of you getting away with changing the subject. That car did not blow up of its own accord. Now this "accident" tonight. What happened?'

I gave him the authorised version.

'I see,' he murmured, when I was done. 'These big gas cylinders, they're in common use, are they?'

I nodded.

'Have you ever heard of one blowing up?'

I shook my head. Then I ventured, 'But I'm sure it has happened, especially if they're not properly stored.'

'Aye, and next time Cisco over there offers me pork, I'm going to ask if I can have the wings, deep fried. This is not right, Primavera. What have you got yourself into?'

'I haven't got myself into anything!' I protested.

'You haven't run away from it, either. Bloody hell, woman, it sounds to me as if you're covering up a murder!'

'I'm not!' I hissed. 'The Spanish state is.'

'In that case,' he asked, in Grandpa Mac's more accustomed tone, 'what are you going to do about it?'

'What makes you think I'm going to do anything?'

'It isn't in your nature not to. Just promise me one thing, that whatever you do, you won't take any risks.'

'I promise,' I said. 'But honestly, Mac, what the hell can I

177

do? I will bet you that by now, not only will the remains of that exploded car have been disposed of, but there won't even be any evidence that it ever existed, far less that Ricky Ross hired it. As for tonight, by the end of this week, they'll be rebuilding the bloody place, and by the end of the month it'll be as it ever was.'

'I'm sure you're right,' he agreed. 'But you'll still find a bone to gnaw on, I know you will.' He sighed; in the light from the square that washed the terrace, casting shadows, he looked older than I'd ever seen him.

'You know, lass,' he went on, 'if it wasn't for young Tom, that masterpiece you created, I might wish that you and my son had never met, for both your sakes. You'd probably be matron of some big infirmary by now, and he'd probably still be taking witness statements for lawyers in Edinburgh, if he'd lived. But you did, and you transformed each other's lives.'

'For the better,' I whispered. 'Even with all that happened, for the better.'

'Maybe you did, but only for as long as it lasted. Now he's gone and you have to raise what he left behind. Do what you have to do, love, but put them first. Okay? Will you promise me that?'

'I promise,' I said, and I meant it. 'Honest, Mac, I don't know where I'd have been if it wasn't for my kids.'

And still I don't.

Eighteen

As you'd expect, I didn't sleep much that night; whenever I did drop off, I was back in the garden at La Bassa, and I didn't hang around there long.

I gave up trying as soon as it started to get light. I got up, put on shorts and a sports bra, and went for a run to L'Escala via the road, as far as the Anchovy Museum . . . honest, there is such a place . . . then back along the walkway that skirts the beach. It has a name, Cami dels Enamorats, although very few expats know that and most of the natives who did have forgotten.

I didn't feel very loved up as I reeled off the kilometres, not even with the distraction of Default, my favourite Canadian rock band, on my iPod. Far from it: I was even more shaken up than I had been the night before, and I was fearful too, afraid of the call that I knew would come, sooner or later.

As it happened it was sooner; it was quarter to eight and I had just stepped out of the shower when my mobile rang.

It showed a UK number that I didn't recognise, but the city code was Edinburgh, so I made an educated guess and took it.

'Is that Primavera?' a quiet female voice asked.

'It is. Alison?'

'Yes. Mr Weighley's just left. He arrived on my doorstep just after six; he's only just gone. He gave me your number and said I should call you. I'm still struggling to believe it. Tell me it's all a joke, please. Tell me that Jack misunderstood you and that Ricky was only injured.'

'I wish I could, Alison, but he is dead, really. The police here are involved. They're satisfied it was an accident and they'll be advising the consulate as soon as it opens. You'll probably have a call from them, or a visit from someone from Ricky's old force, sometime during the day.'

'I'll head them off,' she said. 'I'll make the announcement myself, through my firm.' She gave a deep sign. 'Listen to me; PR professional to the last, eh.'

'You don't have to do that. Tell Jack to handle it; I'm sure his secretary would circulate a statement. Ricky was on his business, after all.'

'I'm sure she could, but he was my husband, so I'll do it. I have to.'

'You're a brave lady. I could barely speak for a couple of days when I heard Oz was dead, and he and I were well separated by then.'

'But you did part on good terms . . . before you were in that plane crash, and had amnesia and everything. I know you did, because he told me.'

That surprised me. 'He did?'

'Oh yes. He and I were pretty close, in our twenties, and later we were in touch through Ricky. He was devastated when you disappeared. He never did accept that you were dead. Things were difficult between him and Susie after that; he got obsessive, and wouldn't speak to her, other than to blame her for coming between you. He made Ricky hire investigators in the US to try to find you, but they couldn't. They said that your body had vanished and they assumed you had been vaporised in the crash, or taken by bears.'

It occurred to me that Ricky's gumshoes had taken him for a ride, but there was no point in telling her that.

'And so he died not knowing you were still alive.' I didn't need to be reminded of that, but since it was helping Alison avoid her own reality, I let it lie.

'Where did it happen?' she asked suddenly, in the tone of an interviewer.

'In a restaurant in a village called Ventallo.' I spelled it out for her.

'What was the name of the restaurant?'

I frowned. 'Alison, please don't put that in your announcement. They'd have ghouls crawling all over the place. They're nice people and they don't deserve that.'

'I won't . . . but I'd still like to know. If they were negligent and caused Ricky's death, I might be advised to sue them.'

Jesus, I hadn't thought about that. But when I considered it I was sure that meticulous little bastard Saviola would have.

'They weren't,' I told her. 'There was nothing they could have done to avoid it. You'd have trouble finding a lawyer to take the case. Even if you did, the mills of God have nothing on the lethargy of the Spanish courts. Did Ricky have accident insurance?'

'Yes, he did,' she replied. 'I hear what you're saying, Primavera, but I'd still like the name of the restaurant. At some point in the future I'm going to want to see the place where he died.'

'Of course.' I softened my heart and gave her the name. 'But give it a month or so; let them rebuild it. You wouldn't want to see the place as it looked last night.'

'What about the practicalities? Getting the body home, registering the death. What's the law?'

'Don't worry about that. I'm sure the consulate will deal with the legal side, and WeighleyAir will bring Ricky home.'

'Will it? Jack never mentioned that, and I was too shocked to ask him.'

'Give him credit for being shocked himself,' I suggested, without quite believing myself. 'I'll make the arrangements and tell him what I've done.'

'Does that mean they'll fly him back in the hold, with suitcases and all?'

'The hell it will. I will also tell Jack that he's sending his private plane to bring the coffin back.'

'You seem to have a lot of clout with him,' she observed.

'Yes, I do, don't I, even if I'm not quite sure why. Since I have, I'm going to use it.'

'How was he?' Alison asked. 'Last time you saw Ricky, how did he seem? Was he happy?'

'Perfectly,' I replied. 'He was doing his job, and he was doing it well. He'd just made the key appointment that will sort out the problem he was sent here to solve. So yes, even though I barely knew him, I'd say he was happy.'

'That's good to know. It's just that with him being so far away when it happened, I'm struggling to get a handle on things. You understand that, don't you?'

'Yes, I do. Now, you go and issue your statement, tell Ricky's kids and anyone else who needs to hear it personally from you, then stop being brave and cry your eyes out for as long as you need to.'

'That's exactly what I will do,' Alison said. 'Thanks for the advice and for the comfort. We've never met, but I feel that I know you. When I get round to going out to Spain, maybe you'll come with me when I visit the restaurant.'

'Of course I will.' *And you will feel like a hypocrite all the way through,* I told myself, sternly.

I finished dressing and went downstairs. The kids were gathered in the kitchen and I was late, but Tom and Janet had everything under control.

'Hello, Mum,' my son said, a little too casually for comfort. 'Did you and Alex get your business done?' He didn't have to say he was unhappy about me leaving the dinner party; his eyes told me that.

'Yes, we did,' I replied.

He wasn't done. 'What was it?'

'I don't want to talk about it. Big people's stuff.'

I knew as soon as the words were out that I'd stepped on a landmine. Having spent thirteen years making a point of never doing so, I'd patronised him. He placed his glass of orange juice back on the table, and looked me in the eye. 'What does that mean, exactly? Are you and Alex having an affair? Is that it?'

I stared at him, open-mouthed, only half aware of Janet shouting at her brother, 'Tom, don't you dare say that!' Then I did something totally unexpected and in our kitchen totally unprecedented. I dropped into a chair, buried my face in my hands and started to cry: the last refuge of the weak little woman.

It was completely spontaneous, and not meant as a tactic at all, but if it had been, it worked. My son was on his feet in an instant, beside me, his strong young arms around me, cradling me, sheltering me. 'Mum,' he whispered. 'I'm sorry. I didn't mean it; I was angry and I was stupid. I'm sorry, I'm sorry, please don't cry.' His guilt made it worse, I cried all the harder.

Janet joined in the comforting. 'Mum,' she murmured in my ear . . . she'd never called me that before, 'we know you're not, but even if you are, it doesn't matter.'

Her sisterhood solidarity helped me pull myself together. My sobs subsided and when they ended altogether, I was aware of wee Jonathan standing beside me, holding a sheet of kitchen roll. I thanked him, dried my eyes and blew my nose, wondering what the hell I must look like, but not being brave enough for a face-to-face encounter with a mirror.

'I'm sorry, Mum,' Tom repeated. He was crouched beside me, his arm still around my shoulders. 'That was an awful thing to say. It was just that we've never had as big a family party, and I was upset when you had to leave.'

'You'd a right to be. I'm sorry that I had to go, and I wouldn't have, but it was a police thing and Alex said he really, really needed my help. He did too, but I don't want to talk about it.'

'Was it the gas explosion in Ventallo?' wee Jonathan asked.

I felt my eyebrows rise. 'How did you know about that?'

'I heard it on the Radio L'Escala news when I was getting dressed. They said it was a terrible accident and that somebody had been killed.'

I nodded. 'Yes, Jonathan, that's right.'

'Wow,' he murmured. 'Who was it?'

'Enough,' a strong voice, the kind that does not leave room for debate, declared from the doorway. Grandpa Mac was awake and in action. 'Your mum had a hard time last night and she's still upset. Press her no further, any of you. I'll be taking you all to school today, so go and get into your neat little uniforms, get your pencil cases packed into your satchels, and be ready to hit the road when I blow the whistle. I don't actually know where the schools are, so you're going to have to guide me. That means we leave here in plenty of time. Go on then, vamoose, or whatever you say in Catalan.'

The three of then gulped down what was left of their breakfast and made a sharp exit.

'Thanks, Mac,' I said, when we were alone. 'How much of that did you hear and see?'

'I heard all of it. I was just outside the door when Tom went off at you. I should have warned you that he was on the warpath. He was growling about Alex last night after you left. I don't think you appreciate just how protective he is of you. Oz was like that with his mother. She and our Ellie had a barney once, Ellie's fault, as always. Before I could stop him Oz had his sister against the wall, by the throat.'

'I'll talk to him this evening,' I promised, 'and straighten him out. Mac, I don't know what came over me.'

'I do,' he retorted, as he loaded the toaster with half a baguette, cut longways. 'It's called shock. I was only a bloody dentist, I know, but I've seen it in my practice. You take out a wisdom tooth, stop the bleeding, patient tells you he's fine; two steps towards the door then he faints. You took longer and you did it in a different way, that's all.'

'Maybe,' I conceded.

'There is no "maybe" about it. You really want to chuck this, you know. You should tell Weighley you want no fucking more to do with him and his airline.'

'I should, I know; maybe I will. But . . .'

'In my long but hopefully still incomplete by some way experience of life, "but" always overrides "maybe". You know what your priorities are.'

'Yes, I do,' I conceded.

'What would you like on your toast?' He looked in the fridge. 'Jam? Honey? Anything you like apart from fucking Marmite. I refuse to touch that.'

I laughed. 'Janet loves it.'

'Must come from her mother's side,' he grunted. 'Go on, what do you want?'

'None of the above, thanks.' I rose from my chair, filled a large plastic beaker with Granini carrot and orange juice and picked up an apple.

'Thanks for volunteering for the school run, Mac. I appreciate it. Now I must repair the damage I've done to my face.' I paused. 'By the way, sorry if I spoiled your evening too . . . although I did wonder if you noticed I was gone. You and Anais seemed to hit it off.'

'She's a nice lady,' he conceded, then to my huge surprise, his weatherbeaten countenance seemed to blush. 'As a matter of fact, she's invited me to lunch at her hotel.'

'Great. When?'

'We didn't set a date, I said I'd have to check with you.'

'No you bloody don't. I've never heard anything so daft. Or,' I said as the obvious reached me, 'did you just stall her because you'd feel guilty about accepting?'

He nodded. 'Mostly.'

'Then you have no reason to. You're doing all you can for Mary, Mac, more than most people would, but she will never be a companion to you ever again. You have a right not to be lonely, just as much as Anais. You're a widower in all but name. You call her and make that date, or not if that's what you decide. Either way, don't hide behind me.' I smiled at him. 'By the way, you're daft if you don't go. I've eaten in her hotel.'

I left him to think it over during the school run, and went up to my room. My eyes were a little puffy, but otherwise there was nothing that I couldn't and didn't repair. I took my apple and my juice out on to the terrace, looking at the developing day and considering what Mac had suggested I do about my connection with WeighleyAir.

He had a point, no doubt, but he hadn't spoken to Alison Ross, so he had less reason to be struggling over her right to know what had really happened to her husband, and balancing that against the possible personal consequences of telling her, and worse, of lighting the touchpaper on the loose cannon that was Jack Weighley.

My apple was down to the core and I was still pondering when I was aware of muted music coming from within my bedroom. I went to investigate the alien sound, following it until I reached my wardrobe, and the jacket that I'd worn the night before.

The miracle mobile that I'd rescued from La Bassa, and forgotten completely until that moment, was trilling away; somehow it had survived the blast. The speaker wasn't at its best but I recognised the vestiges of 'Caledonia'. I'd assumed that it had belonged to Ricky, and that truly patriotic ringtone proved it beyond doubt.

I snatched it from my pocket, looked at the screen and stabbed at the green button that glowed there, faintly.

'Hello?' I ventured.

'Hello back,' a male Scottish voice replied. 'Who is this, please?'

'This is Primavera Blackstone. Now, who is this?'

'This is Detective Superintendent Ronnie Morrow, of

Lothian and Borders Police. Primavera Blackstone? Used to be Primavera Phillips? The same woman I met in the last century?'

'The one and only.'

'Then I have to ask, Mrs Blackstone, although maybe I shouldn't, what you're doing answering Ricky Ross's phone at five to eight in the morning.'

Ronnie Morrow: he'd been Detective Sergeant Morrow when Oz and I came across him in the Leith police station, sixteen years earlier. We'd been in a tricky situation and he had been sensible and helpful, unlike his over-zealous seniors. From what I'd been told, he hadn't been tainted by Ricky's fall from grace, and his prospects had been improved by the defection of Mike Dylan, his erstwhile DI, to the Strathclyde force.

You're going to wish you hadn't, Ronnie, I thought, but I wasn't ready to say that.

'It's five to nine here, Superintendent, past my breakfast time. How come you're calling Ricky when you should still be bent over your All-Bran?'

'How do you know I eat All-Bran?' he asked.

'Most cops are full of shit,' I retorted. 'They need all the help they can get.'

He laughed. 'I can hear you haven't changed, Primavera. I'm calling Ricky this early because what he asked me to do for him isn't exactly part of my remit. Now can I speak to him, please?'

Time to ruin his morning. 'No, Ronnie, I'm afraid you can't.' Then I told him why.

I could almost hear the colour drain from his face.

'Last night?' he whispered.

'Yes.'

'Were you there?'

'No, not at the time, I wasn't, but later. A friend of mine in the Mossos d'Esquadra took me there, to . . .' I paused. 'I'm not really sure why he took me there, but he did.'

But even as I spoke I realised that I was sure after all. Alex had wanted me to see for myself what had happened, before the cover-up machine went into action again, as he had feared it would.

'I saw Ricky's body,' I continued. 'I found this phone at the scene and picked it up. I wasn't asked to identify him formally, and if I had been I couldn't have. It's a DNA job, I'm afraid. But there's no doubt that it was him, not the faintest.'

'An accident, the police are saying?'

'That's right. A gas explosion.'

'Are they fucking serious? Ricky called me yesterday to ask me to check out some names, old customers of his, people he sent to prison as a cop. He told me that somebody blew up his car on Monday. Two days later he's killed in a second explosion and I'm supposed to believe that it was accidental?'

'Yes you are, and so is everybody else. That's what the official report says, and it's what the local media are reporting, for that thing that happened on Monday, that was a vehicle fire, no more.'

'That's not what Ricky said.'

'I know. Ronnie, I was bloody there when his car exploded;

I know exactly what happened, and I know what happened last night too. But there are local, no, scratch that, national politics in play and there is absolutely nothing I can do about it.'

'Are you telling me that a British citizen's been murdered and the police don't want to know?'

'No, I'm telling you that the government doesn't want to know.'

'I'm not having that,' Morrow protested. 'Based on what Ricky told me, I'm going to demand that they investigate. I'll tell my chief what's happened and he'll raise it with the Spanish. He knew Ricky, from way back.'

'And they will send him a polite reply,' I assured him, 'telling him that he's delusional, because there is absolutely no evidence to support his accusation. What's he going to say to you then?'

'So I've got to let it lie?'

'Yes,' I told him, then took a step down the road that I knew all along I would take, in the face of all warnings and advice. 'But I don't. There are things I can do that you can't. I'm not saying I can undo the cover-up, but if I can prove that Ricky's death wasn't an accident and had nothing to do with terrorism, maybe certain people in Madrid will take their heads from up their arses.'

'But what can you do?'

'I have a certain official status in this.' I explained my role with WeighleyAir, the one that Mac had wanted me to give up. 'Yesterday Ricky and I appointed a security chief at Girona

Airport. He's an ex-cop, and he's already primed to investigate the trouble that had Ricky sent out here. His old force has been nobbled, and maybe he has too, but somehow I doubt that. He has a personal grudge against the guys who did the nobbling. I plan to meet him later today. We'll see what happens after that.'

'In that case,' Morrow said, 'you may want to know what I was going to tell Ricky. Those people he asked me to check out; do you know about them?'

'He ran through them, yes.'

'Well, the bus driver's still driving his bus and that's what he was doing on Monday. Grant Donaldson isn't in his vegetative state any more, but only because he died last Friday. The relocated witness is still in New Zealand. James Cockburn died in a hit and run in Paisley a few months ago, one that nobody thinks was an accident, and Billy Rodger's a monk.'

'He's a what?'

He chuckled. 'You heard me. He got religion when he was in the nick, big time. When he got out he joined a monastic order in Gloucestershire, in England. He's Brother William now, and he works in a factory that makes pottery for his order to sell to tourists.'

'So we can forget a Scottish connection to all this?'

'Not quite,' Ronnie said. 'There's another name, one that wasn't on Ricky's list, a man called Hamish Orr. He might have forgotten about him, because the guy got out about nine years ago, and he's never been in trouble since. I know that, because I've spoken to his probation officer. She doesn't see

Hamish any more because his parole period ended three years ago, but he sends her a Christmas card every year. A few months ago she got something else, out of season, a postcard from Spain, with a note to say that he'd found a job, settled there and was enjoying the life.'

'Does Orr have a grudge against Ricky?'

'No, not as far as I know,' he admitted. 'He did his time for culpable homicide, manslaughter; he was in a pub and got into an argument. The other guy came for him with a knife; Orr took it off him and stabbed him, twice. The second one made the difference, and left Ricky with no choice but to charge him with murder, even though the other guy started it, but his QC did a deal and he pleaded guilty to the lesser charge. He got twelve years, but he was released after six. He had no previous and, as I say, nothing since, but the thing that makes him worthy of attention is that he's ex military. He was in the Royal Engineers, and he was a specialist.'

'In what?'

'Bomb disposal, but it's a fair bet that anyone who knows how to take them apart for sure will know how to put them together. Hence the interest.'

'Do you know where he lives?'

'I'm afraid not. The postcard didn't have an address on it, and the other side was just Flamenco dancers, no pictures. The postmark was smudged so that wasn't any help.'

'Is there anywhere you can check?'

'No. He was perfectly free to leave the country. I can try to find his ex-wife and ask her if she knows where he's living. She divorced him while he was inside, but the probation officer might have her address on file. But what can you do if I find him?'

'That'll be up to Hector, my new colleague.'

'Hector?'

'I know, you're going to ask how a Catalan cop got a Scots name. We don't have copyright on it; there are Hispanic Hectors too . . . but no Hamishes that I've ever heard of, which will make our man easier to find, if you can't pin him down. This is a big country, though, and he could be anywhere in it.'

'Sure. I'll do what I can, Primavera.' He sighed. 'It'll be a while before this sinks in, you know. Ricky? Dead? It's not quite Edinburgh Castle falling down, but it's not far short of that.' Then he paused. 'Here, maybe there's another way we can stir up the Spanish. I've got quite a few friends in the media, and one in particular who does exposé features for the BBC. If I had an off-the-record chat with him, and got him interested, what effect would that have?'

'The same thought occurred to me,' I told him, 'but it didn't hang around for long. The Interior Ministry special police would be all over it like a rash. They'd produce very convincing reports with scientific back-up, proving that the restaurant explosion happened exactly as they said it did, and as for the car . . . that won't be logged as anything other than a local fire. Two people were there when it happened, apart from Ricky. I'm one, and the other is the parking attendant, all he saw was a car in flames. Whether you stir up the press or I do, the same thing's going to happen. The funny police will start to look for potential sources, and my doorbell will be the first they ring. The second will be Alex's, my friend in the Mossos d'Esquadra. I can't allow either of those things to happen.'

'No,' Morrow conceded. 'I understand. Listen, I've got some leave coming. How about if I take a week and come over to help you?'

'Is your Spanish any better than Ricky's was?'

'Mmm. No.'

'Then thanks, but leave it to Hector and me. Let me know if you turn up anything on Orr, and I'll keep you in touch with our progress.'

'Okay. Now I must phone Alison. She knows, I take it?'

'Weighley went to see her first thing this morning. She called me a little while ago.'

I left him to it, but not before he'd given me his mobile number, which I patched into my own phone, and I'd given him mine. Then I called Hector Gomez, in his new office at the airport, and told him that I was coming to see him later that morning.

'Good,' he said. 'Maybe I will have something to tell you when you arrive.'

'I will have something to tell you,' I replied, 'but it can wait until then.'

My doubts behind me, I went back to my wardrobe and chose clothes that I deemed appropriate for a business day, grey trousers and a pale pink top that buttoned all the way up to the neck, bottomed off by shoes that weren't too high but weren't flat either.

I was ready for the road when my phone sounded again. I checked the screen; if it had been Weighley I might have let it go to voicemail, but it showed the Edinburgh number that Alison Ross had called from earlier, so I answered.

'Hi, how are you?' I began.

'I've done what needs to be done. I've dictated a statement to my senior account director; she'll issue it as soon as she gets to the office, and she'll deal with all the calls from the media. She has Ricky's bio on file; he was a director of the business. I spoke to Jack again too, and asked him about bringing Ricky's body home. How long do you think that will take?'

'Leave it with me,' I told her. 'I'll speak to the consulate and to the police in Figueres. Hopefully, they'll release the body tomorrow, at the latest.'

'That's good. I was afraid there might be all sorts of red tape to be undone. Primavera,' she continued, 'there's one other matter that has to be taken care of. I'd like to get Ricky's things back; his clothes, his luggage, his laptop, his personal effects. I'm assuming that anything he didn't have on him when he died will still be at his hotel. He told me it was called the something Mar in a town called L'Escala. Do you know it?'

'Yes, I live a couple of miles away and I know the people who own it. I should be able to take care of that without any silly formalities. In fact, I'll do it right now, on my way to my meeting at the airport. I'll send everything back on Jack's plane.'

'Thanks. I owe you.'

'No you don't. We have a bond, you and I, name of Oz Blackstone.'

'I suppose,' she murmured. 'Who'd have thought it? Both Ricky and him gone to Jesus, and you and I left behind.'

'Yup,' I said. 'Our Lord and Saviour can be pretty unpredictable at times . . . that's assuming they haven't gone to the other place.'

'If they have,' she chuckled, sadly, 'they'll be running it inside a week. Satan's not going to know what hit him.'

'Oz has been there for years,' I pointed out. 'He'll have a job lined up for Ricky already.'

After suggesting that she unplug her phone and switch off her mobile, I left her to the wave of grief that she had been fighting off with her activity but which I knew would soon overwhelm her. I considered what I had to do, then made a call, to Alex Guinart.

'How are you getting along?' he asked.

'I've had better mornings; a fight with my son, two conversations with a brand-new widow and a chat with a cop in Edinburgh, who knew I was telling him a fairy story but is enough of a realist to know he can do nothing about it. Now I'm off to clear Ricky's sad leavings from his hotel room. I know your hands are off this thing, but I'd like you to call the management and tell them it's okay with the police for me to do that. Will you?'

'Sure. The tragic accident is a matter of public record already, so I have no problem with helping clear up the aftermath.' (If you're imagining ironic quotation marks around 'tragic' and 'accident', don't. The Catalans do deadpan better than any other people in the world.)

'In that case,' I followed up, 'I want the body released from the mortuary in Figueres. Can you handle that too?'

'Not personally,' he replied, 'but I can speak to the man who can. I'm willing to bet that he'll be only too pleased to help get Mr Ross's remains out of Spain as quickly as possible. You'll need a funeral undertaker, and I doubt that you've ever used one in Spain. Take down this number. It's a company in Girona; explain the situation to them and instruct them. Tell them to make contact with the mortuary and to let you know when the body can be collected.'

'And any personal effects,' I added.

'Of course.'

'Thanks, Alex,' I said, sincerely.

'No problem. All I ask in return is that you and Hector Gomez please do not get me into any trouble. My job and my pension are dear to my heart.'

I promised him that both would be safe. We said 'So long' and I called the number he had given me. The undertaker was as solemn as they always are; he'd been listening to the same news bulletin as wee Jonathan, and so the instructions that I gave him came as less of a surprise than they might have.

'I understand completely, señora,' he said. 'I have dealt with this type of situation many times before. I know what to do. The deceased gentleman will be flown out of Girona, yes?'

'Yes, by private aircraft. As soon as you're ready, I'll arrange for the pick-up.'

'Do you wish to choose a coffin?'

'Not personally, no. You choose something appropriate, and of quality, something that will meet all the regulations for transporting bodies. I have no idea whether there will be a cremation in Scotland or a burial, but let's err on the expensive side.'

'The casket will have to be hermetically sealed,' he told me. 'Also the British consulate must issue a certificate. We will need the Spanish death certificate, but that will be available when I collect the remains, I'm sure. Mmm, can you tell me, do you know, is the gentleman in a suitable condition for viewing?'

'The answer's no, not a chance.' That was one thing of which I was certain. Not even the guy who fixed up Sonny Corleone in *The Godfather* could have made Ricky presentable.

I told the undertaker that the cost of his services would be met by WeighleyAir; I suspect he smiled at that news, and that the bill increased by ten per cent. He promised me action that day, and I moved on.

The consulate was next on my to-do list. I have a couple of contacts there, and called one of them directly. Will Harris is the commercial counsellor, but he can get anything done. As it happened, my news wasn't news. When I told him of Ricky's death and of my locus in the situation, he said that he'd already been informed of the 'tragic accident' by the Spanish

Interior Ministry. If he found it odd that they were doing the informing rather than their Catalan equivalent, he wasn't saying, or asking any questions. Will's smart enough not to shake a tree without knowing whether anything might fall out.

He was also willing to speed the process for me. 'You say you've seen the body, Primavera?'

'Yes,' I confirmed. 'And it is who they say it is.'

'That's good enough for me. Normally one of our people would have to see what we're signing off on before we issued a UK entry certificate, but you're a person of standing with us, so I can take your word for it.'

'Thanks.' I paused as I saw an opportunity. 'Can you do me another favour?'

'Try me.'

'There's a British citizen I'm interested in contacting. Not for personal reasons; it has to do with the airline. He's Scottish, his name is Hamish Orr, and I'm told he's now living in Spain, but that's as much as I know. If he's shown up on the consular network, and you could point me at him, I'd be grateful.'

'I'll see what I can do,' Will promised. 'Hamish Orr, you said?'

'That's right.'

'Age?'

'I'm not sure.' I took a guess, based on the little that Ronnie Morrow had told me. 'Possibly around the fifty mark. It's a long shot, for he could be anywhere in Spain, but you never know your luck.'

'Okay. As you know, ex-pats only get in touch with us when

they have to, but I'll have a look. I can check with the consulate general in Madrid too. I'll let you know.'

I thanked him, and gave him the contact details for the undertaker, so that he could forward the permission for Ricky's repatriation. All that done, I headed for the Nieves Mar, and my mission for Alison.

Mac had taken the jeep for the school run, so I took my posh car, a rather nice Mercedes saloon that Liam and I had bought together. It hadn't seen the light of day since he left.

I felt good in it, at ease with myself again, despite everything that was going on. I realised that I was smiling as I headed out of the village; I couldn't work out whether my pleasure came from the thought of Liam coming back, or was related to the fact that when he was around I didn't get to drive the Merc too often.

It was in good company in the Nieves Mar car park, between a Ferrari and a Porsche. The hotel is the best in L'Escala, even if it does close for the winter. As soon as I walked into the foyer I was clocked by Fredi, the manager and one of the owner family, who was standing by the reception desk. From his grim expression and his nod, I knew that Alex had made his call.

'A terrible thing, señora,' he began as I approached. 'I have often thought that gas cylinders are far more risky than we realise, and yet most restaurants still use them, and very many households also.' He handed me a key. 'Señor Ross's suite is on the second floor, at the end of the corridor.'

I thanked him; I took the lift rather than the stairs, since my legs were still aching from the punishment I had given them on my early morning run.

Ricky had been in the suite after the maid, but the place was still spotless. I had no trouble spotting his suitcase. It was a vivid lime-green colour, probably chosen to stand out from the rest on airport carousels, and it fairly screamed at me from the folding stand on which he'd left it.

I started in his wardrobe: two pairs of Austin Reed trousers, one pair of Tommy Hilfiger shorts and one lightweight suit; a pair of tan shoes, and a pair of flip-flops. No overcoat; people never pack those when they're heading for Spain, and often don't realise until they're caught in it that it can rain harder here than they've ever seen.

I packed the garments in the case, along with a bag of laundered shirts and underwear that was in there, then went through the drawers, where I found two M&S short-sleeved shirts still in their wrappers, and three pairs of jockeys. They all went in as well, as did a pair of cufflinks, emblazoned with the crest of Lothian and Borders Police. It seemed that Ricky had never really left his old force behind him.

When I'd finished in the bedroom, I went through to the bathroom. Ricky had been a blade shaver, and was down to his last Gillette Fusion blade. I wondered whether Alison would want that, or a canister of Colgate shaving cream, or a Rexona deodorant aerosol, but she'd asked me to pack all his belongings, and so I did.

There were only a few things left to find, those personal items he hadn't been carrying when he was killed, and that laptop. I'd been through all the drawers but hadn't seen it. Then the obvious came to me like a cartoon light bulb above my head. I looked in the wardrobe, and yes, there was a safe . . . and yes, it was locked. Of course it was, Primavera; the man had been a security consultant, after all. But I didn't stamp my foot in frustration; instead I went to the bedside intercom and called reception. As I'd hoped, there was an override code for use in emergencies. I noted it on my phone as Fredi read it out to me, then went back to the wardrobe and keyed it in.

The door swung open smoothly, I felt around inside and came up with Ricky's passport, a money clip with two hundred and twenty pounds sterling, a mobile phone charger, and another, larger power supply and plug, for a Sony laptop, according to the label. But no computer. I groped around inside again, but there was nothing left in the safe.

My first thought was obvious. That little fucking creep Saviola! I grabbed my mobile and called Alex. 'Can you get through to that spook?' I asked him, angrily.

'Maybe, with difficulty,' he replied. 'But I'm not keen to try, and anyway, suppose I do, what am I going to ask him?'

'Ask him why the fuck he stole Ricky's laptop. I'm in his room collecting his effects for his widow, and it's missing.'

'Indeed?' Alex murmured. 'And of course you're assuming that he's responsible. Primavera, I have a problem with that. Tell me this. Why would he want to? He achieved his objective last night in Ventallo, when he saw us off and turned the crime scene into an accident. How would he know that Señor

Ross had a laptop in the first place, far less be concerned about what it contained?'

Solid reasoning, I had to concede.

'If not him,' I asked, 'who?'

'The cleaning people?' Alex suggested. 'These things happen.'

'If that was the case, why would they leave over two hundred quid in convertible currency and take a computer that might make them a hundred euro resold, if they were lucky?'

'Good point,' my pal conceded. 'It may be that Señor Ross took it with him last night and left it in his car. I'll try to check that out for you. Meantime I suggest you ask the people at the hotel a couple of questions, since I can't, without involving myself in an investigation that should not be happening.'

'Okay,' I said, 'I will.'

I called my friend downstairs once again. 'Has anyone else been in Mr Ross's suite before me?' I asked.

'Today? No, nobody. The maids were in yesterday, but they haven't even started on today's rounds. Why do you ask, Primavera?'

'No reason,' I replied, thinking on my feet. 'I'm just making sure that nothing will be left behind. It's important that Señor Ross's widow has all of his possessions returned.'

'Sure, I understand,' he said. 'But nothing has left that room that the man did not take away himself. I'm certain of that.'

I took his word for it; I had no choice. I finished my packing (I kept one souvenir for myself: the mobile phone charger) and wheeled the outrageous lime-green suitcase out of the suite, into the lift and down to my car. Then I returned the key to the suite to Fredi, thanked him, and headed for Girona Airport.

I was almost there when Alex called me back. 'No joy about Señor Ross's computer, I'm afraid. In fact, with Saviola's interference and us leaving, nobody was bright enough to wonder how he got to Ventallo. His car would still be there if it wasn't for the mortuary technician who cut the clothing from the body. He'd been carrying his key in his back pants pocket. The force of his impact against the door was so great that it was buried in his ass cheek. The assistant had to lever it out of there. The local police picked it up early this morning. They searched it for his possessions but there was nothing there, other than a credit card slip for petrol. I asked the commandant, who's a friend of mine, specifically about the laptop, but he said there hadn't been one reported.'

I knew better than to ask if he'd believed him. That would have been to suggest that a fellow cop might have been a thief.

'Something else they didn't find,' Alex continued. 'There's no mention of a phone anywhere. Did you find one in the hotel?'

'No.' I was on the verge of telling him the whole truth, but I decided that too much knowledge could be bad for him, given his awkward professional situation.

'Mmm. In which case it's probably buried somewhere inside the poor bastard. If they do a full autopsy in Britain they might find it.'

'They didn't do one here?' I asked, surprised.

'No. Budgets are tight, this was officially an accident and he was a foreign visitor. The death certificate will say "massive blast injuries" or something along those lines. If the home nation wants to know any more, it can pay for it. That's the line these days.'

'Fair enough,' I said. 'I don't really care.'

But Hector Gomez did.

He was waiting for me in his new office. 'How are things?' I asked him.

'Here?' he replied. 'They're not a problem. Overall, the airport is pretty secure. When I toured it yesterday with Señor Ross and the airport manager we identified a couple of security weaknesses. These will be fixed with an extra surveillance camera and some more motion sensors. They'll be installed as soon as possible, and I'll pass the cost on to the airport owner. There will be no more Gaizka Alonso episodes, of that I am confident.

'To tell you the truth, Primavera,' he added, 'I'm not sure there's a full-time job here for me, with these things in place. I'm planning to say as much to Señor Ross when he gets here . . . or has he come to his senses and gone back to Scotland? If someone tried to blow up my car, I'd make myself scarce, that's for sure.'

'He hasn't gone back,' I said, 'but he will, very soon.' I took a deep breath and told him what had happened, in every detail. When I finished, he was staring at me, wide-eyed.

'Jesus!' he whispered. 'So they were really serious, whoever it was.'

'As serious as death.'

'The plainclothes guy, the older one: run his name past me again.'

'Luis Saviola; an offensive little shit.'

Hector frowned and scratched his chin. 'Yes, I know him; I met him a while back, when he was in the mainstream. He's from Barcelona, and he had a pretty heavy reputation. Even then he was undercover. His specialty was infiltrating the gypsy no-go areas, and taking out the top guys in their criminal cadres. He killed a few of them, with questionable grounds; some said he'd gone slightly native. Now that he is where he is, attached to the Interior Ministry, he will have even more freedom of action. I'm not surprised he scared my cousin. But I'm too old to scare,' he added, ominously.

'Gone native?' I exclaimed. 'He's completely off the fucking reservation. Be careful how you deal with this man.'

'I will, but I'm going to deal with him nonetheless. I don't buy this Catalan terrorism shit, not for a minute. In fact as a Catalan I find it offensive, so I plan to disprove it. However,' he added, 'there is no need for you to be involved. It's best that you aren't, so go back to your children and leave this thing to me.'

'I would do,' I replied, 'if it wasn't for one thing. Ricky's actually dead. Somebody killed him. The Spanish government might want to sweep it under the carpet for its own half-arsed reasons, but he has a widow. I spoke to her this morning. She's going to get his body back in pieces . . . that's if they ever found his feet . . . and she has a right to know exactly how it got into that condition. So I'm in, Hector. I'm helping in whatever way I can.'

'What about our employer, Mr Weighley? Doesn't he have a right to know too?'

'Your employer, but my client,' I pointed out. 'I've always believed in telling the client what he needs to hear. In Jack's case, I reckon he's best kept out of this, because I can't predict how he'd react. He might declare war on Spain for all I know.'

'Okay, I've been told that I report to you. Let it be so. I know where the boy Alonso lives. I plan to pay him a visit, today.'

'Then I'm coming with you.'

'Maybe it's better that I talk to him alone. You might see things you don't want to.'

I laughed. 'Hector, I've seen things that would turn your hair grey . . . if it wasn't already under that discreet dye. But we don't need to be threatening when we confront the guy. I have another idea about how to get him to talk to us.'

'What's that? He's already had the police leaning on him, remember, and they couldn't prove anything.'

'I'm not going to lean at all. The opposite, in fact: I'm going to offer him his job back.'

Nineteen

Our man Alonso lived in a small plain town called Flaça. It lies on the road that connects Girona with La Bisbal, although it's now bypassed, so nobody goes there without a reason, the usual one being to catch a train.

In the dim and distant it was a hamlet in the midst of farmland, then the railways arrived and a station was built not far away. That triggered growth; today it's mostly a dormitory for Girona and Figueres, and the most convenient boarding point for tourists bound for Barcelona Airport from the northern Costa Brava resorts.

Gaizka Alonso's address, which Hector had been given by a friend in the social security administration, together with the information that Alonso was still drawing unemployment benefit, was a small terraced house just off the main street, not brand new, but not that old either. In other words typical of Flaça.

We got there at one thirty, in the hope that since he was on the dole he wouldn't be going out for lunch too often.

Although neither of us had seen a photograph of our target, the look on the face of the man who opened the door to Hector's knock told us at once that we had found him.

Furtive, suspicious, guilty; he was all of those things as he looked at my companion. There is something unmistakable about a police officer's knock, and his expression when it's answered. The former Intendant Gomez had taken both into retirement, and it was clear that neither were new to Gaizka.

'Oh not again,' he moaned, without as much as a glance at me. 'Don't you bastards ever give up?'

'No, they don't,' Hector admitted. 'But lucky for you, I'm not one of those bastards any more. My name is Gomez, I work for WeighleyAir, your erstwhile employer, and this is my colleague, Primavera. You may call her Señora Blackstone. Now that you know who we are, you're going to invite us in. Closing the door in my face is not an option open to you.'

Alonso knew the truth when he heard and saw it. He sighed, and stepped aside to let us in.

His house was neat and tidy, and so was he; mid-twenties, clean shaven, well dressed even though he wasn't going anywhere in a hurry as far as we could see, since the telly was on, showing re-tread football on Canal Plus, a game that had another hour and more to run, according to the screen clock.

'You live alone?' I asked him.

He caught my accent, and it made him take note of me for the first time. 'Yes, I do,' he replied. 'I don't have a woman.'

'Or a man,' Hector grunted, roughly. 'I've heard about you cabin crew guys.'

'Then you've heard wrong!' Alonso protested, vehemently.

'Of course,' I intervened. 'You told the police, didn't you, that you were waiting for a woman at the airport, the night when the plane's tyres were flattened.'

'Exactly!' he declared, then frowned at me. 'Are you from head office?'

'You could say that.'

'I don't know you.'

'I'm a new arrival, since you were fired.'

'How come you speak Catalan?'

'My kids do, so it's rather important for me as well. I live in Catalunya, in these interesting times. Catalunya, not Spain, note.' I pointed to a sticker on his living-room window, placed so that it could be seen clearly from the street. It was the banner of Catalan independence, narrow red and yellow stripes with a white star set on a blue triangle on the flagpole side.

Alonso nodded. 'Good,' he murmured. 'Good, good.'

'This girl you were meeting,' Hector chipped in, 'the one whose name you couldn't remember. Has it come back to you since the Mossos interviewed you?'

'Aurelia,' he replied, then nodded. 'That was it, Aurelia.'

'Have you seen her since?'

'Yes.' He grinned, then glanced at me. 'She blew me off then blew me out.'

'Where does she work?'

'I'm not sure: one of the booths beside international arrivals. One of the car rental companies … or maybe she sells tickets for the Barcelona bus. That could have been it. But why are you interested? I told you, man, she's history.'

'I don't believe that.'

'What, that she's history?'

'No,' Gomez said. 'I think she belongs in a different section, namely fiction. I don't think she ever existed. Come on now, Gaizka. If I went to buy a ticket for the bus to Barcelona, there's no chance she'd be selling it, is there? No, not a one.'

Alonso's back straightened as he stared Hector down. 'Let me see your badge,' he snapped.

'What badge? I told you, I'm not a cop any longer. I'm the WeighleyAir security manager at Girona Airport.'

'Then you can fuck off! And sorry, señora, you too. The police tried to pin that vandalism stuff on me, and they weren't able to. You won't be able to either.'

'Because there are no witnesses?' I murmured.

'Exactly!' he said, staring at me as his expression changed into that of a man who has realised too late that he was standing on a trapdoor.

'Why were you fired, Gaizka?' I asked.

'Because some shit of a cabin director said I was rude to a couple of passengers.'

'But didn't they also complain?'

'Yes, but they were a couple of drunk assholes from Birmingham. Other passengers complained about them but the cabin director took no notice.'

'It wasn't the first complaint against you,' I pointed out.

'No,' he admitted, 'that's true. But I don't take shit. You should try working on some of these flights. Often there's a crowd of guys going to Lloret or Tossa with some sucker who's getting married. They're half drunk when they get on the plane and all the way before we leave British airspace. And women too: Jesus, they can be worse than the men, usually are. Once I saw this great fat cow from London, sitting on the lever that opens the aircraft door while she waited to get into the toilet. The front-seat passengers looked nervous so I asked her to get off. She told the cabin director that I'd sworn at her. A lie, but it was recorded and I got an official warning.'

I'd been running a gambit, but to my surprise I was beginning to believe that the guy'd had a raw deal. I told him so. 'Gaizka,' I asked, 'did you ever appeal your dismissal?'

'No, what would have been the fucking point?'

'You might have kept your job if you had.'

He shot me a deprecatory glance. 'So what?'

'So you wouldn't have a dismissal on your CV! So you'd still have had a job! Gaizka, if you want to lodge an appeal even now, I'll make sure that it's heard and I'm pretty sure it will be upheld. You'll be re-employed.'

He took a deep breath and his look became almost sympathetic. 'Señora, you're new to WeighleyAir so you might not understand this, but the truth is I wouldn't get on one of those airborne fucking buckets again if it was the only thing standing between me and a nuclear explosion. I don't want my job back.'

213

'Then why did you spray-paint that aircraft and vandalise those tyres?'

'Who says I did?' he challenged me, but without meeting my eyes.

'I do,' I shot back. 'In fact I'm quite certain of it.'

He gave in, shrugging his shoulders in resignation. 'Okay, between the three of us, and I'll keep denying it outside of this room, I did it, both times.'

'Why? If you weren't bothered about losing your job, why would you do that? Were you just being macho?'

'Macho? Me? Your cop friend here was right, señora, I'm gay. No, I did it because I was paid to do it.'

'You were paid?' Hector repeated. 'By whom?'

'I have no idea, because I never met the guy. A few days after I was sacked, I had a call, here at home, from a man who said he had a proposition for me. He said that he owed Señor Weighley a bad turn, and that there would be four thousand euro in it for me if I could help him do it. I said I was interested, but what did he want me to do. He told me; that was it, what I did.'

'If you never met him, how did he pay you?'

'He said that after I'd done each job, there would be money in my letterbox when I got home. I suppose I took him on trust the first time, but he was as good as his word. Two thousand, each time.'

'Old banknotes or new?' Gomez snapped.

Alonso smiled. 'Old. He's not dumb. You won't be able to trace him that way.'

'Then how will we?'

'Well, for openers, he was British, he spoke English.'

'Did he have an accent?'

'I'm not sure; this was done over the phone, remember. When I think about it, he might have sounded like the señora . . . maybe. No, I can't be sure of that.'

'Did he ask you to do anything else for him?' Hector asked, with more than a suggestion of menace.

'Such as?'

'Such as planting a device to torch a car? Or maybe even demolish a restaurant where WeighleyAir staff might be eating?'

Alonso gasped. 'Absolutely no fucking way!' he shouted. 'What do you think I am?'

'I think you are what you've admitted to being, a man who will commit acts of violence for money. If you're prepared to do it against property, it's a short moral step to doing the same thing against people.'

'You're nuts, cop.'

Gomez chuckled. 'No. I'm many things but not that. Experienced is what I am, experienced in dealing with people like you.' He looked in my direction. 'Are you still willing to give him his job back, Primavera?'

'Maybe not,' I conceded. 'Maybe not.'

Twenty

After that, Hector had gotten tough with Gaizka. To be exact, he cracked his knuckles and asked me to leave the room. That was all it took for our friend to hold up his hands and yell, 'Okay, what do you want to know?'

'Where you were last night will do to be going on with,' I said.

'I was at a gay club in Girona, all evening. Lots of people saw me.'

'Sure,' Gomez grunted, sarcastically, and sounding not a little homophobic as he added, 'I know you people. You all look out for each other.'

'I can prove it,' Alonso declared. 'I took the train there and I caught the last one back. I still have my ticket.' He left the room but came back a few seconds later waving a piece of card before our eyes. 'See? The date is on it.'

'But not the time,' I pointed out.

'Ask the man on duty at the station,' he countered. 'He'll confirm I got off then. Ask the taxi guy I spoke to when I came out. Ask the woman at the ticket counter; she'll confirm that I bought it yesterday evening.'

'Why did you take the train?' I asked.

'Because I don't have a car; I don't drive, not even a scooter.'

More than anything else, that knocked him on the head as a suspect. Whoever had booby-trapped Ricky's toilet couldn't have known he was eating at La Bassa, so they must have followed him there.

Hector must have thought the same, for he said, 'Okay, let's say we believe that for now. Where were you midday Monday?'

Gaizka beamed. 'I had a job interview in Barcelona . . . with an airline, a proper airline. I got the job,' he added, for good measure. 'I start with them next Monday, and I'll be moving down to the city. It seems that some people believe that being fired by WeighleyAir is a plus point for cabin attendants. The woman who interviewed me said she was surprised I had stuck it for so long, among all those drunken British people. So you see, señora, I don't need my old job back.'

'You might not keep your new one,' I threatened, 'if I tell them what you did to those planes, and why you did it.'

All his bravado disappeared. 'Hey, you wouldn't do that, would you?' he murmured.

'Probably not,' I replied, 'unless I find out that you've been holding something back from us this morning. If that happens I will shop you like a shot to your new employers.'

'I haven't, I swear on my mother's life.'

'I'm sure she'd be delighted to hear that . . . if she's still alive, which I'm inclined to doubt.' I looked at Hector. 'Shall we go, Intendant?' I used his old police title just in case there was any part of Alonso left that wasn't rattled.

'Yes,' he agreed. 'We can always come back if we need to.'

'Do you believe him?' I asked as soon as the car doors were closed.

He nodded. 'I'm afraid I do. It would be nice to nail the little queer for the lot, but . . .'

'Hey,' I protested. 'Less of the homophobia.'

He put a hand on my sleeve. 'I'm sorry, my dear, but I'm an old-fashioned, old-school cop, and an old-fashioned, old-school Catholic as well. I've got some prejudices that I'll never shake, so humour me. As I was saying, while it would be convenient if he was our man, he isn't. He might be willing to take a few euro for causing minor damage, but no way does he have the balls to do anything serious. However,' he continued then paused for breath, 'we have made a little ground.'

'How?' I couldn't see it.

'If we believe his story that he was paid to vandalise the aircraft at Girona, and that the commission came from an English-speaking man with an accent that may or may not have been similar to yours . . .'

'Do you believe it?'

'Yes, I do. The guy had run out of lies by then. All he had left to offer was the truth. If that's what it was, it begins to discredit the official version of the two explosions.'

'That's if you can establish a link between them and the vandalism,' I pointed out.

'Of course there's a link. WeighleyAir, that's the link. Somebody has it in for our company, and that's a fact. I interpret it as part of my job to find out who that person is. Thanks to Alonso, we know he isn't Catalan. That knocks seven million people off our list of possibles.'

I made myself think as positively as Hector on the way back to the airport, but it wasn't easy. We were looking for an English speaker who might have had a Scottish accent, but then again might not; even without the Catalans, the list of possible candidates stretched further than the eye could see.

'Why?' I said as I came off the carretera and headed for the airport approach road.

'Why what?'

'Why would this guy do it? What could his grudge have been?'

'Who knows?' my companion replied. 'He could be a passenger with a grudge, somebody who got charged extra money at check-in for an overweight bag.'

'That's pretty lame,' I observed. 'He paid Gaizka four thousand to do it.'

I caught Gomez's crooked grin out of the corner of my eye. 'Maybe it was a lot of extra money. Maybe he got paranoid about it. I've met some psychos in my time who did that sort of thing.'

'Did that sort of thing include murder?'

'No,' he admitted, 'not that extreme. A big-time grudge

then, a big-time grudge against WeighleyAir, or against Señor Weighley personally.'

'If it was against him personally, why kill Ricky?'

'To do maximum damage to the airline.'

'And yet he hasn't done any,' I pointed out, 'thanks to the Interior Ministry and its man Saviola.'

'Indeed. So maybe he isn't finished.'

'Fuck!'

'Eloquently put, Primavera, eloquently put.'

'I'm not having that, Hector. I'm going to tell Weighley the truth.'

'For which there is no evidence.'

'There is now; there's Gaizka Alonso.'

'Are you kidding? A scared little *maricon* who took money to spray-paint a plane and deflate a couple of tyres? Beyond him, there's still no evidence of deliberate explosions.'

'Fuck!'

'There you go again. But ask yourself another question. How did this man with the money know to recruit Gaizka Alonso to do his dirty work? More than that, why did he recruit him?'

'A recently sacked employee,' I murmured, catching on. 'Good point, we could be looking for someone with inside knowledge of the company. Somebody inside with a grudge against it; a mole.'

'A what?' Gomez exclaimed.

'It's an English expression. It means a spy within an organisation.'

'Moles are blind and crawl about in the dark.'

'True, but they know where they're going, and they're very hard to catch. Let's say ours does have access to company records, and knows about Gaizka being fired. He recruits him to stir up minor trouble, but that's all he's capable of. The next stage requires different skills, but clearly he's found the right person there too.'

'Why? Why did he do this?'

'We'll need to catch him to find that out. Until then we can only guess. But maybe Alonso made up the story about the accent, to send us down the wrong track. Remember, there was an independence sticker on his window. Perhaps our man is indeed a Catalan extremist; maybe Saviola knows something we don't.'

Hector shook his head, firmly. 'No, however nervous Madrid might be, I'm not having that. Even if there is a terrorist cell somewhere, we Catalans wouldn't shit on our own doorstep. This creature, this mole of yours, he has an agenda, no doubt of it, but his target is WeighleyAir. It has to be.'

'In that case, there's an anomaly. Why did he steal Ricky Ross's laptop?'

My ex-cop colleague blinked. 'He did? How do you know that?'

I explained that I'd cleared Ricky's hotel suite but been unable to find the computer that his widow told me he had with him. 'Only the charger, nothing else.'

'Now that is interesting,' Gomez said. 'In fact it puts a

different spin on things. How does this fit? Ross, a detective officer in his police career, suspected that more than the physical security of the airport had been breached. He suspected that there was a deeper motive for the sabotage than the mere revenge of a sacked worker, and he set out himself to find your small velvet friend. But the man, his target, realised his intentions and took steps to eliminate him. Then, to ensure that there was no evidence left behind, he broke into his hotel room. He found the laptop and he made off with it. A theory, yes?'

'But no more than that. And now the damn laptop is missing . . .'

He grimaced. 'I agree. We're as blind as your mole. We have no leads to follow. Any ideas?'

'None that are worth a damn,' I admitted, a second before one occurred to me. 'However,' I continued, 'maybe Ricky talked to his wife. If he was a man on a private mission, maybe he shared it with Alison.'

Twenty-One

I had switched my phone to voicemail when we went to visit Alonso, and forgot to reset it until we were back in the airport office. When I did I found a message from the undertaker. Ricky's body would be released from the Figueres morgue at noon on the following day. He would pick it up and make all the exit arrangements, and expected that we could plan for it to be returned to Scotland on the next day, Saturday.

I called Weighley to let him know, and to drop the word that I expected him to send his plane to collect the cargo. I doubted if he'd been planning to volunteer it, but he agreed, at once, with a murmured, 'Yes, of course. I may even come myself, and bring Alison, if she's up to it.'

I had a sudden vision of those iconic images of Jackie Kennedy on Air Force One, in the suit she'd been wearing when JFK was killed beside her. I was a cynic, even as a kid; I wondered why the photographer had to be there at the time.

'History has to be visually recorded, Primavera, wherever possible,' my dear old father replied when I asked him.

'Throughout the ages it's been written by the winners. Now that we have still and moving images of our times they have to be a little more careful in what they say.'

The fact that those who write the history also control the image editing hasn't occurred to him, not to this day, but I love him for his naivety.

'Yes,' I said to the Flying Scotsman, 'I can see why you'd do that. It'll make a nice photo opportunity back in Edinburgh.'

'Oh, come on, Primavera,' he protested. 'You don't think that badly of me, do you?'

'No, I was joking,' I chuckled, but the second or two that had elapsed before his reply made me sure that I'd read his mind. 'How are the Scottish press treating Ricky's death?'

'Quietly, so far. It was the fourth or fifth item in the Scotland television news at lunchtime and it didn't make the nationals. The company wasn't mentioned at all. I've issued a personal tribute of course.'

'Of course.'

I made a bet with myself that he'd issue a press release saying that he was sending his WeighleyAir Force One to collect Ricky's casket, then left him to get on with drafting it and headed for home.

The house was empty when I got back, but when I went out on the front terrace I soon spotted Mac, seated at a table at Meson del Conde. I changed into casual gear and went down to join him.

'I'm sorry,' I exclaimed even as I sat down. 'I've left you all on your own, all day.'

'What are you sorry for?' he chuckled. 'I've made shameless use of your jeep. Once I dropped the youngsters off I went to Pals, to Jonny's. He was just leaving for the practice ground so I went with him. He took an extra set of clubs along and we played a few holes.' He beamed. 'I tell you, lass, there's hope for my golf yet.' Then his smile seemed to change, subtly, to one of pride. 'That said, Jonny's playing a different game from the one I've played all my life. There's light years of difference between an amateur and a top pro, which he is now, beyond doubt. In every respect. The most I ever won at golf was about thirty-five quid in the sweep at our monthly medal. This year Jonny's tax bill wasn't far short of seven figures. He told me that Brush wants him to move to the US.'

'That's news to me,' I said. 'He hasn't mentioned it. Not that he has any reason to,' I added, quickly. 'It's not as if I'm family, really.'

'Of course you are. No, it's something that only came up this morning. He had a long email about tax management, and saying that now he's a member of the American golf tour as well as the European, it's the sensible thing to do.'

'What's he saying about it?'

'That there are more things to life than money, and that he'll do what's best for Selina and him. Sensible boy, eh? If only his uncle had thought that way.'

'Hey, come on,' I protested. 'That's not fair. Oz was never driven by money.'

He looked at me, surprised. 'You think not?'

'I know not. He never even thought about it. Things just

225

happened to him. He never planned anything, as far as I could see. His entire life was an accident.'

'Mmm.' He frowned. 'I never thought of it that way. Or of him, latterly. I stopped understanding him a long time before he died.' He put his hand on mine. 'Yet another regret, Primavera, eh.'

'Don't get maudlin, Mac,' I snapped, impatiently. 'I'm damned if I'm going to let you spend the rest of your life looking over your shoulder. You've got new priorities.'

'Such as?'

'Your five grandchildren, for openers.'

'Five? Jonny's very much his own man now. He doesn't need me any more.'

'Then why did he confide in you about this American move? Mac, you're the closest thing he's had to a dad for most of his life, Alan, the real one, being a complete wanker who never took any interest in him. Of course he needs you.'

'His brother certainly doesn't. Colin's getting it all from Alan now. Jonny says he's never been down here, even though it's only half a day's drive.'

'No. He's still Ellie's son.' I smiled. 'That means he's not beyond rescue.'

'How do I do that?'

'Front him up next time he comes home; get him drunk, get him laid.'

'In Anstruther? Drunk I could maybe manage, Primavera. The other he'll have to sort out for himself.'

'Whatever,' I laughed. 'What I'm really saying is that you

have a hell of a lot to do yet and time to do it. Unlike poor bloody Ricky, who's travelling by private jet on Saturday, and you can't say it's for the first time in his life, because that's over.'

'True, poor bugger. Are you still intent on your quest for truth and justice?'

'Put it this way, I'm going to look under as many stones as I can.'

'Then the best way I can help is by giving you as much time as I can to let you do it. I'll do the school run again tomorrow.'

'Mac, I can't . . .'

He held up a hand, stopping me in mid-sentence. 'Of course you can. I know the way now, and it's what I came out here to do.'

I gave in. 'Okay. Have you phoned home yet?'

'No, and I don't plan to. It's not as if I can ask Mary how she's doing, and the nurses know where I am if things deteriorate.'

'It must be costing you a fortune, looking after her this way.'

'I've got very little else to spend it on, and besides, value comes before cost. I like what I'm doing, that's my point. But I take yours too, that I've still got a life to lead, yes, unlike poor old Ricky.'

As he spoke, his three youngest grandchildren appeared in the square, fresh off the school bus. Wee Jonathan was the first to spot us. He rushed across, eyes wide. 'Can we go, Grandpa? Have you asked?'

'Asked what?' I said, intrigued by his unusual enthusiasm.

Mac looked at me. 'How far is it to Port Aventura?' he asked.

'By car? It's about two and a half hours, but you can do a day trip on a bus.'

'That sounds okay,' he murmured. 'I thought I might take this lot there on Saturday, if that's okay with you. This one here and his sister say they've never been.'

Port Aventura is an enormous amusement park, more Alton Towers than Disneyland, but pretty good nonetheless. It's a little south of Barcelona, but accessible from our place. I looked at Janet. She nodded at me. Behind her Tom was smiling; he had been there a few times, with me, and once on a school trip.

'Then go for it,' I told him. 'At this notice you'll probably need to drive, though. Is that okay?'

'Of course. I'm sure your satnav will get me there, no problem.'

In truth I was grateful for Mac's proposal. I'd realised that I would probably need to go to the airport on Saturday, to give Ricky a proper send-off, and if the kids were off base, I wouldn't be under pressure to explain to them what it was all about.

'So,' he continued, breaking into my thoughts as he waved to a waiter, 'who's for what?'

Janet and Tom didn't have anything: they headed home, to take Charlie for some exercise, but I realised that I could murder a canya, so I asked for one. Wee Jonathan had a cola.

He settled himself into a seat next to his grandfather. I was pleased to see how well the two of them seemed to be bonding.

When our drinks were done, Mac nudged him. 'Hey,' he whispered. 'Fishing?'

The wee chap's eyes lit up as he looked at me for approval. 'Okay,' I said, 'but off the beach or close to the shore. Don't go to the end of the jetty without Tom being there.'

He didn't protest at my restrictions. 'What would you like us to catch tonight?' he asked, as if his rod could discriminate.

'Well,' I replied slowly as I pondered his question, 'this evening we're having the sea bass you caught yesterday for dinner, so if you could manage sea bream this time, that would be good. Or squid, or monkfish, or a small tuna, or maybe shark . . .'

'Hey!' Mac exclaimed. 'There aren't sharks in that bloody sea, are there?'

'Yes, there are,' I told him, 'but they don't come inshore. I've never heard of one being seen around here.' I have seen a photo of a dead great white washed up on the beach at Tossa del Mar back in the nineties, but I didn't see the need to share that.

'Pity,' he sighed. 'I've always wanted to catch one of those.'

We headed home to collect their rods. When they'd gone I tried to call Alison Ross, as I'd told Hector I would. I was taken aback slightly when another woman answered. 'I'm not sure she's available,' she croaked in a thick, strained voice. 'We've had a . . .'

229

'Yes, I know. Tell Alison that it's Primavera, and that I'll understand if she'd rather not speak to me right now. It can wait.'

It didn't have to, though; she took the call almost immediately. 'That was Judy,' she told me, 'Ricky's daughter. We're still trying to get hold of his son. It's the middle of the night in Australia.'

'When you do,' I said, 'you can give him a complete update.'

I outlined everything I'd done, and the arrangements I'd made.

'So he really is sending his beloved Gulfstream,' I heard her murmur. 'Either Jack's had an unprecedented fit of niceness, or you must have great powers of persuasion.'

'Give him the benefit of the doubt. Mind you, he may offer you a seat on the plane on the way out. I don't need to tell you why.'

'No, you don't. I'd be amazed if he doesn't. One man's tragedy is another man's photo opportunity. If he does, I'll think about it. Primavera, Judy and I, we can't thank you enough for sorting all this out.'

'It's not just me: you can thank the company as well. Jack's taking care of all the bills, here at least.'

'Does he know that?'

'Not yet, but he's put me in a position to authorise them, and be sure I will do just that.'

'Will all Ricky's things be on the plane as well?' Alison asked.

'They will, all of them that I found, at any rate. The laptop's missing.'

'It wasn't in his hotel room?'

'No. Nor was it in the airport office. I had them search for it this afternoon, just in case he'd left it there; no joy.'

'What can have happened to it?' she wondered.

'God knows. I could report it missing, but without knowing where he had it last . . . you get my drift?'

'Yes, of course.'

'Maybe one of the hotel staff would admit to nicking it,' I said, 'but if nobody did, the only result would be resentment. Was it valuable? That is, was the data on it valuable?'

'No, not really. All Ricky's company data and files are stored in his office. All that would have been on it would be the files he was working on, personal emails, music and suchlike.'

'Alison,' I ventured, 'those files? Could Ricky have been looking into something else when he was in Spain, other than just the security issue?'

'Such as?'

'I don't know.'

'To do with WeighleyAir?'

'Possibly.

'Nothing that he ever mentioned to me, I'm afraid. Not that I can recall. But Ricky did have a tendency to keep his cards close. Would you like me to have a look in his office for anything relating to his trip?'

'If you could.'

'I will do,' she promised, 'but why? What's this about?'

'Nothing, really; I've got my company hat on just now, and I'm simply crossing the Ts and dotting the Is, that's all.'

'You're not trying to tell me that Ricky's death might not have been accidental, are you?'

'Hell no!' I exclaimed. 'Ask the consulate and they'll get you the official police report. It'll show beyond all doubt that it was. All I want to ensure is that he didn't have any business out here that was left unfinished. There's still a degree of official uncertainty over who vandalised those planes on the ground. The police weren't too interested, so I'm thinking that Ricky might have looked into it himself. Would that have been typical of him?'

'Absolutely,' his widow declared. 'He never really got over not being a cop any more.'

'Who knows, Alison?' I said. 'Maybe he never stopped being one.'

Twenty-Two

It was as well that I hadn't been relying on Mac and wee Jonathan's Thursday catch to feed the family, for they came back empty-handed, apart from a small, sad creature that might have been an aquatic mongrel, if such things existed. It was as far away from a shark as a sparrow is from a golden eagle.

'Sorry,' the chastened grandparent said as he held it up. 'Best we could do.'

'Moby Dick it is not,' I laughed. 'Why didn't you throw it back?'

'Because it was dead when we took it off the hook; I suspect the poor bugger committed suicide.'

By contrast, Wednesday's sea bass was ace, and the three fish fed five of us easily. Tom and Janet cooked it, Basque style, in the oven with garlic and sliced potatoes, then took it off the bone, so expertly that even I was surprised.

'Where did you learn to do that?' I asked.

'Antonio in Esculapi,' Janet replied. 'He taught us.'

'Cedric in Can Coll said he might give us jobs as waiters there next summer,' Tom added. 'So did Teresa at VaiVe. What do you think, Mum?'

'I'm not sure,' I said. 'I think you might still be a little young next year. There's this also; you don't actually need the money. I'm not saying you'll never need to work, for I believe that everybody should if they can, but at this stage of your lives if you took those jobs just for fun, you'd be depriving people who really do need them. Plus there's this. Do you really want to be carting trays around when you could be swimming or surfing?'

'Maybe not,' Janet conceded.

'No brainer,' Tom laughed.

The rest of the evening dwindled away into a sort of nothingness. The kids did their school stuff, Mac went down to the square for a nightcap, and I settled for an early night.

I had made no firm plans with Hector for the following day, but I decided to go to the airport anyway, to tell its general manager face to face about Ricky's removal on Saturday morning and to make sure that it happened on the one corner of the standing area that can't be seen from the departure lounge windows.

I was almost there when my ringtone sounded through the Bluetooth speakers. I said 'Yes' to accept and found myself in the disembodied company of Will Harris, my friend from the consulate.

'Primavera,' he began. 'I detect road noise. Can you speak?'

'Sure, Will, I'm alone.' I chuckled. 'Story of my life.'

'Come on, that's a rare occurrence, I'll bet.' He paused. 'I've got something for you on that chap you asked me about, Mr Hamish Orr. I've found him, and you've come up lucky, in that he's a lot closer than he might have been. He lost his passport earlier this year and renewed it through the consulate. We posted it to the address he supplied, a post office box number in Figueres. It doesn't pinpoint him for you, but it does give you a starting off point.'

'It does indeed,' I agreed. 'Thanks, Will. That's very helpful, and very interesting. Given Mr Orr's past, it opens a line of inquiry.'

'Into what?'

'I can't say, not at this stage, but let me ask you a question. What's your take on Catalan nationalism, and the independence movement? Is it simply a reaction to an unpopular government in Madrid or is it for real?'

The car was silent as he thought over my question, then the speaker crackled once again, as he spoke. 'It's always been there, to an extent,' he said, 'and the government in Madrid is never very popular in Barcelona. But this is new and it's for real. The Catalan people are more restive and resentful than I've ever seen them, and I've been in Spain for a fair few years now, as you know.'

'And how do you see the governments reacting, here and there?'

'Another good question,' he murmured, slowly. 'Madrid is autocratic, always have been and always will be. No previous Catalan administration has ever been truly for independence and I'm not certain this one is either. But it's seen what's happening and it's sailing with the wind, possibly in the hope and expectation that it will blow itself out.'

'Do you detect any signs that it might turn violent?'

'None whatsoever, but I know that both governments are bricking it over that eventuality.' He paused. 'Here, are you trying to tell me that there might be more to the death of your Scottish friend in that explosion on Wednesday than we've been told?'

'Will,' I assured him, 'I'm not trying to tell you anything.'

'If you were, and it was being covered up, we would have to get involved. You know that, don't you?'

'Yes, but I'm not telling you that. All I can say to you for sure is that it had fuck all to do with Catalan independence.'

'Even so,' he said, 'you're fishing and there's a reason for it. Whatever it is, don't drop me in it, there's a love.'

'I promise I won't.' I paused. 'Do you feel like doing me another favour?' I asked.

'In return for being kept completely in the loop from now on.'

'Okay, that's a deal. Hamish Orr,' I continued, abruptly. 'Do you have a copy of his passport photo in your office?'

'I don't know. I'd need to check. Do you want it?'

'It might come in handy, if we go looking for him.'

'We?'

'My colleague and I. It's a business matter, Will.'

'Is it?' He paused, then added, 'What is your remit with WeighleyAir?'

'Loose. You might all me a troubleshooter.'

He laughed. 'Bloody hell! In my experience trouble usually shoots at you. Talk about setting a thief! Very well, I will cast around for Mr Orr's official likeness. No promises but if I do find it I will scan it and send it to you. Give me your email address.'

I recited it, slowly, thanked him and told him that I looked forward to hearing from him.

Hector was a little surprised to see me when I walked into the WeighleyAir office, but he was also pleased. I found him in heated conversation with Jose Ramos, the operations manager, who was questioning an order for several motion sensors and two CCTV cameras when I walked in on them.

'You don't have the authority to do that,' he bellowed, waving the paperwork in the air. It struck me that was a dangerous thing to say to a man who had exercised authority for much of his life, often with a gun on his hip, so I weighed in.

'Trust me,' I said, quietly, 'he does.'

The unfortunate man turned on me. 'Who says?' he barked.

'I do.'

A blue vein pulsed on his forehead. 'And who the hell are you to do that?'

'I believe that was explained in an email that head office circulated earlier this week. Did you read it?'

'Yes, some guff about you having floating responsibility for public affairs, whatever the hell that means.'

'Public affairs and operations,' I corrected him, 'with executive powers, reporting directly to the CEO. It's a pretty loose description, I will grant you, but what it means is this: I say, you do. You have a problem with that, you call Edinburgh and talk it through with Mr Weighley.'

'And I bloody well will!' he declared. 'This is my operation. I'm the man in charge here.'

'Fine,' I said, 'but when you do call him, keep this in mind. Señor Gomez is here because of a sequence of events. It began with a WeighleyAir aircraft being painted with, alongside the obscenities and the independence slogans, the words, "Fit only for fucking cattle", in English, the language of choice of all good protesters, since that seems to guarantee the widest audience.

'Obviously that plane had to be taken out of service, with the knock-on effect that for the rest of the day, several of the company's flights were compromised all over Europe, such is the nature of its scheduling and crew movements. Some were so badly delayed that compensation had to be paid to passengers.' I looked him in the eye. 'Is that fact, or is it not?'

He nodded, sullenly, but the truculence stayed in his eyes.

'A few days later,' I continued, 'there was a second incident on the tarmac, here, at this very same airport. Another aircraft had two tyres burst, deflated then ripped open so that they were unserviceable. The consequences were exactly the same in terms of financial loss and damage to the company's reputation. As a result, Ricky Ross was sent here by Mr

Weighley to review security and take any necessary action to make this place secure.

'The orders you're querying are a result of his recommendations. They will be implemented, but that will be of no interest to him,' I let my voice rise, 'because he's going home in a box tomorrow!'

I stared Ramos down, and then added, 'While the airport owners bear some responsibility for these lapses, there are a few questions that nobody has asked up to now. Why the hell didn't WeighleyAir's operations manager address the issue after the very first incident? Why did he sit on his arse and wait for another fuck-up instead of leaning on the airport owners to plug the leak straight away? Why did Jack Weighley have to send someone across from Scotland to sort out a problem that could and should have been sorted out in Spain by an operations manager who turned out to be asleep at the fucking wheel?'

'But . . .' he began to protest.

'But nothing!' I snapped. 'This is what you are going to do. You're going to wind your neck in and make sure that not only are those items on site today, but they're installed and working as well. Otherwise I'll be making a phone call to Edinburgh to clarify that I have the authority to replace you.'

For a moment I thought he was going to carry on the argument, but he subsided. 'You're wrong,' he said quietly, 'but to be honest I don't give a shit any more. This is an awful company run by an awful man. Just as soon as I can find another job, I'm out of here.'

Something in his demeanour made me regret that I'd blown my stack, but it was too late to do anything about it. Who wouldn't have resented Hector and me being parachuted into his territory? Still, my point had been a valid one, except . . . I sensed a nagging inconsistency in it but I couldn't pin it down.

I stopped trying as soon as I switched on the computer on the desk I had commandeered and checked my email.

My in-box showed one new item, from Will Harris. I opened it and read: 'You've come up lucky, my dear. We don't usually keep passport photographs here, but Mr Orr supplied more than were necessary for his application and I found one clipped to his file. By the way, his box number is Apt. 9103.'

There was an attachment. I opened it and saw a full-face head shot of a middle-aged unsmiling man with dark receding hair, and a scar on his left cheek. I went into the menu, found a printer, selected the 'photo quality' option and programmed two copies.

'There,' I said to Hector with an air of triumph as I planked a copy under his nose. 'That is Mr Hamish Orr, whom Ricky Ross put away for a twelve stretch, and he's not far away, not at all.' I read out the number that Will had given me. Incidentally, it's quite common in Spain for individuals to have post office boxes, since delivery services are not quite as reliable as in some other countries. 'It's at the Figueres office, so he must be living within easy distance of there. A man of your resources and contacts should be able to get a street address for him. Yes?'

'And more than that,' he replied. 'If he's employed, as we believe he is, I can probably find out where. Leave it with me.'

'Good, call me when you get something. I have something to do here and then I'm off to St Martí, to chase up a long shot.'

'I think I can guess what that is,' he murmured. 'No chance.'

'But worth the effort.'

I went off to see the airport general manager, to explain what was happening next day and what I would like him to arrange. He was as helpful as Jose Ramos had been obstructive, and I left happy in the knowledge that one thing at least was going to work out properly.

My mind was buzzing as I headed up the carretera. It's not that I'm too mean to pay the autopista tolls, but its traffic can be frenetic, I found that I wanted a little peace and quiet, some time to contemplate, even if I was at the wheel, so I chose the back road home instead, where all I had to worry about was being stuck behind a tractor towing a load of harvested apples.

I found myself wishing that I was Doctor Who, and that the Merc was a timeship that could take me back seven days, to a time when Ricky Ross was still a figure from my past, and Jack Weighley was no more than that pain in the arse I'd sorted out in Barcelona.

For all the silly money that WeighleyAir were paying me, a large part of me would have preferred to have been shopping in Girona on the morning poor old Ricky came into the square on spec, with a view to looking me up. Yes, it would have meant that he was toasted in his car there and then instead of being spread all over an outhouse door two days later, but either way he was doomed.

The lesser part of me that recognised she was in the situation like it or not and had to deal with it out of some sense of duty to the dead that I didn't quite understand, knew that there was something about the business that didn't add up.

Somebody had wanted Ricky removed, but why? Was it linked to his past life as a gang-busting police officer, or was it something else entirely, something from the present rather than the past. 'Fuktifano,' I whispered, smiling as I remembered the tale of the legendary Scottish football commentator who misunderstood the answer to his question about the name of a foreign striker and broadcast his version to the nation.

I put the car in the garage when I got back to the village. The house was empty, Mac having said that he was bound for Pals again to play a final few holes with Jonny and to have lunch with 'them'. I'd wondered idly whether the plural might have included Anais, but I'd kept it to myself, not wanting to be over-pushy on that front.

I wandered down to the car park. Marc was on duty in the hut, as I had expected. Business was slow and so he was studying something on his computer, putting his time between tickets to good use. I noticed that the scorched trees had been removed, roots and all, and that new saplings had been planted in their stead.

'Hello, Primavera,' he greeted me amiably. 'How is your friend? Has he recovered from his lucky escape?'

He didn't know. But then again, why should he? The dead man in Ventallo hadn't been named.

'Not really,' I replied. 'He's going home tomorrow.'

'Never to return, I imagine. I wouldn't, if something like that happened to me.'

No, I thought, *he won't be back.*

I reached behind me and drew the passport image of Hamish Orr from my back pocket. 'Marc,' I ventured. 'Think back to Monday morning. Do you recall seeing this man then?'

He looked at the photo for quite a while, then shook his head. 'Sorry. I don't.' He handed me back the mugshot. 'That's a passport photograph, so the guy's looking straight at the camera. If drivers here make proper eye contact with me, in the way that the immigration people always do at airports, there's a good chance I will remember them, even on a busy day, but if they don't, then probably I won't.'

'I understand,' I said, putting Mr Orr back in my pocket. 'It was worth a try.'

'Who is he, then?' Marc asked, with a half smile. 'Do you think he might have had something to do with the spontaneous fire in your friend's car?'

He's a very smart guy. I should have known he would be curious.

'He's a person of interest,' I replied.

'To whom? The police? I don't think so. My boss was told

very firmly that they've made up their mind. Primavera, are you playing detective?'

I made proper eye contact with him, like an immigration person. 'Marc,' I chuckled. 'You should know by now that I never play.'

'Then I wish I could help you, but on the basis of that photograph, I can't.' He stopped, as if he was thinking something over, then came to a decision. 'If you had given me his registration number, that would have been different. We don't tell people this, but we have a clever little camera in the back of the hut, well hidden, that photographs the rear plate of every car that comes in here, and the front plate as they leave. The images are stored on my computer. You don't have his number, do you?'

'No, sod it,' I admitted. 'I don't. Thanks anyway.'

I headed back to the village, pausing on the way to talk to Ben Simmers in his wine shop, and to buy a couple of bottles of something red that I thought Mac might like to try. Because of my involvement with my brother-in-law's wine business, most of my home stock comes from there, but I like to keep an eye on the opposition, and learn where I can.

I was almost home, passing in front of the church, when my mobile stopped me in mid-stride.

I took the call there and then, staying outdoors to ensure an adequate signal, unhampered by thick stone walls. 'Primavera, it's Hector,' Gomez announced. 'I've got the goods on Orr. He lives in a town called Vilamalla, in an apartment block, which probably explains why he prefers to have a post office box. He works in a quarry in the hills behind Verges, on the far side of the main Figueres road. He's a demolition man; he blasts the rock from the face.'

'Why does that not surprise me?' I whispered. 'Anything else?'

'Sure. He drives a Renault Berlingo van, registration FLL7779.'

I stiffened. 'He what? Are you sure of that number?'

'Absolutely.' He repeated it.

'Hector,' I said, 'that's excellent. I'll call you back in a few minutes.'

I didn't even bother to put the wine in the house but turned on my heel and went back down to the car park.

Marc saw me coming; my urgency must have been obvious, for he smiled and tilted his hat back on his head. 'You have something?' he asked.

'A Renault Berlingo; half car, half van.'

His eyes widened. 'Red, or close to it?'

'I don't know about the colour, but I have the number.' I recited it.

'Let me look.'

As he leaned over his computer, I went round to the door of the hut. He flipped through a series of images, one after the other quickly, until he paused, leaned back and turned the screen so that I could see.

'There you are,' he exclaimed. 'That's your man.'

He was more or less right about the colour. Renault might call it plum rather than red, but it's in the ballpark. The rear plate was clear on the image: FLL7779.

'I remember him now,' Marc said, 'because he parked well away from all the other cars; formed a line of his own.'

'When did he leave?'

'That's another thing I remember. After your friend's car blew up and he flattened me when I went to put out the fire, when I got up and could breathe again, I saw that he had gone. Without paying,' he added, as a postscript.

'Did he, by God.' I laughed, not far short of exultantly. 'That gives me all the excuse I need to go looking for him.'

Twenty-Three

I phoned Hector as soon as I got back home, and told him what I'd discovered.

'Hey!' he exclaimed, genuinely delighted, 'have you never in your life thought about becoming a cop? When I was active and got a result like that I used to throw a party for my whole team.'

'Do you want to pick me up or meet at the quarry? I know where it is.'

'Hell no!'

'Will we go to his home instead? Would that be better, more private?'

'No, no, no, no, no,' he said insistently. 'Hold your horses. We've got the drop on Señor Orr. We can call on him any time we like. When . . . if . . . we do that, I want to know the whole story. I'm going back to see our boy Gaizka. Maybe he spoke the truth when he said he never met the man who paid him, but maybe he didn't. I want to show him Orr's picture, to see if it stirs his memory.'

'You think Orr paid him to damage those planes?'

'According to Gaizka his accent could have been like yours. This man Orr is Scottish. To me, that's an interesting coincidence.'

'But why would he do that?' I asked.

'I have no idea. However, I will never know one way or another unless I ask the question.'

'Then wait for me. I'm not missing out on this.'

'There's no need.'

'Maybe not, but I'm coming.'

He sighed. 'Okay. I know better than to try to talk you out of it. I'm going to have some lunch, I suggest that you do the same, then go straight to Flaça. I'll meet you at the end of Gaizka's street, two thirty sharp. Okay?'

'Fine by me. But Hector,' I added, 'you said "if" we confront Orr. Given what we know why wouldn't we?'

'Work it out. We've got a clear suspect for a murder, and also for an attempted murder. Once we've seen Alonso, we have to ask ourselves whether we should hand this over to the police.'

'To Alex?'

'No. He's been warned off. It wouldn't be fair on him to burden him with this. I would go to Barcelona, to show the director general of the Mossos what we've found. That little bastard Saviola scared my cousin. I would dearly love to have his nuts in a vice with my hand on the lever, but only the top man has the authority to put them there.'

He had a point, and I told him so. 'Let's go see Alonso, then decide.'

Action agreed, I made myself some lunch, nothing fancy, just half a baguette stuffed with tuna, tomato and mayo, and devoured it in the kitchen, thinking all the time. Yes, Hector was right; what we knew about Orr made it a police matter. On the other hand, we'd done the spadework, and my dangerous vanity gene felt that it would be nice to go the rest of the way. I wasn't worried about confronting Orr, not with Hector at my side; the guy was a bomber not a shooter, and he wasn't in the first flush of youth either. Plus, I'd seen that photograph and I was pretty sure that while the scar made him look tough, aside from that I could read a different message.

'It's not the scars and the broken nose you want to worry about,' my poor dead friend Mike Dylan had said, once upon a time, 'it's the guy that put them there.'

Hamish Orr might have done time for killing a man, but those eyes looking straight into the camera lens told me that somewhere along the line, maybe in jail, he'd acquired a heavy dose of fear.

I checked my watch as I finished my chunky sandwich: two o'clock, plenty of time to get to my rendezvous with Senor Gomez. I picked up my keys and headed down the stairway to the garage.

Plenty of time, I'd thought, but I hadn't counted on one of those pesky tractors gathering a convoy behind it on the twisty road beyond Parlava. As a result it was two-forty before I reached my destination. Hector's car was parked at the end about fifty metres away from Alonso's front door, but there was no sign of him.

'Bugger!' I cursed and drove on, pulling into a space between two vehicles just past Gaizka's house. I'd noticed that the door was ajar as I passed it. As I stepped out of the Merc, still fizzing over my colleague's impatience, I saw him emerge, backwards.

'Hector!' I called to him. At first I thought he hadn't heard me, but he stopped, turning his head to look in my direction and I could see that he was wide-eyed, shocked.

'What is it?' I asked him.

'I took a walk along while I was waiting for you, just to check the place, you understand. I saw that his door was open, very slightly, but it wasn't normal that it should have been left like that, and so I went in to check it out.'

'And?'

He didn't answer so I decided to see for myself. 'No,' he exclaimed. 'You don't need to . . .

'Too late for that.' I stepped through the door, and even if I hadn't known from Hector's demeanour that something was wrong, I'd still have twigged straight away. It's not something most peace-loving people know or consider, but blood, a lot of it, has a smell; it's metallic, distinctive and in a contained environment it can take a long time to dissipate. It's much the same with piss.

My nose led me into the kitchen, and I could see at once what had shocked Hector. Gaizka was lying face down in two pools, one from his voided bladder and the other from a massive head trauma, the kind from which there is no recovery. As I moved closer I could see that there were several wounds, his skull had been cracked open and the grey stuff was visible. The poor lad had been beaten to death.

He'd been there for a while. The urine was mostly dry, and the blood was sticky and congealed. I leaned over and touched his neck. He was stone cold.

'Quite a mess, eh.' Hector had followed me indoors. 'It gave me a hell of a turn. I never liked the messy ones.'

'But this isn't,' I pointed out. 'There's nothing frenzied about it. No bloodstains on the ceiling, nothing like that. Look at it; this was done very efficiently. His killer hit him often enough to do the job and no more.'

'No, you're right,' he agreed. 'This was not a lovers' quarrel. I saw a couple of those in my career and they were both awful, much worse than this. There was a man in Girona who beat his wife's brains out, literally. Whoever killed Alonso stopped when he saw them, because he knew he didn't need to go any further. Señor Orr, do you think, getting rid of a possible witness?'

I didn't believe that for a minute; I told him so, and why. 'Yes, Orr did time for killing someone, but it was a fight, and many a jury might have called it self-defence and let him walk. I don't see this as his style. Besides, why would Orr pay Gaizka to damage those planes, and even if he did, why wait till now to kill him?'

He frowned as he gazed back at me, then nodded, conceding my argument.

'You know what I do think?' I continued, suddenly certain. 'We're being tailed in some way. The man who hired Alonso found out that we've spoken to him and he's taken him out of the picture. If he knows also that we're on to Orr, then . . .'

'Jesus, yes. Primavera, we have got to find him and warn him.'

'Agreed. But what do we do about this?' I asked.

Hector's forehead set in even deeper ridges as he considered my question. 'I phone Alex Guinart,' he said, finally. 'He's been warned off the explosions, but this is different. I'll tell him that I came to question Alonso about the vandalism, and that when he didn't answer the front door, I went round the back and found that the rear door into the kitchen had been forced . . . which it has, look.' I followed his pointing finger, and saw that it had indeed been jemmied. 'Obviously the killer broke in here, took Gaizka by surprise, then left through the front, being a little careless when he closed it.'

'Okay,' I agreed. 'We should do that.'

'You needn't be involved. I'll wait for him here. You go and find Orr.'

'What do I say to him when I do?' I asked.

'Nothing. Find out where he is, that's all I'm saying, then just keep an eye on him. Call me when you've tracked him down and I'll join you; I don't want you tackling him on your own. That's not for negotiation; do as I say.'

Twenty-Four

'**D**o as I say' has rarely worked with me, but there are times when you don't need to be told.

I left by the back door. It opened into a lane that allowed access to all the houses in the terraced block, feeding back out into the street. I glanced around before stepping out, but the place seemed deserted so I hurried to my car and stepped in.

I sped out of there, and out of Flaça. I took the same route by which I had come, but when I reached the roundabout in Verges, I carried straight on instead of making the right turn for home. The quarry where Orr worked was big, and visible from several kilometres away. The approach road was wide, as it had to be to accommodate the enormous trucks that were needed to carry away its rocks, but not as rutted by their weight as I had feared it might be.

As I neared the entrance, two things occurred to me. The first was that I had no idea how I was going to determine whether my man was there or not. The second was that it was very quiet for a place where enormous chunks of hillside are blasted loose then broken up.

When I got there, I discovered why. It was deserted. 'Oh shit,' I whispered as the reason came to me.

The Spanish calendar is littered with saints' days. They're not all school and public holidays, but many of them are celebrated by individual trades. You name it, butchers, bakers, candlestick makers, they all have a celestial watchdog. Quarry-men too, it seemed. I'd noticed in *La Vanguardia* earlier in the week that Friday was the Feast of St Someone-or-other, but it hadn't been of great interest to me, not until then.

I sat there, frustrated. So what next? I could see only two options. One of them was to let Hector know, then wait for him to catch up with me. The other was to press on and try to pin down Orr's address in Vilamalla. There was no harm in taking a look, I persuaded myself.

I made my way back to the main road and rejoined it, heading in the direction of Figueres. I knew roughly where I was going, for I had noticed the name on signposts often enough, but I'd never had occasion to visit there. I took the indicated turn-off and found it soon enough . . . then paused, as I found myself in a very small, very old village; Orr's address was an apartment yet there wasn't a block of flats to be seen anywhere.

I fed the destination into my satnav. It looked at me blankly, and then said, in Castellano, for we'd never bothered to change the installed operating language, 'Where the hell is that?' or words to that effect.

It took me a while to find the place, because it wasn't really in Vilamalla at all. Having exhausted all the possibilities in the village itself, I headed along the Figueres road, in the direction of some buildings I could see in the distance. When I got there I found that they were residential and that quite a few were multi-owned.

I had no street name to go on, only the name, 'Apartmentos Santa Rosa'. I had to identify each block individually, but I persevered. The Spanish equivalent of the Law of Sod applied. Orr's block was the last I checked.

It was a relatively new construction, three storeys high, with what looked like half a dozen apartments to each floor. It might well have been designed to be unhelpful to callers; there were no letterboxes . . . Spanish postmen can refuse point blank to deliver to flats, and if they deign to, they aren't usually too fussy about whose mail goes where . . . and there was no residents' address board in the entrance hallway either, when I took a look in there.

I stood there and listened, just listened, for sounds of life. Someone was watching television, an afternoon quiz programme from the sound of the audience laughter. Behind that but still audible there was music.

The hallway had a rear door. I opened it and looked outside: there was a small back garden with a couple of swings and a slide for kids, and a community barbecue built into one corner.

Beyond that there was a parking area, and there I saw a very big clue: a plum-coloured Renault Berlingo, registration FLL7779.

'Now I know for sure,' I murmured.

'Can I help you, señora?' A man's voice came from behind me. I turned to find its owner, a big curly-haired guy in his early thirties, looking at me with a friendly smile on his face. 'Are you looking for someone?'

That was the point at which I could have, should have, talked my way out of there. I could have told him that I'd gotten confused and was in the wrong block.

But I didn't. Instead I replied, 'I'm trying to find Señor Orr. Can you tell me which is his apartment?'

The smile widened. 'Ah, the Scottish man; sure, he's on the same floor as me. Come on, I'll show you. My name's Ramon, by the way.'

Again, I should have declined his offer and left, like those *News of the World* reporters of old. Again, I took the option that Hector had warned me against. If we were right then Orr was in danger, and he needed to know it.

'Why are you looking for Hamish anyway?' Ramon asked, as we headed for the stairs. His pronunciation of the name made it sound like a synthetic pork product, but it was a damn good question and one that I had not expected to face.

I pride myself on being a fairly quick thinker, but I've never bettered the answer I produced in that instance, straight off the top of my head.

'I'm Scottish too,' I replied. 'I'm interviewing other ex-pats from my country for articles in the Catalan Society magazine, and somebody told me about him. I'm going to ask him if he'll take part.'

'You'll be lucky,' he said. 'Hamish never talks about his past.' He chuckled. 'In fact, he doesn't talk much about his present either.'

'You're friends?'

'Of a sort; we go to the bar together,' he grinned, 'when my wife lets me.'

'You ask permission?' I exclaimed. 'I could have sworn you were Catalan, but apparently not.'

'Señora, we're not all relics from the Franco era.'

We stepped out on to an open walkway that stretched the length of the block, with three apartment doors on either side and wide enough for washing machines to be sited outside, common practice in Spain.

'My place is number four,' Ramon said. 'Hamish is number two. His car's there so I guess he's in, unless he's gone to the bar, but that's not likely, not this early, not even on a holiday. Let's see.'

He led the way along to the second door on the left, and banged on it, rather than just ringing the bell. 'Hey, Hamish,' he yelled, 'open up. There's a lady journalist here to see you.' He grinned again. 'That should bring him running.'

But it didn't. We waited, allowing time for him to have been on the phone or on the bog, but nothing happened. We stood there, in silence, until Ramon shrugged his shoulders and grunted, 'Must have gone to the bar after all.'

As he spoke I thought I heard a sound, coming from inside. 'Hold on a minute,' I murmured, holding up a hand for silence, and putting myself close to the door. After a few seconds, I knew I'd been right, for it was repeated: a cry, a moan, a wail, whatever, unintelligible, yet clearly meaning 'Help!'

I tried the handle; it was unlocked. 'Come on,' I said, not even pausing to consider that anyone other than Hamish Orr might be inside, and taking it for granted that my burly escort would be as reckless as me and would follow. As it happened he was, and he did.

The kitchen and a bedroom were nearest to the door. I was going to check them when the plea sounded out again. We followed it into the main living area, and there we found its author.

'Hamish!' Ramon cried out. All his jovial bravado had gone; he seemed less chunky, and very scared.

Orr was lying on his left side, on a rug that had once been grey but had become two-tone. He was twitching, but that seemed to be all the movement of which he was capable. I pushed my companion out of the way and knelt beside him.

He had been bleeding from the head, but it had stopped. His injuries were different from those inflicted on Alonso. I leaned close, took his hand and peered at them.

'He's been shot in the head,' I said, glancing over my shoulder. 'Ramon, I know what I'm doing here. What I want you to do is go back downstairs and call this number.' I recited Alex's mobile. 'Got it?'

'Yes, hold on.' I watched as he patched it into his own phone. 'Got it. Who is it?'

'Intendant Guinart, of the Mossos. Tell him where you are, what's happened and that Primavera is here. Remember the name: Primavera. Tell him we need an ambulance, give him the address and directions and then wait for him at the gate.'

'Yes, yes. At once.' He bolted from the room, out of his depth and glad of an excuse to get back into safe waters.

I took a longer look at Orr's cranium. As far as I could see he'd been hit there three times, and yet he was still alive. 'Don't move,' I told him; unnecessarily, because he couldn't.

I searched around the place until I'd found a couple of towels, then went to the fridge freezer in the open kitchen, shook loose the contents of a cube tray, and made an impromptu icepack which I wrapped around his wounds, as I turned him gently on to his back.

He looked up at me, eyes flickering and rolling. Maybe he could see, maybe not. One bullet had exited, through his cheekbone, just below his left eye. Presumably the other two were still in there.

'Can you speak, Hamish?' I asked.

'U-huh,' he grunted.

'Did you make two bombs recently? We may not have much time and I need to know. The worst has happened already so you might as well tell me.'

The eyes rolled again, but finally locked on to me. 'Uh-huh,' he grunted.

'Did you plant one in Ricky Ross's car last Monday? Actually you don't have to answer that, for I know you did. When that failed, on Wednesday you followed Ricky from his hotel to a restaurant. You put another bomb in the men's toilet and when he went in you detonated it.'

He blinked, wildly; I don't think he was capable of any other movement by then. 'Nuh, nuh,' he grunted. His teeth were clenched, with the effort of his denial, or in frustration at being unable to shake his head.

'Then who did?'

'Man.' He whispered it. 'Man Ah made the bombs for.'

'He planted the second one, not you?'

'Right. He said he wanted to be sure it was done . . . right.'

'You were paid to make them.'

'M-hm. Ten grand. Said Ah wouldnae at first. Then he told me who they were for. Made it different.'

'Who was he?'

'Dinnae ken. Never telt me.'

'Can you describe him?'

'Nah. He was a Brit, ordinary lookin' but a hard man. He never smiled, no' ever.' His voice was growing even fainter. 'Just yer average hitman, that's a' .'

'Was it him who shot you?'

'Aye.'

The sound came out as a sigh, then his eyes closed and I thought he'd gone; until they opened again. Only as slits, but they did open. He whispered something but I couldn't make it out.

'What?' I leaned as close as I could.

'Ross is dead, then?' he gasped.

'Yes.'

'Good.' The word rattled at the back of his throat, and then he joined him.

Twenty-Five

I felt like legging it, getting my shapely arse away from the scene of the crime before Alex arrived, but there would have been no point for he'd have found me soon enough, and besides, it wouldn't have been fair to leave poor terrified Ramon there on his own, given that even the best of homicide cops look first at the guy who finds the body.

Instead I left the newly deceased Mr Orr to cool his heels, and everything else, and took myself outside on to the walkway, as a self-appointed door warden. I hadn't been there long when the superfluous paramedics arrived, a man and a woman.

'Where's the customer?' the guy asked, abruptly.

'I'm sorry,' I answered. 'You're too late. He's dead.'

'We'll be the judge of that,' he snapped and would have brushed me aside if I had been in the mood to let him.

I stepped across, blocking the doorway. 'No, you won't,' I said. 'I have an honours degree in nursing, which means I'm better qualified than you are to determine whether someone's dead or not. The man in there is. He's been shot, that makes it a crime scene, and it's been contaminated enough already.'

'So who's going to pay us?' he grumbled.

'I'm not,' I assured him. 'You can discuss that with the cops when they get here, which should be pretty soon. I suggest you wait in your vehicle until they arrive.'

The woman paramedic saw the sense in what I was saying. She took her colleague by the arm and eased him away.

They hadn't been gone long when two uniformed Mossos patrol officers arrived, a sergeant and a Mosso, their equivalent of a PC.

Sarge was a woman. 'You are Señora Primavera?' she asked. I nodded. 'The intendant said we would find you here. The ambulance crew said the man's dead.'

'Yes. Three bullets in the head usually does it, eventually.'

'But you called an ambulance.'

'Yes, he was just about alive when we found him. I made him as comfortable as I could, but he never had a hope.'

'Did he say anything before he died?'

'Nothing you could understand.' I believe that was technically true, very few Spanish people, even those who have some English, can cope with a Scottish accent, and even fewer when its owner is in extremis.

She reached into a pouch on her equipment belt, produced paper overshoes and gloves, put them on and went inside, leaving her colleague to guard the door, and me as well, I guess. She wasn't gone long.

'You put the towel and the ice round his head?' she asked.

'Yes. Just to make him as comfortable as I could.'

'A good thought. It must be terrible to die alone.'

'We all die alone, Sergeant,' someone said.

I looked to my right, towards the source of the voice, and saw Alex approaching, in uniform, with Ramon at his heel.

'Primavera,' he said, 'come with me. The rest of you wait here.'

He stepped into the apartment, then paused to put on sterile footwear and gloves.

'So I need those?' I asked.

'No. You've already left traces in here, from what I've been told. Your friend outside was pretty incoherent when he called me, but eventually I got the message.'

'Is Hector with you?'

'No. He has no reason to be here. Any more than you have,' he added, 'but I'm stuck with you.'

We walked through to the living area . . . a misnomer if ever there was one . . . where Orr was staring sightlessly at the ceiling.

'Jesus Christ, Primavera,' Alex sighed. 'What are you doing to me, dragging me from one homicide to another? Who is this guy?'

'He's the man who didn't blow up Ricky Ross's car on Monday. He's the man who made the bomb that was never in the toilet at La Bassa on Wednesday, when Ricky died in that miraculous gas explosion.'

'Are you sure?'

'I'm certain of it,' I said, firmly. 'He admitted it before he died.'

'Did he pay Alonso to vandalise the aircraft?'

'No, someone else did that.'

'Who?'

'Are you being dumb or just cautious?' I asked. 'The person who paid Alonso also paid Orr. Then he killed them both, for safety's sake.'

'Who is he? What's his name? You seem to know everything else.'

'Not that, though; I don't have a clue who he is.'

'And do you have any evidence that Alonso did the damage at the airport?'

'Not now he's dead,' I admitted, 'no.'

'Do you have any evidence that this man . . . what's his name? Hector told me, but I was so steamed up that I forget.'

'Orr, Hamish Orr.'

'That this man Orr made the bombs that Saviola says never existed?'

I sighed. 'No . . . but maybe you'll find evidence here, explosives traces, that sort of stuff.'

'Of course we will. Hector said that the man worked as a blaster in the quarry along the road. Almost certainly we'll find such traces here, and it will prove nothing.'

'Ricky put Orr in jail,' I volunteered, 'back in the nineties.'

That got his attention. 'Did he now?' he murmured. 'That's a strong link, I'll grant you. But I fear that Saviola will say it's not strong enough. He will say that if Orr made the bomb, singular, for he will deny the existence of the first one, then it's possible that he did it for Catalan nationalist terrorists. If I can't produce the man who paid him, this will go nowhere. The cover-up will still be in place and I will be in the shit for digging the whole thing up again.'

'What about Gaizka?' I protested. 'Doesn't his murder add to the evidence?'

'If I could place the same person at both crime scenes then maybe it would. But I'll bet you I can't do that. Without it . . . there's no similarity between the murders. Alonso was battered to death. Saviola will call that, to use an English phrase, a queer-bashing. Orr was shot; he'll put that down to his mythical terrorists.'

'So what are you going to do?'

'My job, my duty; that's what I'm going to do. I'm going to open two separate murder investigations, then go where the evidence takes me. If it links the two crimes, fine, but if doesn't, then they stay separate.'

'And what do we do, Hector and I?'

'Are you seriously asking me that?' he retorted. 'Hector believes that this killer found out by some means that you two were on his trail, and so he wiped his tracks clean. I've said this to Hector, and now I'm saying it to you. You should accept that and drop this thing, otherwise he might . . . that's if he exists . . . decide to wipe you away as well.'

That possibility had occurred to me, but to hear my friend come flat out with it, that was pretty grim. He wasn't finished ether.

'Primavera,' he continued, 'I'm really worried about you, and not just about the fact that you might be putting yourself in danger. Most people, given the afternoon you've had, would be in pieces, but you're not. You're handling it far too well for my liking. I'd rather see you shaking, like you were on Thursday night at La Bassa, than being as cool as this.'

I turned on him. 'Do you think I'm not shaking inside? Do you really believe I can look at the inside of a man's skull, then have another die in my arms without being affected? I wish I'd never heard of these people, Alex, but most of all I wish that Ricky Ross wasn't dead and being denied justice by your chickenshit fucking government. I could go on for an hour without repeating myself about the things I wish hadn't happened and that I wish I hadn't done, but that wouldn't make them all disappear. Instead I have to go into Figueres and buy another shirt, one that doesn't have Hamish Orr's blood on it, then go home and face my kids and their grandad and pretend that I've had just another day at the office, when all I really want to do is lock myself in the fucking toilet. Oh God,' I cried, 'I wish Liam was here!'

He put his gloved hands on my shoulders and held me. 'Okay,' he said softly. 'I'm sorry. I was out of order. You're too good an actress, that's all.'

'A scared actress. What you said earlier about this man, taking out all the witnesses. It's all very well Hector and me backing off, but we can't be certain that he hasn't already decided to come after us. No, Alex, we've got to find him before that happens.'

'Then how can I help? Our friend Ross asked me for a firearm, and I couldn't give him one. But for you . . .' He unbuttoned the flap of his holster, took out his service pistol, and offered it to me, butt first. 'Just for a day or two. Nobody will notice.'

I shook my head. 'Thanks, but no thanks; not with the kids in the house. Besides, I'm not without protection.'

'Christ, you haven't bought another Taser have you?' A few years ago, I kept a stun gun in the house; Alex found out about it. 'Don't tell me!' he pleaded as he reholstered his automatic. 'Don't tell me!'

Twenty-Six

I hadn't, but it did no harm to let him think so. My protection was the fact that I live in a fortress, in a village where every stranger who isn't a restaurant customer stands out like a Stevenson lighthouse. My alarm system lets me set it so that anyone who tries to force any door or window will set it off.

That didn't mean I wasn't nervous. Normally I'd have taken the family out on a Friday, but that night we stayed indoors, hiding behind Mac's outing to Port Aventura and the fact that I had an early start next morning.

Indeed I had, for I wanted to be at the airport to see Ricky off. I left before the family, and was on my way there when I had a text from Hector. I had called him the afternoon before, as soon as I'd got home, but I'd only just had time to give him the story before I was interrupted by the returning tribe.

The road was quiet so I sneaked a quick look. 'We need to talk. See you in office.'

As soon as I got there I checked with the air traffic people, and found that Weighley's plane was on the way, with an estimated arrival time of ten thirty. Then I called the under-taker to check one last time that all the paper was in place and that everything was ready.

It was. 'We will leave for the airport now, Senora Blackstone,' he announced in the solemn funeral director tone that seems to work in any language.

As it turned out, Ricky and Hector arrived simultaneously. 'Primavera,' the live one began, but I headed him off.

'Let me get this over with, please. In fact you might want to come with me; an extra pair of eyes will come in handy.'

'What will they be looking for?' he asked.

'Anyone who shouldn't be there; I've tried to keep this thing as private as possible.'

The Beechcraft arrived on schedule, and the yellow reception car led it from the exit from the taxiway across to the area where we stood. I'm sure the pilot could have figured it out for himself, since ours was the only hearse on the tarmac, but it's standard procedure.

I watched and waited as the plane came to a halt, and the engines were switched off. Their noise still hadn't faded completely when the door opened and the in-built steps began to deploy.

Part of me was expecting Jack Weighley to appear and come bouncing down the steps, but he didn't. Instead a woman emerged; she was around the forty mark, her face was pale and drawn and she was wearing black. I walked towards her as she came down the stairs, quietly cursing the fact that I was in my usual Saturday denims, and not in something more suitable for the occasion.

'Alison?' I ventured. She nodded. 'I'm Primavera.'

'Good to meet you,' she replied, then her mouth twisted as she realised that the circumstances couldn't be any worse. 'I decided that I had to come, to bring Ricky home myself.'

I moved on quickly, introducing the undertaker. They shook hands, and he extended condolences in a language she did not understand, but which were clear enough.

He looked at me. 'I must speak with the crew about the best way to place the deceased on board. Probably we'll have to use a catering hoist if the coffin is to travel in the cabin. The lady may think it is not dignified, so perhaps you would like to take her somewhere else.'

That was sensible, so I asked Alison if she would like to come with me. 'I've brought Ricky's effects, but there's some paper I have to give you. We can run through it in the office.' I glanced at Hector. 'My colleague will stay to supervise.'

'Okay,' she agreed. 'I've brought my passport.'

'You won't need it. We're airside.'

We had come out in a buggy. I commandeered it, offloaded the lime-green suitcase and we headed for the terminal building.

'Would you like a coffee?' I asked, when we were inside.

Alison winced. 'Actually, Primavera, would you think the worse of me if I asked for something stronger? This is a bit of an ordeal.'

'Of course,' I said. 'Let me see what I can find.'

I wasn't sure where to look, so I tried Jose Ramos's office. He hadn't bothered to show up for the occasion, another black mark that I would make sure went against his name. To match it, he had a bottle of Johnny Walker Black Label on his sideboard. I opened it, poured a good-sized shot and took it, and a bottle of still water, back to the other room.

Alison thanked me profusely. As she watered down her drink, fifty-fifty, I opened the folder I was carrying and laid the contents on my desk. 'There's Ricky's passport,' I began. 'Next, that's the consular authorisation for the entry of the body to the UK. Also, you'll find the Spanish death certificate. I'm not sure what the registrar in Edinburgh will want, but I've had a translation made, with a certification stamp. Next, the police report, also officially translated. The consulate got that for me. My contact said you will need to give it to the coroner, but he's an ignorant Englishman and doesn't know there's no such person in Scotland and that it should go to the procurator fiscal instead. So should this,' I added, handing over the final document. 'The autopsy report. I've included two copies of the English version, one for the fiscal and the other for you, if you can bear to read it.'

'Have you?'

I shook my head. 'I didn't need to, Alison. I saw him.'

'Are you telling me not to open the coffin?'

I met her gaze. 'I'm afraid so, yes.'

She took a deep breath, as she absorbed what I'd told her.

'Does all this mean,' she continued, 'there'll be a fatal accident inquiry?'

That possibility had not occurred to me, but I saw its attractions at once. The idea of Saviola being summoned to Edinburgh sheriff court was so appealing that I had trouble keeping a smile from my face. 'I don't know,' I replied, truthfully. 'If you insist on it, maybe there would have to be.'

'Are you suggesting that I should?'

The prospect of throwing a rock into that little spook bastard's millpond was too good to resist. 'I would, in your shoes. In the circumstances there should be absolute transparency.'

'Then I will.'

I gave her one more item, in a small envelope. 'Ricky's wedding ring,' I murmured. The undertaker had passed it to me. I'd taken a look inside, and it was gleaming; he'd polished it and it looked brand new. She took it out, and slipped it on to the third finger of her right hand. It was loose so she switched it to the second.

'What about his wallet?' she asked. 'I gave it to him for his last birthday . . . not that I knew it would be,' she added sadly.

'You wouldn't want it, Alison,' I told her.

'No,' she conceded with a frown, 'maybe not. But thanks for all the rest. Now I have something for you. You asked me if Ricky had been working on anything else I didn't know about. I had a good look around his office, but the only thing I could find that was out of the ordinary was this.'

She took a piece of paper from her handbag and gave it to me. I looked at it and saw that it was a short handwritten note, or memo. Two names, two numbers, that was all: 'Weighley 20, Raymac 80'.

'Who or what is Raymac?' I asked. 'A company? Shorthand for somebody's name?'

'I've no idea.'

It was a puzzle, but I knew one thing. 'The numbers equal one hundred,' I pointed out. 'Per cent? If so, of what?'

'Again, I couldn't say.' She paused. 'The only thing I do know that isn't general knowledge is that Jack's planning to float WeighleyAir on the London Stock Exchange. There's no timetable yet, but it's on the way. When it happens . . . Jack's made a few million already from the business in salary and bonuses, but when it goes public he will be very, very rich.'

'Indeed.' My mind was whirling again, and I couldn't stop it. 'Are you in touch with Ronnie Morrow?' I asked.

'Of course. He and Ricky were very close. I'll be seeing him later today, in fact. I'm having a reception, a sort of wake, at the Scotmid Funeral Home, when we get the coffin there.'

'Then do something for me, for both of us, indeed. Ask him to find out everything he can about this Raymac entity. If Ricky was concerned about it, then it must be worth knowing about.'

Twenty-Seven

I offered Alison another shot of Ramos's Johnny Black, but she declined. 'I know Jack all too well,' she said. 'For sure he will have press at the terminal when we touch down, and it wouldn't do if the grieving widow got home rat-arsed and fell down the steps. You see, Primavera?' she added, sadly. 'I'm a PR professional to the last.'

We talked a little about old times, about Oz, and when it was time for her to leave, I took her back to the plane, and went into the cabin with her. Ricky had been spared the indignity of a luggage hold return. His elegant oak coffin was secured to two seats, by thick straps.

I gave her a quick hug and a whispered, 'Good luck,' and left.

Back in the office, Hector was waiting, seated at his desk. 'So,' he said. 'Señor Ricky has gone home, his fellow country-man Orr has taken his place in the Figueres morgue, and Gaizka's in the cooler in Girona. Now, where the hell are we and what are we going to do?'

'Alex says we should do nothing,' I replied, 'other than we should cover ourselves and leave him to investigate the murders.'

'I think that is very good advice and is exactly what you should do. Obviously Alex and the Mossos have to investigate the crimes.'

'And obviously,' I added, 'they must do so on the basis of provable evidence, which ours isn't, thanks to Gaizka and Orr both being dead.'

'Exactly, and also against the background of previous circumstances as they are officially; neither man stood accused of any crime, especially not Orr, since the state itself says that he never made any bombs.'

'You've told me what I should do,' I observed, 'but what about you?'

'I have something else to consider. Alonso wasn't killed until after we had been to see him. Maybe that's a coincidence, but maybe not. On my first day here, I instituted a rule that all employees must maintain diaries on the company computer showing where they can be contacted when they are not on site. Not just how, but where; mobile phones can go out of range, and their batteries can run down.'

Gomez smiled. 'Since I introduced this measure, which will not be universally popular, clearly I must be exemplary in observing it myself. So, when we went to Flaça, I entered that on the log, including the address. You see? There has to be a possibility that our killer, or someone working for him, was able to access the company's computer system, to check up on me, the newly appointed ex-cop, the troubleshooter. As security officer, I can't let that go unresolved.'

'And as the person who's supposed to be Jack Weighley's personal troubleshooter, neither can I. Do you have anyone in mind?'

'No. The most obvious suspect might be Jose Ramos, who's been antagonistic to both of us since we arrived here. The guy has a chip on his shoulder that's so big he must have trouble standing up straight. But he's too obvious.'

'He's also Spanish,' I pointed out. 'The only thing Orr could tell me about the man who shot him was that he was a Brit.'

'No, but he could be providing information. Only in theory, though. Your moles, Primavera, your little velvet creatures, they don't draw attention to themselves. Ramos does; he's full of bluster.'

'He's not dead yet either. His secretary told me she spoke to him this morning. That could mean it's not him.'

'It's not,' Hector insisted. 'I promise you.'

'So where do you go next? What do you do?'

'If I was an IT man, I could look at the entire history of the network, and see who has accessed the availability logs, but I'm not, so I'd need to hire specialists. That would be noticed, and it might be useless, for it would have been easy for our man to cover his tracks.'

He looked up at me, and then lapsed into police-speak. 'We have very few lines of inquiry, Primavera, and only one that is really viable, given that we have no official status as investigators. You told me last night that the dying Orr denied planting the second bomb, the one that killed Ricky.'

'That's right.'

'Then we must go back to La Bassa, for if we're to find our killer, that's where it will be.'

'If you say so, let's do it.'

'Good. We take my car, yes?'

'No,' I replied, 'I'm not coming back here afterwards. We take both and we meet there.'

He grinned. 'Very well, but just remember, it isn't a race. I can't keep up with your flying machine.'

He needn't have worried, for I wasn't in any hurry. Part of me was still thinking of Alison on her unbearably sad homeward flight, and another part was still holding Hamish Orr's bloody head and watching the last faint light go from his eyes. The part that was in the present knew that while Juan Manuel and Tess lived on the premises, the restaurant would be closed and they might be anywhere. However, when I shop I'm always back for lunch, and I hoped they would be the same, so I chose the carretera again, kept my foot light on the throttle and made sure that I didn't get there until well after one.

Hector must have been thinking along the same lines. When I turned off the trunk road and headed for Ventallo, I saw his car emerging from the autopista exit. He fell in behind me and followed me for the last few kilometres.

The first thing I noticed as I approached the restaurant was a builder's skip, full of rubble. I parked before I reached it, then took a closer look. There was shattered porcelain mixed in with the stones and wood.

'They've been quick off their mark,' I told Gomez as he joined me. 'Saviola said they'd be open again within a couple of weeks. This is debris from the explosion, and it's only been two days. Have you ever known an insurance company to settle that fast? Somebody must be pulling strings to make it happen.'

The place was new territory to my colleague, so I led the way past the sign that read 'Closed for renovation' and along the path that opens into the garden. They really had been working. The folding tables and chairs were all stacked against the far wall. All of the wreckage had been cleared away, so the skip outside could not have been the first. Building materials, including copper pipes, cement bags and timber were stacked in a corner, ready for work to begin.

Both of the restaurant entrance doors had been reglazed, or even replaced, possibly. Whatever, I was pleased to see that the one on the right was open, and to hear voices from inside.

Juan Manuel must have heard us too, as our feet crunched on the gravel, for he appeared in the doorway as we approached.

'Primavera!' he exclaimed, looking a lot happier than the last time I'd seen him. 'Good to see you. You're looking a lot better than last time, but we were all pretty shaken up on Wednesday. Come on in. Tess and I are eating, so why don't you join us. It's not much, no cooking involved.' He turned to Hector, hand outstretched, and I did the introductions.

Inside, Tess was just as welcoming. She rushed off and

brought up two more chairs so we could join them at their round table, then went off again and came back with a tray bearing another loaf, and two of everything else, plates, glasses and cutlery.

'They're cracking on with the work,' I remarked, as I ripped off some bread and cut myself a slice of cold tortilla.

'They surely are,' Tess replied. 'That policeman said they would. I didn't believe him, but he was as good as his word. Mapfre, the insurance company, was in touch the next morning and people arrived that afternoon.' She paused as if she realised that her smile was not one hundred per cent appropriate. 'It is still tragic about the poor man, though.'

Juan Manuel nodded. 'Yeah, sure is.' He sighed. 'It might be callous to say so, but I'm pleased that we're insured for him too. Our policy even has accidental death cover in it, so if his family do come after us for compensation, we'll survive.'

I sensed that Hector was about to jump in, and forestalled him by the old-fashioned method, a kick under the table.

'You're convinced that it was an accident, then,' I said, quietly.

'Yes, we are. The cop said it was, the guy in plain clothes. You heard him, you were here. I've learned my lesson about keeping gas bottles in such a place.'

'How many did you have in the store?' I asked, casually.

'I thought I just had one, but I must have been wrong. There must have been two. How the other didn't blow I will never know. That would probably have taken down the restaurant wall.'

'But you might have been right.'

Husband and wife both stared at me. 'Why do you say that?' Tess asked.

'I dunno,' I said. 'It's just . . . it occurs to me there was something missing at the scene if that had happened. The gas bottle, it was metal. The explosion would have generated tremendous heat, but it wouldn't simply have melted, would it?'

'No,' Juan Manuel admitted. 'It wouldn't.'

'Right.' As I spoke, I remembered something from my nursing in Africa, the aftermath of a mortar strike in a war zone. 'There would have been shrapnel, lumps of hot jagged metal flying around everywhere, into the bar next door, everywhere. You and your customers, some of you would probably have been hit. Yet there wasn't any. There were no metal fragments at all that I could see. Stone, wood, glass, bits of toilet, but no metal debris.'

The restaurateur frowned, and leaned heavily on, the table. 'That's true. So what are you getting round to saying to us, Primavera?'

Hector couldn't stay quiet any longer. 'We're saying that there was a bomb, and that the target was the man who was killed. The man who made it, he's dead too. He was shot dead yesterday.'

Tess stared at him. 'So why did the police guy say differently? He assured us that it was a gas explosion, that it was our fault. Why would he do that if he knew it wasn't?'

'The answer to that is politics; a lot of people in power are very scared at the moment.'

'They don't like to think of bombs going off in Catalunya?' Juan Manuel ventured.

'Exactly!' Hector exclaimed. 'You understand.'

'But the bomber, the man who did it, you say he's dead.'

'We only said that he made the bomb. We believe it was detonated by someone else, when Ricky . . . the man who died . . . went into the toilet. And to do it, that person must have been watching.'

The couple stared at each other, then Tess turned to me. 'There was another man,' she said. 'He arrived not long after Señor Ross, but he never came inside. I served him at a table in the garden. He was the only person out there, for it had turned chilly in the evening. I asked him if he'd be warm enough, but he said he'd be fine. He ordered patatas bravas, croquettes and a bottle of Rosado. He . . .'

Hector interrupted. 'Where he was seated, could he be seen from inside?'

'No, he was in the one spot you can't see from the bar.' Suddenly she gasped. 'I remember now! I did see him!' She looked at her husband again. 'Juande, I never said. When Señor Ross went outside to the toilet, I watched him to make sure he went into the right one. Sometimes people who don't know, they get it wrong, and the men go into the ladies' place. I don't like that because they're . . . messy. If they're going to get it wrong I'll call out and stop them. Senor Ross, he got it right. But just as he closed the door, I saw the man outside moving, heading for the way out.' She paused, wide-eyed. 'I thought, "Hey, he's leaving without paying," and I was going

281

to tell Juande to go after him when . . . boom! . . . the place went up.'

'I guess he did leave without paying,' I said, 'but he was actually going into the lane to get out of the line of the blast that he was about to trigger, remotely.'

'Wow!' Juan Manuel whispered. 'We need to tell that cop, don't we, that he's got it wrong.'

'Hah!' Gomez grunted. 'He wouldn't like to be told that, so maybe not. Let's gather up everything you know, and then we'll see what to do. Tess, you saw him; can you describe him?'

'He was British,' she volunteered immediately. 'He wore dark clothes. He was tall but not a basketball player or anything like that. One metre eighty, one eighty-five maximum. Does that help?'

'Everything helps when you know nothing, señora.'

'But we can do more than that,' she exclaimed. 'What am I thinking about? Juande, do we still have the video from Wednesday?'

It was my turn for the goggle eyes. 'You have video?'

'Yes,' her husband confirmed. 'We have a camera; it's set on a pole beneath the garden floodlight, just at the entrance. I installed it so I can see what's going on outside when we're very busy and I'm tied up behind the bar. Wait here,' he instructed, rising.

Thanks, God, for our over-scrutinised society, I thought, remembering the image on Marc's computer.

He walked through to the other room and returned almost

immediately carrying a laptop, open and making booting-up noises. He set it on the table, and then went to work with the track pad, frowning as he concentrated, until finally his face set in a smile.

'That must be him,' he declared, 'for it can't be anyone else. That's about ten seconds before the explosion.'

He spun the computer around so that Hector and I could both see it. He had frozen the video on a single frame. The garden floodlight was good enough for us to see the subject clearly. He was as Tess had described him and he was holding a small box in his right hand.

Hector shook his head, then muttered, morosely, 'I don't know the son of a bitch.'

But I did. I'd had lunch with him four days before. We were looking at Jack Weighley's driver, Cedric Jenkins.

Twenty-Eight

I know I should have, but to this day I don't know for sure why I said nothing to Hector. Looking back, it may have been because my first thought was to tell Weighley before I shared with anyone else, because the mess was going to splatter all over him for sure. Idiot. I should have told him, then called Alex and screamed bloody murder at him to put a 'Stop on sight, shoot if resisted' bulletin out to all his troops.

Not that it would have done much good, given the way that things worked out.

'Still,' Hector continued, 'it gives me something to go on, a place to start.' He turned to Juan Manuel. 'Señor, is there some way you can give me a print of that image?'

'Sure.' He spun the laptop around, did some more fiddling around, then clicked. 'Give me another minute,' he said as he left.

He was back in less than that time with two copies of the frozen frame, one for me, one for Gomez.

My colleague folded his and slipped it into a jacket pocket. 'I'll show this around the office,' he said to me.

'Is that wise?' I asked. 'If this guy does have a contact inside WeighleyAir, won't they stay tight-lipped and tip him off that he's been rumbled?'

'Primavera, I know when people are holding something back from me.'

Oh no you don't, I thought.

'But maybe you're right,' he continued. 'Maybe it is time to bring Alex into this. After all, this relates to two open murder inquiries, apart from the one this photo reveals. The two of us could go down to Barcelona and tell the director general the whole story. I'll call him and ask him to meet me. You, you should go home, and leave everything else to us.'

That's what we each did, after sharing the rest of Juande and Tess's lunch.

'I'll let you know how my meeting with Alex develops,' Hector said, as we reached our cars. 'One thing you could do, perhaps. Can you send faxes?'

'Yes, I can. I have an all-in-one printer that will do it.'

'Then send the image to your friend in the consulate. They may be able to identify him, as they did with Orr.'

'If I can,' I replied. 'Consular staff guard their weekends jealously.'

All I was doing was stalling, of course. My initial impulse, that I had to tell Jack Weighley before anyone else, was growing weaker. I needed to be alone, to think about the situation, and I did, all the way back to St Martí.

Cedric Jenkins? Why him? Was he a loose cannon? Possibly, but was that likely? The man worked for Jack Weighley; he was his driver, and probably, apparently, a whole lot more. So . . .

Jack? Behind the vandalism of his own aircraft? Ordering the murder of his own security officer? No, surely not. What possible motive could he have?

I wrestled with the riddle all the way home. By the time I got there, I had made a decision. As soon as I got in, I was going to phone Alex myself, and tell him the whole story, as far as I knew it . . . but only after I had faxed Jenkins' image to Will Harris, as Hector had suggested, together with a covering note explaining who he was and what he was in the act of doing.

I took the low road into the village, and drove straight into the garage. I parked the Merc in its usual spot, jumped out and ran upstairs, up the three flights that lead through the cellar levels to the door that opens into the kitchen.

As I threw it open, I realised that I'd left Jenkins' image on the passenger seat of the car . . . and the thought went out of my head in that same instant, as I saw . . .

The man himself was facing me, dressed in black, his favourite colour, it seemed, or maybe he had chosen it to match the pistol he was holding, lengthened by a suppressor.

I was seized by a terror far greater than any I'd ever experienced, even in the moments when I knew that plane was going to crash and that almost certainly I was doing to die. It wasn't the pistol that scared me; I've had guns pointed at me before. No, it was the fact that Tom was close beside him, looking sideways at me with his arms stretched round behind the chair on which he was sitting, with his hands tied.

But he didn't look afraid, not in the slightest. He looked angry, and his eyes were darker than I'd ever seen them.

'Welcome home, Primavera,' my enemy greeted me. 'How are things at La Bassa?'

'How did you know . . .' I began.

'I put a tracker on your car two days ago. I've known where you were ever since, and where you were headed. I knew your kid was in, because I've been watching your house, so when it was clear you were coming back here, I rang your doorbell and the lad answered.'

As I listened to him speak I realised why Gaizka Alonso had confused his accent with mine. It was Welsh but not heavily so, just as my Scots tones aren't as strong as they were twenty years ago.

'You hacked into the WeighleyAir computer,' I said 'to check Gomez's movements. Didn't you?'

'I didn't have to hack into anything. I have a global WeighleyAir staff access pass. I went into the office at night and logged on to the system. Simple as that.'

From where I was standing that was all that was simple. 'What's this all about?' I demanded. 'Why did you murder Ricky?'

He smiled. It was the first time I'd seen him do that, and it wasn't nice.

'This isn't one of your ex's movies, lady,' he said. 'This isn't one of those scenes when you delay me by getting me to reveal the whole plot. You're going the same way as Ross, and so unfortunately is your son. I don't have time to indulge you. Now sit down, like the boy, and put your arms around the back of the chair.' He waved the gun at me. 'Go on. Do it.'

I thought about rushing him, but not for long; it wouldn't have ended well. Instead I did exactly as ordered. As he tied me, I turned to Tom. 'Why are you here?' I hissed. 'You should be at Port Aventura.'

'I decided not to go. I have a wing shun belt grading tomorrow, and I need to be ready for it. Plus I didn't know when you'd be back, and I didn't want to leave Charlie on his own.'

'Oh, Tom,' I moaned, feeling hot tears, in my eyes, and spilling down my cheeks. 'I'm sorry I've done this to you, by getting involved in stuff I didn't need to.' I looked up at Jenkins as he stepped back round in front of me. 'Let him go!' I wailed. 'Don't hurt my boy, please, I'm begging you.'

'Too late for that,' Jenkins murmured, although he wouldn't make eye contact with me.

'Don't cry, Mum,' Tom said, with a calmness that astonished me. 'It's okay. My wing shun grading's been brought forward a day that's all, and I've got a live target instead of a dummy. I'm going to kill this fucker.'

Our prospective assassin laughed. 'Brave to the last. Your dad would have been proud of you, I'm sure. But it's the other way round. I'm going to kill you, and this is how it's going to happen.' He looked down at me once more. 'There's enough wood in this kitchen to build a decent bonfire, and all sorts of flammable stuff besides. The table, the chairs, the rug they're sitting on, the parquet flooring, sugar, and half of the rest of the stuff in your larder, I'm sure. The ropes you're tied with, they'll go first. They're clever, made from paper, not hemp or nylon, so no trace will be left. So you see, this place is actually a tinder box. Question is, how do we start it?'

He lodged his pistol in his belt, then stepped across to the hob and turned the two biggest burners full on. 'It's widely believed that cooking oil isn't a flammable liquid. That's true, up to a point, but the vapour it gives out is different. It's just the same as diesel; in fact it can be used as a substitute.' He took the larger of my two woks down from its hook and put it on one of the rings, then half filled it with corn oil from a large can that I keep, carelessly, on the work surface. The rest of its contents he splashed all over the hob, letting it drip down on to the floor.

'It will take a little while for what's in the pan to start giving off vapour,' he continued. 'But in fact, the stuff itself can catch fire at a high enough temperature. For example, if I tip it on to a naked flame.'

He reached out, took hold of the handle of the wok, which had begin to sizzle, and started to tip it over, towards the second burner. As I closed my eyes, I felt Tom tense beside me. I prayed for a miracle . . .

Two of them happened at once.

The first came from the hall. There was the sound of a key

in the lock, then the door opened and a voice called out, Liam's wonderful, lovely voice, 'Honey, I'm home!'

As I opened my eyes, I beheld the second miracle. Jenkins had his gun in his hand, but too late, for Tom had sprung from his chair. A lightning fast, whirling left-footed kick caught the killer square on the wrist and sent the weapon flying across the room.

Jenkins cursed, then lunged at him, his face twisted with shock and pain, but he was met with a right-footed strike, so powerful that when it caught him, flush on the kneecap, the crack could have been heard in the square outside.

The guy was finished, even without the final roundhouse kick to the temple that cut him off in mid-scream, knocking him unconscious.

As he lay on his back, Tom stood over him and raised his foot, shaping the outside like a blade. I don't know what he was going to do, but I'm dead sure that Jenkins wouldn't have survived it, had it not been for Liam grabbing him from behind in a half-nelson hold and pulling him back. It took a bit of doing, but he managed.

'Easy, buddy,' he whispered. 'Your man is down. No need for more.'

I stared at them both. I couldn't speak and my heart rate must have been dangerously high, for I felt as if I was about to black out. I calmed down, though, when Tom came across and began to untie me.

'How did you . . .' I croaked.

'He might have been good at starting fires,' he murmured,

'but he was crap at tying knots. I've been free for a while. Even if Liam hadn't walked in, I'd have got him anyway.'

'Is he dead?'

'Would you care?' my large, dangerous, hero, nearly adult son asked me, looking so like his father that I was scared all over again.

'Yes, I would,' I told him, 'but only because I wouldn't want you to have killed him. Besides, he has a lot of questions to answer.'

'Before we wake him up so he can get started,' Liam drawled, looking delightfully bewildered as he stood there with Jenkins' silenced automatic in his hand, 'would someone mind telling me what the pluperfect fuck is going on here?'

Twenty-Nine

Cedric Jenkins was unconscious for five minutes; not nearly long enough for me to explain to Liam everything that had happened, but it let me give him an outline. Ricky's death shocked him; they had met on that film project in Edinburgh.

The killer rejoined us in stages, and by the time he was fully conscious, Tom had tied his hands tight, with his belt, not paper, and he was sitting in the chair that I had vacated. He came round in agony. His left knee was shattered and I wasn't in the mood to administer painkillers.

'What happened?' he winced, when his eyes could focus properly.

Liam jerked his thumb in Tom's direction. 'He did,' he replied. 'This boy left me behind in his martial art quite some time ago, and I was a pro. If he was a couple of years older he'd have broken your neck.'

He took the gun from behind his back and pressed the suppressor muzzle, hard, against the other man's forehead. 'If

I'd been here, though, I'd have broken every limb in your body before I got there. As it is . . .'

Taking the gun from Jenkins' skull, he moved round behind him and put it to the inside of his left elbow. When he pulled the trigger there was a soft, crumpling noise. Jenkins must have been too shocked to scream; his eyes bulged and his mouth opened wide, but he made no sound.

'. . . I can't not leave my mark on you. You were going to burn my woman and her boy alive. Say what you like about that arm; my story will be that it happened during the struggle and nobody will question me. In fact, knowing the cop who's coming here, you'll be lucky if he doesn't shoot you as well.'

Alex and his sidekick Maria arrived ten minutes later. By that time I had staunched the flow of blood from the Welshman's wound, packed it with gauze and bandaged it tight.

'Who are you, señor?' Alex asked him, in English. He wasn't my jovial friend, not then. I'd told him the whole story when I called, but he'd known most of it by that time, for Hector had dropped in on him at home.

'I'm saying nothing until I've had proper medical treatment,' Jenkins replied. His face was white with shock and pain.

'Your arm has been expertly treated. Your leg isn't bleeding, so it can wait. I repeat, who are you?'

'I'm sure the lady has told you.'

'She's told me who she thinks you are. I'd like to hear it from you, and then I'd like you to prove that you are who you say you are, since you don't appear to be carrying any personal papers.' He paused. 'Not that it really matters: I have your pistol and I know that I'm going to prove it was used to kill a man named Orr, yesterday in Vilamalla. You're going to prison, and whether it's as Cedric Jenkins or Mickey Mouse, that's of no concern to me.'

'Let me have a minute with him,' Liam growled, 'and he'll give you his grandmother's National Insurance number, and anything else you care to ask him.'

'I'm sure that he would,' Alex agreed, 'and that's why I'm going to take him out of here now. He's going to need hospital treatment; we'll take him to the Trueta in Girona and then to the cells there. Primavera, can we carry him downstairs and out through the garage? I don't want a big excitement in the square.'

Neither did I, so I agreed. In fact I didn't want any excitement, ever.

Two paramedics arrived shortly afterwards, via our discreet back entrance, and a doctor, who gave Jenkins a shot of diamorphine while his knee was immobilised in a padded splint. When it was done they carted him down the stairs. I found myself hoping they would drop him but they didn't, worse luck.

I was okay, right up until the moment when the garage door banged shut, noisily as always, and Tom shut the stairway door. Then I folded. If Liam hadn't caught me I'd have hit the floor but he did and I sobbed my heart out against his chest. I tried to speak, but I couldn't. All I could think of was Tom and all I could see in my mind's eye was the two of us helpless in the midst of an inferno.

'There now,' my lover whispered. 'It's okay.'

But it wasn't, and I knew that it never would be again: that vision will always be there in my darkest dreams.

When I regained my self-control and my dignity, I saw my son hard at work, mopping up the oil that Jenkins had intended to use to kill us.

'What are you doing?' I asked him, weakly.

He looked at me as if I was daft. 'They'll all be home soon,' he replied. 'If they see this mess they'll ask questions. You don't want them to know what happened here, do you?'

I cupped his face in my hands. 'Tom,' I said softly, kissing him on the forehead, 'it's all right to let your feelings out. Don't bottle them up, it's all right to be afraid.'

He took my wrists and put them by my sides. 'I'm not afraid, Mum. It's all over. Yes, it was scary at the time, but I was too angry to think about it. He was going to hurt you; when I said I was going to kill him I meant it, because my hands were free and I knew I could. If you want to know how I really feel now, I'm a little bit ashamed, because we're trained not to let anger overcome us.'

Liam ruffled his hair. 'Sometimes you need anger, kid. The trick lies in controlling it.'

Tom looked at him, raised an eyebrow, and smiled. 'Like you did when you shot the guy?'

I walked across to the fridge, took out three Coronita beers, uncapped them and handed them out. 'I know you don't drink,' I told my home again man, 'and I know you shouldn't,' I told my son, 'but I think we all deserve these.'

Tom killed half of his in a single swallow, with an expertise that made me wonder, just as the noise of the garage door reopening came from downstairs. He poured the rest down the sink. 'If Janet sees me with this . . .'

Liam handed me his, untouched. 'Me too,' he said. 'Anyway, after what's just happened, I wouldn't stop at one.'

A few seconds later, the stairway door crashed open, and an animated wee Jonathan burst into the kitchen. 'Tom,' he yelled, 'you should have come, it was great, far better than staying at home.'

Thirty

They didn't twig that anything out of the ordinary had happened. Mac and Janet . . . and wee Jonathan, when he noticed his presence . . . were delighted to see Liam, and claimed all his attention. That gave me the opportunity to slip off unnoticed, up to my room, where I stripped off and stood under the shower for a good ten minutes, as if I was trying to wash away my fear.

As I dried myself off I realised that I was starving. Also, I knew that I needed something to keep me occupied, and hauling Liam off to bed was not a possibility at that time. 'Let's go and eat,' I declared, as soon as I was back downstairs.

I always try to share our custom around, and the kids like the novelty of the kebabs in Can Coll, so that's where we went. All that wee Jonathan wanted to do was talk about Port Aventura, and even Janet was showing that she still had something of the kid left in her. I let them dominate the dinner table discussion and that suited me very well, because within me, the doorway to hysteria was still ajar, and I wasn't capable of behaving normally.

I think that Mac realised that but put the wrong inter-pretation on it, assuming that I wanted Liam all to myself. Whatever his thinking I was pleased when he said that if he was knackered, Janet and her brother had to be as well, and that given Tom's exam in the morning, they'd best all bugger off home.

'So,' I murmured, once we were alone and I had ordered a very large Bailey's, 'what did bring you back?'

'You did. After we sent each other those texts the other day. I found myself wondering how I could have been such an arse, and what the hell I was doing to us, sulking in fucking Venezuela.'

'Is that what you were doing, sulking?' I asked, provocatively.

'More or less, yes. I've done all the photography and research I need to write this damn book. I didn't need to stay away any longer, and once the two of us had cleared the air, I found that I couldn't. So I packed, went straight to the airport and caught the first flight to Barcelona, via Madrid. I was stupid, love, to think that us being married is important. I've never been happier and I'll never be happier than when I am here with you.'

'And three kids?' I necked some of the Bailey's. 'And a loyal if slightly idiotic dog?'

'For sure.'

'Then ask me to marry you again.'

'You mean it?'

I nodded.

'Will you?'

'If you still want to in a few months, say next Valentine's Day, when we're all less emotional . . . and when you've finally finished your book. If you still want to then, I will.'

He beamed at me, and I'll swear his eyes were misty behind his round blue specs. I'd never seen him smile like that before.

Then he winked. 'And how about another kid?'

'At my age,' I told him, 'that'll be a miracle, but if you're not joking and that's what you want, I'll try as hard as I can . . . and as often.' I smiled, for the first time in hours. 'Hell, I'll do that even if you are joking.'

I was about to add, 'Starting as soon we've paid the bill,' when I became aware of someone heading in our direction. It was Alex, out of uniform and looking stressed.

'Beer please,' I said to our waiter, even before he'd reached our table.

'How are you?' he asked, as he eased himself into a chair beside me.

I reached across the table and squeezed Liam's arm. 'A lot better now he's back,' I told him.

Alex nodded. 'I'm glad to hear it. She's been impossible since you've been away, Liam.'

'I haven't!'

'No?' he challenged. 'Just ask around.'

'Well, I'm fine now. Okay?'

His canya arrived and he paused to savour it. 'By God I needed that.' He looked at my partner again. 'I've spent two

299

days following a trail of dead bodies and mayhem, leading to her.'

'The last one was alive, though.'

'What's he saying?

'Virtually nothing: only one thing. He's still in the Trueta, under guard. The surgeon who saw him says that his knee will need two operations, the first to pin his broken patella, the second to repair ruptured tendons.' He frowned. 'Did Tom really do all that damage?'

'Yup.'

'Holy Mother of God! The surgeon asked if the man had been hit by a car.' He paused. 'Then there's his elbow; that's more surgery, and he'll be lucky if he can ever straighten that arm again. The doc was in no doubt about what caused that; a gunshot, he said, right through the joint.'

'Indeed?' Liam murmured. 'And what does Jenkins say?'

'Nothing. To be frank I don't care what he says. His gun went straight to our lab and it ties him beyond doubt to the murder in Vilamalla. We identified his car very quickly through the unlock button on the key, and we have a sighting of it in the vicinity, by the wife of the man Ramon, the guy who showed you where Orr lived. He will be charged with murder and will be found guilty, whether he chooses to talk to us or not. Maybe we'll be able to convict him for the Alonso murder also, but that's more doubtful. So far we have no weapon for that one, no forensic evidence and no way of placing him at the scene. It doesn't really matter, though. Killing Orr; that will be enough. He'll get at least thirty years for that.'

'But what about Ricky?' I protested. 'What about his murder?'

'I'm sorry, Primavera,' Alex said. 'That's not going to happen. The cover-up is in place, and even though we know there was no reason for it, that there were no free Catalunya terrorists, it would be too embarrassing for Madrid to admit that it happened, and also for the Catalan Justice Minister to admit that he went along with it.'

'Bollocks to that!' I protested. 'I'm not having it.'

'You have no choice, and neither do I. Make no mistake, I don't like it either; I never liked it. Besides—'

I cut him off in mid-sentence. 'What if I went to the press? Not here, but in Edinburgh.'

'Then you would build a big hill of grief for yourself. You live here, remember, not in Edinburgh. You piss off our present national government, and they will get even, for they are not nice people. You must know that; you've met Saviola, and he's a minor nuisance compared to some of them. Your tax affairs would be audited, and those of your brother-in-law's wine company. You'd be hassled by the Guardia Civil every time they saw your car on the road. Your life here would cease to be pleasant. And I could do very little to help, for I'd be in the same boat myself.'

I was convinced, but he continued. 'This too: the evidence isn't strong enough. What is there? An image of Jenkins heading for the restaurant exit with a little box in his hands, that's all. The camera doesn't cover the toilets, so even if it is accepted that there was a bomb, it cannot be proved that he planted it. Be content with what he has coming to him already.'

He finished his beer and waved for another. 'Of course,' he continued, 'there is also the question of his attack on you and Tom. On the basis of your statements I could still charge him with attempted murder; strictly speaking, I should. The case would take at least a year to come to trial. When it did, you and Tom would be reliving the experience all over again, under cross-examination from his lawyer. At that point the court would take a real interest in how he got shot.'

I was doubly convinced. 'No,' I said, 'let's not go there.'

'Good, for it would only get in the way of the next stage of the investigation, and our pursuit of our next target.'

I stared at him, my brain fuzzy from the after-effects of stress, shock and fear, and from the growing effects of at least a bottle of Pesquera and a canya-sized goblet of Bailey's. 'Who's that?' I mumbled.

'Who else? Your new client, the man you told me Jenkins works for: Señor Jack Weighley.'

I shook my head, to clear it as best I could. Assuming that the human brain is capable of processing only so much at a time, mine must have been fully occupied with the deaths of Alonso and Orr, my own mortal peril, Tom's heroism, and Liam's perfectly timed return. I guess so, because I had completely blanked out the potential consequences of Jack Weighley's driver doubling up as a ruthless psychopathic multiple murderer.

'His master's fucking voice,' I whispered, but most of me was unable to believe it. 'Surely not.'

'That one thing I mentioned earlier,' Alex said. 'The one thing that Jenkins is saying. When I asked him whether he was carrying out Mr Weighley's instruction, he replied, "Absolutely not." He even laughed as he said it, in spite of his pain, as if it was the silliest thing he could imagine.'

'Do you believe him?' Liam asked.

'My mind is open, and will be until I have spoken to Weighley face to face. My problem is, with Jenkins denying that he is involved, I have no power to order him to come here, and none to ask that he should be brought before me.'

'Hah!' I laughed. 'No worries about that.' I took my mobile from my bag and selected a number from my directory.

Weighley picked up on the third ring. 'Yes, Primavera,' he snapped, sounding simply grumpy, not out of breath as he had before.

'Did the photocall go all right, Jack? Was Alison up to it?'

'Yes. Yes she was. The media were interested and respectful too. Is that why you called, to ask me that? If so . . .'

'No, that was just a warm-up. I'm calling to tell you that the shit has hit the fan here in the smelliest way imaginable, and that if you want to have an airline left, you will fuel up the Beechcraft and get yourself out here first thing tomorrow morning, Sunday or not. I will be there, and I won't be alone.'

'Primavera, what . . .'

'No questions; I am deadly serious, so just do it.'

Thirty-One

'Did you sleep all right?' I asked Tom, as he fed four slices into the toaster.

'Of course, Mum. I have to be fresh for my grading today.' He handed me a mug of tea. 'I know why you're asking, but I'm all right. Look forward to the good, not back at the bad; that's what Dad said when I talked to him in my head last night.'

He was never as sensible when he was alive, I thought.

Weighley had tried to call me back a couple of times after my ultimatum, but I had rejected both attempts, and switched my phone off after the second. I didn't want to speak to him, and besides, I had priorities.

The first of these was to show Liam how much I'd missed him. Once he'd shown me in return, we had time to talk and I gave him a detailed account of everything that had happened in his absence, from my conclusive investigation of Oz's death, through our little ceremony on the beach, and right up to that moment. When I was done, there was nothing he didn't know, and I was asleep.

When I woke, he was out on the terrace, looking at the sun. I slipped on a robe and joined him. 'You know,' he said, as he slipped his arm around my waist, 'I saw some fantastic places when I was away, but when it comes to sheer niceness and peace, nothing came close to this.'

'I'll accept niceness,' I laughed, 'but there hasn't been much peace around here since last Monday.'

When I switched on my phone, after we were showered and dressed, there was a text from Weighley. *Expect me Girona 12:30 CET*, I read. *This had better be good.*

I forwarded it to Alex's number. He called me back almost immediately, on the landline. 'Thanks,' he said. 'I thought you'd be interested to know, we found Jenkins' phone in his car. I instructed that it be left on, but there have been no calls or texts from Weighley since you spoke to him, and none for the last five days. We also found his wallet and a card key for a hotel in Estartit. I have people checking his room now.'

'Tell them to look out for Ricky Ross's laptop. It was missing from his hotel suite when I cleared it on Thursday. I thought that one of Saviola's people might have taken it, but now I'm not so sure.'

'Jesus, there's so much about this investigation that I don't know.'

'That's not your fault. Is there any way Jack can know that Jenkins has been arrested?' I asked.

'None that I can think of: we haven't made any announcement about him being in custody. His identity is being kept secret in the hospital, especially from the porters. They're frequent media sources.'

I had to laugh. 'That's an international truth. Alex, I'll be at the airport by midday, just in case Weighley's plane has a strong tail wind.'

'You don't have to . . .'

'Yes I do. He has no reason to talk to you, but he won't ignore me. I should meet him off the plane, and escort him into the office. You'll be a nice surprise for him.'

'What if he insists on leaving and gets back on his plane? I can't detain him.'

'Liam will be with us. He'll persuade him to stay, if necessary.'

The idea must have amused Alex. 'I'll have to leave the room if that happens,' he chuckled.

I had been worried that Grandpa Mac might have been reluctant to be stuck with the kids for another day, but I couldn't have been more wrong. 'Primavera,' he declared, holding a plate laden with toast, cheese and ham, that Tom had just given him, 'that's why I'm here. This break is doing me the world of good. Will you be back by tonight, though?'

'Absolutely.'

'That's good.' He hesitated, then added, quietly so that the kids couldn't hear, 'Thing is, I've got an engagement. I'm having dinner with Anais, at her hotel.'

'That's great, Mac,' I said. 'Now stop looking so bloody shifty about it.'

'Ach, lass, I can't help it. I feel as if I'm cheating on Mary.'

I'm not much of a giggler but I did then. 'Hey, I doubt if you're going to get to that stage after just one dinner, but suppose you do, lose the guilt. Mary left the building some time ago, and she isn't coming back.'

'I know, I keep telling myself that, but it's difficult. Mind you,' he added, 'Anais is a very attractive woman.'

'And you're not exactly Quasimodo either, so tonight, sparkle and see what happens.'

'What was all that about with Mac?' Liam asked later, as we drove down the motorway heading for the airport. He was behind the wheel; my fun times in the Merc were going to be restricted, but it was worth it to see him there, relaxed and happy.

I hadn't explained the Anstruther situation, so I brought him up to date. 'Oh dear,' he murmured, when I was finished, 'the poor old guy; poor lady too. But Anais is just the woman to bring him out of himself. And you're just the person to be giving him advice.'

'Me? Why?'

'Think about it; you lived through years of refusing to admit to yourself that Oz was dead.'

He had a point . . . and also, the good sense not to labour it.

Weighley did indeed have that tail wind, but by the time his plane was on approach, Alex was there, in civvies, in Jose Ramos's otherwise empty office, with Hector Gomez and with Liam, who had been issued with a staff pass. Obviously Alex didn't need one; his gets him anywhere he likes.

I was waiting in the empty baggage hall as Jack emerged from passport control. 'Where's the fucking fire?' he asked.

'In the circumstances, Jack,' I retorted, 'that's not funny.'

'What are you talking about? Primavera, I seriously do not like my chain being pulled.'

'Let's go to the office and I'll explain.' I studied him as we walked. He wasn't nervous, or shifty, or guilty: none of the above.

When I opened the door of the office and he saw the others, he turned on me, furiously. 'Who the hell are these guys? What game are you playing, you fucking twat?'

All three of my escorts started out of their seats, but I waved them back down. 'The big one with the blue-tinted glasses is my partner, Liam Matthews,' I told my client. 'He's a retired wrestler, and he's likely to rip your sack off if you ever talk to me like that again. Alongside him is your new security manager, Señor Gomez. The other's my friend Alex Guinart.'

Weighley took a deep breath. 'Okay. I apologise for my intemperate language. Now what's going on, and what's the threat to my airline that you mentioned last night?'

'When we met on Tuesday,' I began, 'you had your driver with you, Cedric Jenkins.'

'Yes.'

'But the general aviation flight records show that you went back alone.'

'That's right. Cedric was due a few days' holiday, and since we were in Spain, he asked if he could spend them here.' For the first time, I sensed a wariness about him.

'Do you know what he did on his holidays?'

'No,' he replied, very quickly, then added, 'why would I? It was his own free time, nothing to do with me.'

'Then let me tell you what he got up to. He murdered a former employee of yours, Gaizka Alonso. You may remember him. He was accused of damaging two of your aircraft on the ground here in Girona.' I smiled. 'Actually, he wasn't just accused, he did it, but the police couldn't prove it. What they didn't know was that he was paid to do it, by Cedric Jenkins. That's right, your driver bribed a disaffected former employee of WeighleyAir to attack your own planes.'

'How do you know that?' Weighley demanded. 'How can you possibly prove it?'

'We know it because Gaizka told Hector and me. We can't prove it because Jenkins found out we'd been to see him, and took him out of the picture.'

'So what you're saying is that none of this stuff is substantiated.'

'That's what it amounts to,' I conceded, 'as far as Alonso's concerned. But it doesn't stop there. We know also that whatever the official record may say, Ricky Ross's car didn't catch fire spontaneously on Monday. A man called Hamish Orr tried to kill him. When he failed, he made another bomb and gave it to Jenkins, who had paid for the first one. He followed Ricky on Wednesday to the restaurant where he died, planted it in the toilet and detonated it remotely when he saw him go in. We do have an image and a video of him getting ready to do it, but it's not conclusive.'

'But you assured me, and poor Alison,' he added, 'that it was an accident.'

'No. I told you that was the official verdict.'

Jack shook his off-blond mullet. 'Whatever, if you can't prove otherwise, you're not doing too well so far, Primavera, are you?'

'No, but it doesn't matter, because the police can prove, for sure, that Jenkins killed his bomber, Orr.' I paused and looked my 'boss' in the eye. 'And do you know what he did after that? He tried to kill me, and my son.

'He was going to burn us alive in our own kitchen, Jack, was your friend Cedric. He came damn close, but not close enough, and was pretty badly hurt in the process. Now he's in hospital in Girona, being patched up so he can be transferred to prison, where he'll stay for a long time. All that's going to look very bad for WeighleyAir when it hits the Scottish press.'

Weighley turned to face me, to look me in the eye; that was a mistake on his part, for it let me see that he was afraid. 'Primavera,' he exclaimed, 'I swear to you that I knew nothing of this.'

'I'm sure you didn't, Jack,' I agreed. 'You're far too clever to put yourself in a position of knowledge. Deniability rules, isn't that right? But you know what? Suppose you are absolutely lily-white in this, I am still quitting as your consultant, because I don't like the company you keep.'

'Me also,' Hector said, throwing his staff pass on the table. 'I do not like you, señor, and I do not trust you.'

'Well, fuck you, then,' my ex-client grunted. He threw a sneer in Alex's direction. 'How about you? Are you going to quit too?'

He laughed. 'Most certainly not; I like my job. Primavera didn't explain what that is. I am the ranking detective police officer in this area, and your driver, Jenkins, he is in my custody.'

'What's he saying?' Weighley snapped. Too quickly? I wasn't sure.

'Nothing,' Alex replied, casually, 'but I have barely begun to question him yet. When I do, he will have the right to maintain his present silence, but it won't impress me. I've been around long enough to know how these things work. Men like him, ruthless, efficient professional killers, they're usually good at what they do, but they are rarely self-starters. Always, they follow orders.'

Jack shrugged, with an expression that was meant to convey indignation. 'I'll take your word for that. As far as your allegations are concerned, his so-called orders weren't mine. All I can say about Cedric is that he always takes me where I tell him. He's my fucking chauffeur, that's all.'

'No, señor,' Alex countered. 'I know what he is, and very soon, when your Metropolitan Police come back to me with his complete life history, I will know where he came from. He is only your driver, you say? No, I don't think so, not for a minute.'

'Okay, okay!' Jack shouted. 'He's my bodyguard as well. What's wrong with that? I'm a very important man, and I need personal protection. He's ex-army. He served in Iraq and in Afghanistan.'

'I see.'

'You see what? Tell me, detective. What do you see? That he's been trying to sabotage my airline? Why in God's name would he ever do that?'

'That's not what he's saying, man,' Hector Gomez exclaimed. 'It's only a very small piece of the story. He's . . .' He stopped. 'I'm sorry, Alex. For a moment there I thought I was still in the job.'

'That's all right,' his one-time subordinate said. As he spoke, his mobile sounded; he took it out and looked at the screen. 'I have to take this; you carry on. You were my boss once, and we are of the same mind, as we usually were before.'

'If you wish.' As Alex put his phone to his ear, Hector turned back to face Weighley. 'We do not believe this has anything to do with your airline. No, as we see it, it is all about Señor Ross. Someone wanted him dead, wanted that very badly. But it had to be done . . . discreetly. Señor Ross was a well-known man in Scotland, a former policeman, a man of influence. If he had been murdered in his home city, there would have been a lot of noise, and the investigations would have been very thorough.

'So,' he continued, 'a plan was devised. Incidents took place in Girona, at the airport. They were minor, really, but a great fuss was made, and Señor Ross was sent over here, to deal with it and put everything right. When he arrived it was an important occasion and his mission received publicity in our Catalan media. Some of that, I am sure, was stimulated by your company.' He paused. 'You follow?'

'Go on,' Jack murmured.

He did. 'The incidents, the supposed vandalism, the independence slogans, they were contrived, to make it seem as if WeighleyAir was in some way being targeted by extremists. It was the beginning of a smokescreen to hide the truth.

'Señor Ross was meant to die on Monday, but he escaped, by pure luck. It was only a short reprieve though, for Señor Jenkins made certain two days later. And that smokescreen worked even better than anyone had hoped. The people in power fell for the nationalist deception, and they took measures to conceal it. A bomb explosion became a gas explosion, and Señor Ross's murder became an accident, both here and in his own country. That was the hope all along; that it should pass virtually unnoticed, or at least without questions being asked in Scotland.' He glanced at his one-time protégé. 'Isn't that correct?'

Alex's phone call had ended. He nodded, but he was frowning, and I detected a subtle change in his manner, and his bearing. 'It's what I believe,' he declared, 'given the chain of events.'

Weighley was still standing. He seemed to draw himself up to his full, modest height as he faced up to the cop and said, 'Let me get this straight. You're accusing me of conspiring to have Ricky Ross murdered. Is that it?'

'No, sir,' he replied, 'but only because I do not believe I have enough to ask our prosecutor to lay such a charge.

Jenkins was your man, your ex-soldier bodyguard. I know what he did, because Señor Orr, the bomb-maker, told Primavera the whole story before he died, but I do not have his signed statement of that, or the two other pieces of evidence that I need. I don't know why you would order Mr Ross's death, and I do not have Jenkins' admission that he was acting on your orders.'

'It's early days yet, though,' I said to him in Catalan. 'Once Jenkins has time to think about it, he might be willing to do a deal for a lesser sentence.'

'No, Primavera, he will do no deal.' Then he switched to English. 'I have some very bad news for you, Señor Weighley. Your employee, Señor Jenkins, is dead. He decided to take the easy way out.'

'What?' I thought I was dreaming. 'You're joking,' I gasped. 'He'd a broken leg, a smashed left elbow, and he was under close police guard in hospital. How the hell could he have managed to kill himself?'

'He was being taken to the operating room,' Alex said. 'In the preparation area they paused his trolley beside a tray of instruments. He was left alone for a few seconds, long enough for him to grab a . . . an operating knife, whatever you call it in English . . . and cut his neck.'

'And they couldn't save him, not even in the operating theatre?'

'No.' He touched both sides of his own neck, where the carotid arteries lie. 'He cut each of the main veins; he was very determined.'

I looked at Weighley; it seemed to me that he was struggling to keep a smile from his face, but he managed.

'So,' he said, 'this is where we're at. You think that I ordered an attack on my own airline and the murder of my own security consultant, but you don't have any evidence, or any witnesses. Fine. Now this is my position: if I ever hear a whiff of any of this defamation having left this room, I will ruin every last one of you, including you, Mr Matthews, just for having been here.'

He looked at Hector, then at me. 'Mr Gomez, Mrs Blackstone, your resignations are accepted, without compensation. Now, all of you, get the fuck off these premises or I will call security and have you removed.'

Thirty-Two

'It doesn't get any better, Primavera.' Alex sounded mournful.

'But can it get worse?' I countered.

It was Monday morning, the kids were at school, and Mac had gone with Liam to cast his eye over some boats that were for sale in L'Escala marina. My partner had arrived home with a sudden desire to take to the sea, and Mac, who knows something about the subject having been commodore of his local sailing club in his middle age, was with him at my request, to stop him from buying something completely impractical. Almost every day I see people from my terrace, cruising around in Sunseekers and Oceanmasters and the like, with no clear idea of where they're going, and even less of what they're doing, which is in fact the equivalent of chucking fifty-euro notes into the Mediterranean.

While they were doing those things, I was in the Mossos office in Girona, making a formal statement of events in Orr's apartment, including his dying deposition. With Jenkins' death the case was closed, but the law required that Alex submit a report to the prosecutor nonetheless.

'In terms of finding out why it all happened, yes, it can,' he said, dolorously. 'My people recovered Ross's computer from Jenkins' hotel in Estartit. There was nothing on it that related to his business; only music, photographs, books, his personal emails. Any files and spreadsheets were purely domestic.'

'I suppose Jenkins was bound to have erased the business stuff,' I sighed, gloomily.

'No, there was no evidence that he did. Computer experts will usually find traces of deleted files, and believe me, our people are expert, but they could find nothing.'

'Was there any reference to something called Raymac?'

'No there wasn't, not unless it's a song title, or a book. I can have them check again, but that name hasn't been reported to me. Why, what does it mean?'

'Probably nothing. It was a name on a note that Alison Ross found in Ricky's office.'

'Then I will have my guys look again,' Alex promised, 'but don't hold out any hopes.'

'We're sunk, aren't we?'

'Yes and no; we know who killed Señor Ross, Alonso, and Orr, and he is now before the ultimate judge, the one we all face.'

'Craig Revel Horwood?' I murmured. He didn't get the joke; not surprising, since they don't show *Strictly Come Dancing* on Catalan telly.

'Where we've failed,' he continued, 'is in, one, establishing any chain of command, any link in the whole business between Jenkins and that awful little man Weighley, and two, finding out why Weighley found it necessary to have Ricky killed. Those are the pieces of evidence that I need, but do not have.'

'That's assuming he did order it.'

He stared at me. 'You doubt it?'

'Yes, I do,' I admitted, 'just a little bit. It's because of the "Why" part. I can't get my head round that. Weighley's a calculating, manipulating little bastard, the kind who does everything for a reason.'

'That reason being business, and the good of his airline: Ross must have been a threat to it.'

'But was he such a big threat that it got him killed? Surely not. WeighleyAir is successful; even through the recession its profits have climbed steadily. It's done its business shrewdly, and openly. Jack even bought a failed Spanish rival out of liquidation to get his hands on its routes, and became a hero in this country in the process, even though he used that status to bludgeon ridiculously low landing charges from airport operators. All over Europe he ran a good PR operation; everything WeighleyAir did, he did openly and put a positive spin on it. The man had no secrets, so what could Ricky have found out that got him killed?'

'I don't know,' Alex conceded, 'but he found out something.'

'Okay, but this too: I don't doubt that Weighley's clever enough to have put together the plan that got Ricky out here, but does the man have the balls actually to give the order for someone's murder? I've met a couple of killers in my time, including a long time ago one of your fellow cops. To be what they were, that took courage. The way I see our Jack, he's a coward at heart.'

'Then who did, Primavera?' he challenged me. 'Who gave Jenkins his mission?'

'I do not have a single, tiny clue,' I sighed. 'How about you?'

'Not really, but in situations like this, us cops, we go back to basics, we fall back on our preconceptions, and one of those is this. Most homicides happen within the family. What do you know of Mrs Ross?'

'Enough to laugh that notion right out of the water; I met her on Saturday, remember, and I knew of her long before that. She and I had one thing in common, that being Oz Blackstone's prodigious trouser snake. Oz treated her like dirt, and she took it. He used to call her "Tomorrow", because he said she never came . . . ignoring the fact that it was his fault.

'Alison's a mouse, and anyway, she loved Ricky, I'm sure of that. Not only that, when I asked her if she knew of anything else that he was working on, she helped me. It was her who mentioned Raymac to me.'

'Could she have done that to put you off her trail?'

'No!' I laughed, yet as I did, in spite of my own instincts, I was thinking, *could she?*

I dismissed the idea as quickly as Alex had put it there, changing the subject to put an end to it. 'Have you established how Jenkins broke into the Nieves Mar to steal the laptop?'

He smiled. 'He didn't,' he replied.

'Then . . .'

'He was a cool one, Señor Jenkins. He arrived at the hotel very late on Wednesday evening, just after ten, and registered as a guest. When he had his key he asked, casually, about a friend of his, Señor Ross, and whether they could tell him what room he was in, so that he could surprise him.

'A little later the manager saw him in the bar. He asked him if he'd found him, and was told no, that he hadn't answered. A couple of hours later, Jenkins called reception. He said that he'd locked himself out of the safe in his room, and asked, could they give him a release code. Of course, the night porter did just that.'

I whistled. 'Clever bastard, but how did he get into Ricky's suite?'

'Too easily, so don't tell anyone else. We found a device in his room that can open a door with a card entry system, just like a burglar can open a lock with picks.'

'Bloody hell! Alex, this man Jenkins wasn't a run-of-the-mill driver cum bodyguard. You remember the guy Susie and Oz employed, Conrad Hunt?'

He nodded. 'Yes. I met him once, when he brought Tom home from a visit to his sister and brother in Monaco.'

'Right. Conrad was pretty specialist, a top-end security man, but I doubt if he could have done stuff like that.'

'He probably could,' Alex snorted, 'but he wouldn't be telling anyone.'

'Be that as it may, why the hell would Jack Weighley employ someone with that sort of capability?'

'I can't imagine,' he replied, 'but to be honest I've had quite enough of that man. If you want to know, you'll have to ask him yourself.'

'It may come to that,' I said.

Our business was done, so I headed home, or rather I started out for home, only to be redirected by a call from Liam. 'Can you come to the marina?' he asked. 'There's something I'd like you to look at.' He sounded excited, like a kid in a sweet shop.

He and Mac were waiting for me beside the restaurant, where he'd told me to park. They weren't alone; a salesperson was there too, eyeing me up as I climbed out of the Jeep, with the nervous air of a bloke who suspected that a chunk of commission depended on my yeah or nay.

'Show me,' I said, poker-faced. I sneaked a look at Mac; he was grinning, but he'd been doing a lot of that since his dinner date, from which he'd returned just after midnight, volunteering only that he'd had a 'very nice time'.

The boat salesman led the way; we had to walk quite a distance, round past the apartments that face the sea, then past the block with the shops and bar underneath. I know the marina quite well, Tom having been to sailing school there when he was younger, so I twigged fairly early on that we were heading for the bigger moorings. *No wonder the sales guy's nervous*, I thought.

Finally we stopped. 'What do you think?' Liam ventured,

and I realised that he was as edgy as the agent.

I stared at the vessel in question. Today I wish that someone had taken a photograph, for my expression must have been worth capturing.

'Liam,' I said. 'You told me you were coming here to look at boats. This isn't a boat: this is a fucking yacht!'

It was a Menorquin, all sixty-odd feet of it, a motor yacht with beautiful lines to its deep blue hull, and not a hint of the boy speedster about it. I fell in love with it at first sight . . . but no way was I letting Liam know that.

'We don't need anything this size,' I protested.

'We don't need a Mercedes either,' he pointed out, 'but you enjoy that.'

'But the kids . . .'

'The kids will love it, as you well know. This thing has long-distance cruising capacity, it's ultra stable and it's economical to run; it's built for comfort not for speed.'

'It'll cost a fortune.'

'No, it's not that expensive, and anyway, I'm not poor.'

'But you don't know how to . . . how to drive it.'

He laughed out loud. 'Who says?' He took off the tinted specs, laid his hands on my shoulders and looked me in the eye.

'My darling, my love, my wife, whether officially or otherwise,' he said. 'Since it's practically impossible to lure you out of Catalunya, you've never come with me to Toronto, so you don't know that I have a boat on Lake Ontario that's as big as this, if not bigger . . . or rather I had a boat there, 'cos

I've just sold it. I'm qualified, and I'm experienced. This one is a bargain, it's only just over a year old and I want it. Please?'

I hugged the big idiot, hard as I could. 'As long as you don't change its name to Primavera,' I murmured.

'You haven't looked at the stern yet,' he whispered in my ear. 'I won't have to.'

Thirty-Three

Too right the kids loved it. As soon as I showed them the photo I'd taken with my phone, they insisted on being taken down to the marina to see it for themselves. Liam had paid a deposit there and then, so I was able to take them on board and show them around.

It was family-sized and then some, beautifully fitted, and I couldn't wait to see the look on my friend Shirley Gash's face when I showed it off to her.

'Can I have my own cabin?' Janet asked.

'As far as I can see,' I told her, 'you can have a choice of two.'

Later, much later, when Liam and I were alone, fed, watered and sitting out on the upstairs terrace in the moonlight, I asked him a simple question. 'Why? And don't give me any nonsense about boys' toys. It's more than that, I know.'

He gazed across the bay, towards the marina where his new pride and joy was moored and guarded. 'A couple of days ago, honey,' he murmured, 'I could have lost you and

Tom. He says no, that he would have taken Jenkins regardless of me surprising him, but the man was armed, so he might not have. Can you imagine what that would have done to me?'

'I wouldn't like to try,' I admitted.

'It's made me realise truly what I have with you, and Tom, and Janet, and wee Jonathan, and even Charlie. I have a family, and that's something I have never had as an adult, or been part of for most of my life. So that's what the boat's about; it's for us as a unit, something we can all enjoy together, how and when we like . . . apart maybe from Charlie,' he chuckled, 'when we go on cruises, for there will be nowhere on it for him to do his stuff.

'I will teach the youngsters how to handle her, and you too for that matter. It's for fishing, it's for holidays, and more than likely in years to come it's for us on our own, when this house is full of young adults and their partners and we fancy somewhere to bugger off to for some peace and quiet.'

'You're a lovely man,' I told him, 'and I'm lucky to have you, boat or no boat.'

The next day was normal; I could hardly believe it. Mac and Liam went off to Gualta to play the par three course and I was left on my own, with only Terri the buzz-bomb cleaner for company.

I hadn't shaken off the events of the weekend completely, and still felt more than a little fidgety. I barely knew what to do with my hyperactive self, but eventually I decided to catch some of the autumn rays. I took my backpack and my mat and jogged with Charlie along to El Riuet, where I lay on the nudie beach for an hour, trying but failing to doze off.

I swam for a bit, then went for some lunch at VaiVe. I wasn't sure whether word of the Saturday excitement in our house had leaked out, but if it had I would probably find out there. It seemed that it hadn't, for all that Teresa said when I asked for a sobresado sandwich, a cortado and a bottle of water was, 'I hear Liam's back,' with a smile and a look in her eye that added, *you lucky sod!*

I smiled back, probably with a look of my own that said, *and don't I know it.* 'Yeah, he is. He's done his wandering, and his research.' Then I told her about the boat. 'Would you believe it has FOUR bathrooms, including the one in the crew quarters. Not that we will have a crew, other than ourselves.'

She laughed. 'I never saw you as a sailor, Primavera.'

I threw her a quick salute. 'I'll be quite happy just to be the cabin girl.'

I took my lunch across to a table, and as I did so, my mobile sang 'New Kid in Town'; I'd changed the ringtone in Liam's honour.

I thought it might have been him, begging me to come and rescue him from being trounced by Mac on the golf course; he has perfect co-ordination in most things so you'd assume that he could hit a golf ball straight, but he can't.

It wasn't; it was Superintendent Morrow.

'Hello, Ronnie,' I answered, curiously. Was more interest being taken in Ricky's death? I wondered.

'Primavera, hello,' he echoed. 'I hope I haven't caught you at a bad time.'

'All my times are good from now on, Ronnie,' I told him. 'What can I do for you?'

'Nothing. It's just that Alison said you wanted me to check out an entity called Raymac. I can't get hold of her just now; her assistant says she's having a few days' seclusion . . . her word . . . before Ricky's funeral next Monday. So I thought I'd call you direct, since the message is for you anyway. Raymac's an investment company, based in Liechtenstein. That's all I can tell you about it. You could probably have found out as much yourself on Google.'

I'd forgotten all about Raymac; from what Ronnie was saying I had no need to remember it. I thanked him, wished him good luck as a pallbearer at the funeral, and went back to my serious sandwich.

And yet, it wouldn't leave me alone. Ricky had made that note for a reason; Raymac had meant something to him.

It niggled away at me all day, and through the evening. 'What's up?' Liam asked me eventually, after dinner, when the kids had gone to do their homework and Mac had gone to Meson del Conde for a coffee. 'Are you having flashbacks?'

'No,' I assured him. 'Not in the way you mean, anyway.' I told him about Ricky's note and what Morrow had reported. 'It's just not right. Ricky was murdered because of something he was working on, I'm certain of that, but Raymac was the only lead I had left and it turns out that it's a dud.'

'What do you mean, that you had left? You have to let this go, love. It nearly got you killed.'

'But it did get Ricky Ross killed. You knew the man too, Liam. Do you think it's right that somebody should get away with doing him in?'

'You mean that Weighley should get away with it?'

'No. There's more to it than Weighley; I'm convinced of that. I'd hoped that this Raymac connection might prove it, but Morrow's given them a clean bill of health, as clean as Ricky's fucking computer turned out to be.'

'Mmm.' He sat there, silent, for a minute or so, in what I had come to recognise as his 'ponder' mode. 'Let's say you're right,' he ventured, when he was ready. 'The Ricky that I remember was a careful man. He was disciplined, methodical. If he was working on something he'd be unlikely to have kept it in his head. If his laptop was clean then where else would he have stashed a file?'

'Search me.'

'I will later, but for now, gimme some ideas.'

'Safe deposit box?' I suggested, more in hope than with conviction.

'Nah, I don't fancy that. But how about . . .' he put his hand in his pocket, took out his phone and held it up '. . . one of these? If I wanted to make a note, or a record, so I could have it with me all the time, that's where I'd put it. If you could find out what happened to Ricky's mobile . . .'

I sat bolt upright. 'I don't need to,' I exclaimed. 'I've got it!'

I had it, but what could I do with it?

When I retrieved it from my desk, where I'd stashed it, and took a good look at it, I realised that it was a miracle that it had been able to receive a call, given the mess it was in. The casing had once been all white, but it had been scorched by the blast. The thing was noticeably buckled too. It looked like a piece of the sad detritus that can be seen in the TV coverage of an aircraft disaster. The only thing that could be said for it was that the LCD screen was intact.

It was an iPhone, like mine, so I knew its capabilities and how to operate it. I pressed the on button and the screen glowed very faintly, showing me 'Slide to unlock', but when I tried to do that the slider wouldn't budge. I found Ricky's card and dialled the number on my own phone. It rang and, once again, I was able to accept the incoming call by pressing the faint green stripe. I'd hoped that might let me in through the back door, but no such luck.

'Try connecting it to your computer,' Liam suggested.

'Okay,' I said, but I was doubtful from the start. I could barely force the connector into the base, but I managed it, and connected it to a USB port. The iTunes application started and recognised that there was a device attached, but as far as it was concerned the thing was blank.

'Too bad,' he murmured, but in a way that made me think that as far as he was concerned it was no bad thing at all.

'Not quite,' I countered. 'There's one last thing I can try, and I will, tomorrow morning.'

Thirty-Four

There's a little shop in L'Escala that doesn't belong to any of the big chains but to a guy who sells phones with and without SIM cards, and who has a reputation for doing a whole range of the techie stuff that the big boys tell you is impossible, as they sell you a replacement for your actually fixable mobile.

I called in to see him just as the bells in the church nearby rang eleven times. He turned out to be a little man with a round head and a straggly beard. If he'd had 'nerd' printed on his forehead nobody would have thought anything of it. There was nobody else in the place, yet still he managed to look harassed.

'What can I do for you, señora?' he asked, eyeing me up as if he thought I'd walked into the wrong shop.

'The impossible,' I replied. 'My son's school pals say you do.'

'Nobody will do that . . . but I get as close as I can.'

'In which case, I'd like you to try this.' I took two iPhones from my pocket and laid them on his counter, then pointed at Ricky's. 'I want you to take all the information in that, and transfer it into mine.'

He whistled. 'All the memory?'

'I'm not too bothered about his music library or his contact list, but apart from that, yes.'

'I don't know, and I won't till I get in there.' He picked up the damaged phone. 'But from the look of this I'm doubtful there'll be anything to transfer. What happened to it anyway?'

'Let's just say it was mishandled.'

'Okay, leave them both with me. Can you come back tomorrow?'

I smiled my sweetest. 'I can come back in an hour.'

He gasped. 'No chance; I have other work.'

I took out a fifty-euro note and laid it beside the phones. 'If you're ready when I come back just after twelve, I'll put another one alongside it.'

'I can't promise.'

'I'm not asking you to promise, just to do your best. See you after the clock strikes twelve,' I said, then turned on my heel and walked out.

Liam and Mac were waiting for me in Caravella, one of the cafés that ring the town beach. They had just been to complete the deal on the boat.

'Signed and sealed?' I asked.

'You're looking at L'Escala's answer to Captain Jack Sparrow,' my other half replied.

'Does that mean you're going to look like Keith Richard when you get old?'

'Now there's a visual metaphor too far, I reckon.'

'I'll settle for Captain Liam,' I told him. 'When are we going for a sail?'

'For a proper one, on Saturday, seven of us. Mac's coming and so is Anais. But today, I thought we might have lunch on board, then maybe take her out into the bay, if the weather stays fine.'

'Can you handle her on your own?'

'I won't be on my own, I'll have you to cast off, and tie up when we're finished.'

While I had a coffee and a croissant, they went off to the Lacoste shop, looking for boating shoes. There must have been quite a range on offer; just as they returned I heard the town clock striking midday.

We all headed towards the car park, but I took a detour just before we reached it and went back into the phone shop. Señor Nerd was waiting for me, looking pleased with himself. Before he had a chance to say a word, I took out another fifty and put it on the counter.

'Thank you,' he said. 'I've done what you wanted. The iPhone is a very tough animal; the memory and the SIM card on the damaged one were both intact. It wasn't easy, though. I couldn't copy the data across to your phone, so what I did was take them out and fit them into yours. When you're ready, I can reverse it.' He grinned for the first time since we'd met. 'No extra charge.' He gave me back my mobile and a small envelope. 'That's your insides,' he said. 'What do you want me to do with the old one?'

'If you can ever make it work again, it's yours.'

His eyes gleamed. 'Now there's a challenge.'

I put phone and envelope in my bag and forgot about them as I enjoyed my first lunch on board the new family yacht. Mac had brought a bottle of champagne, but he wouldn't let me smash it against the bow. Instead we drank a toast to the motor yacht *Guardiola* . . . the skipper had been joking about the name.

Once we had eaten and the cabin girl had cleared up the debris, Liam eased us away from the mooring and we put to sea for the first time, moving slowly out of the marina, then turning to face the open water.

'Where do you want to go?' he asked.

'Not far,' I answered. 'Anywhere there are no rocks. How do we know where there are rocks?' I admit it, I'm a novice sailor: remember, I was brought up in Auchterarder; that's about as far from the sea as you can be in Scotland.

We settled on Montgo Bay as our maiden destination; it was accessible and it's easy to moor. There was a breeze and the sea was a little choppy, but the *Guardiola* didn't notice as she moved serenely and steadily along. I sat beside Liam as he steered; he was just as he'd been the first time we'd been out in the Merc, getting used to the new layout but completely confident. He knew what he was doing, all right, but no wonder. Lake Ontario's a big stretch of water.

The voyage didn't last long; the mouth of Montgo Bay was

just around the first headland, only a couple of kilometres, but it was enough for us to get the feel of it. 'Can I steer on the way back?' I asked Liam, as Mac secured us to a mooring buoy.

'Next time,' he promised. Then he looked me in the eye, eyebrows slightly raised. 'Well?' he said.

'Well what?'

'Well . . . are you going to see whether or not you've wasted your money on that phone?'

'Yes, all right I will; might as well get it over with.' I picked up my bag, as Mac rejoined us. 'Let's go up to the fly bridge,' I proposed.

'Fly bridge' is a fancy name for what is effectively an open viewing gallery above the main deck, with a second wheel and controls, so that the driver . . . sorry, helmsman; must get used to these terms . . . can steer the vessel without being stuck in the enclosed cabin. We climbed the steps and took seats around the table.

I took out my phone, with its new innards, and switched it on. The screen looked different; Ricky's lock screen wallpaper was a photo of his wife, and when I slid the bar to open up I saw the same face in the main menu.

I flicked through the pages to check what apps he had installed. Not many, I discovered: Google Earth, Sky Go, Kindle and a word processing package called Pages, which I recognised because I have it myself. I opened that, and found absolutely nothing other than a document headed 'Getting started'. It seemed as if Ricky hadn't bothered.

I found another app called Dropbox, one I don't have but had heard about. It allows file management and sharing. It could have been a location for a document, so I opened it. Its only content was a folder of photographs of Mr and Mrs Ross on holiday, somewhere with lots of palm trees set around a swimming pool, he wearing only red satin Speedos, and she clad in much the same, with her considerable jugs on show.

'Bloody hell!' Liam murmured. I hadn't realised that he was looking over my shoulder.

I closed the app quickly, to protect Alison's privacy and also before he could start making mental comparisons.

The only thing left to check was a standard iPhone facility called Notes, which allows the user to leave memos for him or herself. When I looked there I found a reminder to buy 'Bog rolls,' 'tuna', 'red w', 'milk' and 'Flora'. Nothing else, though; no secrets.

'That's it,' I declared. 'Money wasted; there's nothing on it. It was a long shot anyway.'

'That's if you're looking for a written document.'

We both turned to peer at Mac. 'Uh?' Liam grunted.

'I thought you could record voice memos on those fuckers,' he said. 'God knows, they can do everything else.'

I frowned. 'I think you're right.' I had seen a record facility, but where? I closed 'Notes', and looked at the screen. Alongside it was a square box labelled, 'Utilities', and within it, a tiny blue microphone icon. I clicked the main folder, selected 'Voice memos' from the four options, and opened it.

There was one file: it was twelve days old, and it was called 'Raymac'.

I winked at Mac. 'You clever old sod,' I whispered.

'Less of the old,' he grunted.

'Are you going to play it?' Liam asked. 'If you are, there's an audio system in the main cabin with an input that will let you use its speakers.'

He and I trooped back downstairs; Mac declined to join us. 'I like it up here,' he said. 'Besides, I'm not keen on dead men's voices. Elvis is okay, but not people that I've known.'

I knew exactly what he meant. Tom, Janet and wee Jonathan are all fine about watching their father's movies on Blu-ray and DVD. I encourage them, but when they're on, I always find something else to do.

I felt a little funny as I plugged the phone into the console; it had only been five days since I'd last spoken to Ricky Ross, but on the other hand prior to that we had been fifteen years between encounters so the frisson disappeared once I'd pressed the play icon.

'Okay,' the dead man's voice boomed from the speakers.

'How d'you work this fucking thing?' it continued, as Liam lowered the volume. 'Is that dial reacting to my voice? Aye, fine, seems to be. Let's go.'

We heard him draw a deep breath.

'This is a memo to me, to summarise some inquiries I've been making off my own bat, into WeighleyAir plc, the low-cost airline which is my client. Cedric Jenkins, Jack Weighley's fucking driver, no less, has just told me to drop everything, all my other clients, all my other business, and get out to Spain right away and wipe some shit off the windows in Girona, so I'm doing this quickly, just to set down some stuff, 'cos I don't want to leave a paper trail.

'It's widely assumed that Weighley as chief executive, chairman and everything else in WeighleyAir, is the beneficial owner of the company. He's stated this many times in speeches and interviews, and nobody's ever questioned it.' Pause.

'Me neither. When I was engaged as its security consultant I asked Weighley for certain assurances about WeighleyAir's probity and its financial position. I did this for two reasons. As a former police officer and current recipient of a police pension I won't allow myself to be associated with an outfit that is in any way dodgy, and as a businessman I don't believe in committing my time and that of my staff if I'm not going to get paid at the end of the day.' Pause.

'He assured me that the company was everything it claimed to be, and let me see a set of management accounts that showed its cash position to be extremely healthy, with a reserve of twenty-odd million. He told me that the company's profit-ability was underwritten by advantageous landing charges negotiated with airport operators in the twenty-three countries where it flies to and from and also by subsidies paid by national and regional governments to underwrite routes that might not be viable otherwise. He told me also that the money to found the company came from within his own family, from the sale of his previous business, a motor dealership and bus company, and from a family trust set up by his father, who was involved

337

in the travel and leisure industry when he sold his companies. On the basis of all those assurances I went to work for him, and even let my wife follow me by bidding for his Edinburgh PR account and winning it.' Pause.

'I've never had any money problems with Jack and neither has Alison. He's a complete arsehole for some of the time and just a pain in it for the rest, but he pays his bills and he runs a very successful company, no question about that. Setting up his main operating base at the old East Fortune airport, bang on the railway line and half an hour from Edinburgh, that was a stroke of genius, especially since the Scottish government gave him a grant for the terminal buildings and the local council resurfaced the runway and taxiways for him. As far as I and anyone else can see, he's built a top-class airline from scratch, and when he told Alison a few months back to draw up a plan for the flotation of the company on the Stock Exchange that's going to value it at two hundred million, "Good luck to him" was my reaction.' Pause.

'I'd have thought no more of it, had I not been at a Chamber of Commerce piss-up in the Merchants' Hall a few Fridays ago, and bumped into a guy I hadn't seen in years, an old fellow called Pete McDougal, retired now, but used to be an adman. We got talking; I asked him what he was doing, he said "Fuck all," and asked me the same. I told him what my business was and gave him a rundown of my clients, ending with WeighleyAir. Out of the blue, old Pete said, "I often wonder where the money came from to start that outfit. Young Weighley did all right selling his first businesses, but it must have taken a lot more than that." I told him what Jack had told me, and old Pete said, "Hold on a minute, I knew his old man, well. He was a gambler, big time, and not at all good at it. By the time he sold his business, he'd borrowed so much against it to pay off his bookies and the casino that he got fuck all for it, net. He died soon after that and his daughter actually borrowed money off me to help pay for the funeral; so, family investment trust, my arse." I asked him why the Scottish press didn't pick up on it at the time, and he said they were conned into believing that old Weighley was trousering all the money they were told the deal was worth, when in fact he didn't walk away with enough to put a fiver each way on the favourite in the three thirty at fucking Plumpton.' Longer pause.

'I thought about it over the weekend, saying nothing to Alison, so as not to undermine her faith in Jack. She never says as much but I know she thinks the sun shines out of his fundamental orifice. I know also that she spends far too much personal time on his account, given the fee she's on. Back in the office on Monday, I went to the Companies House website and searched for the records of WeighleyAir. I found nothing at all. So I went up to the office in Fountainbridge and searched in person. It took me twenty minutes to find that WeighleyAir is a trademark belonging to a company called Weighley Aviation Limited. Its only shareholder of record is John R. Weighley. However, his personal holding in the company is only twenty per cent. For the other eighty, he's a nominee shareholder; that means he fronts for the beneficial owner of the shares. Now, there's no way Companies House would tell me who that is, but the company itself can be made to tell the Inland Revenue. As it happens, I have an old pal there, who let slip the fact that behind four-fifths of Jack Weighley's airline, you will find what they call an Anstalt company, registered in Liechtenstein, a lovely place, they say, that Alison and I must visit some day. Its name, my HMRC contact said, is Raymac. As it happens I have another mate who's a corporate lawyer, doing a lot of business in Europe. He told me that the actual owners of these companies can maintain their anonymity, but the names of their directors are public. I had to apply in writing to the public Registrar's Office in Liechtenstein, to find out who Raymac's directors are. They made me jump through all sorts of fucking hoops, but eventually, a week ago, I received a formal reply, recorded delivery. There are three of them; two of the names were Liechtenstein nationals, legal requirements. They meant nothing to me, but the third did, big time.' Pause.

'Rayner Maxton is a lawyer, but not just any lawyer. There are two major, long-term figures in organised crime in Scotland: Kenny McLeish, the Weegie Godfather, and Ronnie Roy, the uncrowned king of Edinburgh. They gave up fighting each other twenty years ago and became even stronger for it. The police never get near them, but if any of their associates is ever lifted, not that it happens very often, the man who will turn up in court as their brief is Rayner Maxton.' Pause.

'They have legitimate businesses as well, naturally, kosher companies with auditors and annual accounts and all that stuff. They have a few accountants, but only one lawyer: Rayner Maxton. He is their Vicar on Earth.' Pause.

'So, that one name tells me who really owns WeighleyAir, and who's pulling our Jack's strings.' Pause.

'That letter from Liechtenstein went straight into the shredder. However, I've been thinking about it ever since. I am quite certain that WeighleyAir is in fact a money-laundering scheme for major-league criminals, and that when the company goes on the stock market, they will be in line for a lift of one hundred and sixty million.' Pause.

' "What are you going to do about it, Ricky?" I ask myself. I'll think about that while I'm away, but probably I'll do nothing. If I pull down WeighleyAir, a lot of people will lose their jobs, plus I'll be looking over my shoulder for the rest of my life, and I don't fancy that.'

As the memo ended and the cabin went quiet, Liam and I stared at each other, wide-eyed.

'Those names,' I whispered, 'Roy and McLeish. Ricky mentioned them, in the square, after the car incident. He might have said more then, but Alex interrupted him.'

'What do you think?' Liam asked. 'How could . . . ? Who? His wife? Ricky said she thought Weighley was God. Could she have set him up?'

I was ahead of him. 'Not Alison. It was her who told me told me about Raymac. No, it's far more likely that Mr Rayner Maxton was advised, officially or otherwise, by the public registrar in Liechtenstein that Ricky had been making inquiries about him and the company, and that he told Jack to sort it.

'But maybe it wasn't Jack; maybe I'm crediting him with more clout than he actually has. More than likely, Gareth Jenkins wasn't Jack's man at all. It stands to reason that he was put in place by Maxton, or directly by his clients, so they could keep an eye on Jack, and make sure that their involvement stayed undetected. When Jenkins was caught, he realised that he'd made himself a risk by knowing too much, so he beat the bullet, or more likely the knife in the ribs in jail, by killing himself. It's possible that Jack knew very little of what was going on, if anything.'

'What are we going to do with that recording?'

'Nothing. We have three kids; they rate above anything else, and I'll never put them at risk. Jenkins killed Ricky; Jenkins is dead himself. It can end there.'

Thirty-Five

It would have too, but for Ronnie Morrow's last phone call.

Rather than have my year-old mobile taken apart again, next morning I talked my nerd pal into a discount on the newest iPhone and transferred my SIM card into it. The rest of the memory didn't matter, since it was all backed up on the Cloud or synched through my computer. The other one, the one with Ricky's story, went into my safe.

Liam and Mac and I were out on the boat again when the Eagles played for the first time in their new home.

'Hi, Ronnie,' I answered, having seen who it was. My immediate assumption was that word of the weekend carnage must have made it back to Edinburgh, that Orr's murder or Jenkins' suicide might have been reported.

I was wrong; his tone told me that as soon as he spoke, for he was excited. 'Something's come up that I thought you'd be interested to hear. Remember Hamish Orr, the guy I told you about. I pulled his complete record, just for fun. It has all sorts of personal information on it, including the name of his

343

ex-wife, the one who divorced him when he was inside. Guess what? She's Jack Weighley's sister.'

I had been missing one piece of the jigsaw. There had been one riddle I couldn't solve and I had thought I never would.

How did Jenkins know to recruit Hamish Orr?

The answer had fallen into my lap.

Jack Weighley told him.

Jack must have known of the plot to assassinate Ricky Ross, all the way along the line. He was in as deep as everyone else.

I came close to dropping my brand new Apple over the side, but Ronnie wasn't to know that. 'Is that so?' was all I said in reply. 'It's a tiny world, and thanks for telling me, but you know, I don't think I ever want to hear anything about that little bastard, ever again.'

And I didn't, for my mind was made up. Apart from my continuing involvement with Miles's bodega, which is family business, I am going to be a full-time wife and mother from now on.

It's Valentine's Day tomorrow and Liam and I are being married in the foresters' house, next to the church. Tom, who's five feet ten now, will be best man, Janet will be my bridesmaid, and wee Jonathan will be usher. The civil ceremony doesn't call for me to be given away but if it did, my father would do it, for he's here too, with the rest of my family, and Mac, who's being partnered by Anais, I'm pleased to say.

Full-time wife and mother, I said, but not quite, for I plan to fill my spare time by writing. In fact, I've finished my first project already. It's a screenplay and I showed it to Miles yesterday morning. He studied it overnight and he says he loves it, so much that he wants to film it.

The plot? You've just read it. The names, apart from one, and the locations are all changed. I've set the story in Italy rather than Spain. The airline and the characters around it are all Dutch, not Scottish. The central character is a widowed Irish schoolteacher mourning her dead footballer husband. All different, but step by step, event by event, line of dialogue by line of dialogue, the story is the same.

I haven't pulled the wool over Miles's eyes. When he'd finished reading, and given me his verdict, I told him the truth, and I played him the recording. That made him all the more determined to go ahead with the movie project.

As I've said, he knew Ricky from the old days, and Miles is definitely not a man who believes in letting people get away with murdering his friends.

And as he said, 'What's Weighley going to do when the movie is released? Sue us?'

Who owns the name I left unchanged? Luis Saviola. He deserves it, and for sure he will not cry 'Libel!'

The flotation of WeighleyAir takes place at the end of March, with one hundred per cent of the equity on offer. It will be fully subscribed, of that I am certain, so Jack and his gangster backers will walk away with their two hundred million pounds.

When that has happened, WeighleyAir will be in the hands of other people, and no historic scandal will affect the jobs of its workforce.

When that has happened, and Miles's movie is ready for release, I will visit Ronnie Morrow, I will tell him the whole story and I will give him the phone, with Ricky's first-hand tale of how he came to sign his own death warrant.

What will he do with it? I have no idea, but he and Alison should know the truth.

It may not matter anyway, for on the day after I meet with Ronnie, a copy of the recording will be in the morning mail of Mr Rayner Maxton, first class, postmarked Edinburgh, in an untraceable envelope, with no covering note.

What will he do with it? Again, I have no idea but I would like to think that whatever he does will be very bad news for Mr Weighley.

By the way, I figured out a long time ago why he hired me: he knew me and so, when he found out I was on the scene, he followed the old Edgar Hoover principle, that it was better to have me inside the tent pissing out, than the other way around. Jack, you were wrong about that one.

It's all part of my past now, or very nearly.

Tomorrow, Primavera Blackstone will become Primavera Matthews, and, with her new husband, will take her first tentative steps towards living happily ever after, or for as long as fate allows her, watching her kids and Oz's grow into the people they are destined to be.

So long . . . maybe. Wish me bon voyage.